Daniele Varè was born in 1880, the son of an Italian nationalist exiled with Mazzini by the Austrian régime. Although he was brought up in Scotland where his parents met, Daniele Varè returned to Italy when he was still young and entered that country's diplomatic service. He served in Vienna, Geneva, Copenhagen and Luxembourg. However, his chief posting was in Peking where he arrived in 1908 and where he served for twelve years. During his time there he saw the overthrow of the Manchu dynasty, the country swept by civil war and the effects of the Russian Revolution and the First World War as exiles fled into China from abroad. Many of these experiences became the subject matter of his novels and tales.

Daniele Varè left the diplomatic service in 1932 in order to devote himself to writing. Many of his books were published in both Italian and English.

The Maker of Heavenly Trousers was first published in 1935 and was reprinted several times: it was followed soon after by its two sequels *The Gate of Happy Sparrows* and *The Temple of Costly Experience,* and by the author's autobiography, *The Laughing Diplomat* in 1938. Daniele Varè died in 1956.

Also by Daniele Varè

THE MAKER OF HEAVENLY TROUSERS
THE GATE OF HAPPY SPARROWS

and published by Black Swan

THE TEMPLE OF
COSTLY EXPERIENCE

'Dreams are the heralds of eternity'
BYRON

Daniele Varè

BLACK SWAN

THE TEMPLE OF COSTLY EXPERIENCE
A BLACK SWAN BOOK   0 552   99309 3

Originally published in Great Britain by Methuen & Co. Ltd.

PRINTING HISTORY

Methuen edition published 1939
Methuen edition reprinted 1939
Black Swan edition published 1988

This book is set in 11/12pt Century

Black Swan Books are published by Transworld Publishers Ltd., 61-63 Uxbridge Road, Ealing, London W5 5SA, in Australia by Transworld Publishers (Australia) Pty. Ltd., 15-23 Helles Avenue, Moorebank, NSW 2170, and in New Zealand by Transworld Publishers (N.Z.) Ltd., Cnr. Moselle and Waipareira Avenues, Henderson, Auckland.

Made and printed in Great Britain by
The Guernsey Press Co. Ltd., Guernsey, Channel Islands.

Dedicated to the
BARON DE CARTIER DE MARCHIENNE

LE SAINT:

> Des profondeurs, des profondeurs
> j'appelle votre amour, Elus!
> Chaque flèche est pour le salut,
> afin que je puisse revivre.
> Ne tremblez pas, ne pleurez pas!
> Mais soyez ivres, soyez ivres
> de sang, comme dans les combats.
> Visez de près. Je suis le Cyble,
> Des profondeurs, des profondeurs
> j'appelle votre amour terrible.

C'est le râlc dans la gorge transpercée, le dernier soupir, le dernier sourire, le suprême appel. La belle tete s'incline sur l'epaule polie comme le marbre cynthien frotté de parfum: les ailerons d'un dard vibrent encore à l'aisselle. Le corps admirable s'affaisse, étirant les bras retenus par les liens.

LES ARCHERS D'EMESE

> —Seigneur!
> —Bien-aimé!
> —Seigneur!
> —Bien-aimé!
> —Bien-aimé!

—LE MARTYRE DE SAINT SEBASTIEN
By Gabriele d'Annunzio

(last act)

Contents

Foreword

*'I am always at a loss to know how much to believe of
my own stories.'*

WASHINGTON IRVING:
Tales of a Traveller

I have written books about Peking and our life there,
but in none of them have I told how and why I came to
make my home in China. This is because I find it
rather difficult to explain, and I feel that I might not be
believed. Also it has nothing to do with subsequent
events. Indeed, I once thought of making a separate
story out of it, writing as if it had happened to
somebody else. But the result did not satisfy me. It was
too absurd and inconsequent.

Even so, the story has a moral, for it was the
absurdity and the inconsequence of it all that
fascinated me, and made me wish to settle in a country
where life moved on lines so delightfully irrelevant.

If this were an eastern tale out of the *Arabian
Nights,* it might begin: 'Once in days of yore and times
and tides long gone before, there was a porter in
Baghdad, who was a bachelor and would remain
unmarried . . .'

I like the opening. It promises so much! The
opening of my story concerns, not a porter in Baghdad,
but a shoe-black in Paris. He had his stand in the Rue
Saint Honoré, close to the church of St. Roch, at the
opening of the Passage St. Roch, which is a footpath
leading round into the Rue des Pyramides. There is a
newspaper kiosk there now, and in the morning you
may also find a couple of handcarts, backed up against
the wall of the church and belonging to two old women
who sell fruit.

The shoe-black is long since dead, for 'he plied his
sable brush for hire' in the eighteen-seventies, when
Monsieur Grévy was President of the Republic, and the

Paris of Baron Haussman still showed here and there traces of the older Paris, of Balzac and *les Mystères*. Certainly by now he would be long forgotten, but for the sign that formed part of his outfit. There is no one left alive who can remember the shoe-black himself, with his blue blouse, and his box and his brushes. But still among the old houses in the Rue St. Roch and round about the church there lingers the legend of that remarkable sign. For this is how he advertised himself and his trade:

Charles de Valois
Cireur de Bottes

The poor shoe-black bore a name famous in history. And he boasted that in his veins ran the blood that gave to France thirteen kings! So it was that many people who might have been content to let their shoes remain muddy for the rest of the day, would stop for 'a shine', held as they were by the arresting antithesis between the humble calling and the name that recalled the Dukes of Burgundy, of Alençon, and the golden lilies!

Perhaps because of his name, Charles de Valois the shoe-black married a lady of property, proprietress of a shop on the other side of the Rue St. Honoré. This shop ('Robes, Manteaux et Articles pour Dueil') specialized in widows' weeds, veils and ornaments of mourning. And it must have prospered, for *la patronne*, some time after she became Madame de Valois, acquired a piece of land west of what is known now as l'Etoile, and did well out of it. So much so that, when she and her husband died within a few months of each other, in the year 1889, their only son, Henri de Valois, who was then a boy at the Jesuit school at Grenoble, inherited a not inconsiderable fortune, which was administered for him, till he came of age, by a guardian.

Among Henri's school friends at Grenoble were

several young scions of the French aristocracy, thanks to whom it became possible for him, when he grew up, to enter into the best society of the capital, *le beau monde,* and to be made welcome even in the more conservative salons of the Faubourg St. Germain. He had the good taste not to be ashamed of his father's profession, but to tell everybody that he was the son of a shoe-black. And he would point out the precise spot, at the opening of the passage of St. Roch, where Charles de Valois had plied his trade.

On the other hand, it amused him to add point to the monarchical evocations of his name, by taking an apartment in the Palais Royal, not far from the Comédie Française. His apartment consisted of one big room on the ground floor (this space has now been converted into shops), and a bedroom and bathroom on the floor above. To a young man calling himself Henri de Valois, it must have been gratifying to use the Palais Royal as an address.

But he impaired the suitableness of his dwelling by the incongruity of his favourite pursuit. And the whimsical element in the profession by which the father made his living reappeared in the choice of a hobby by his son. For Henri de Valois's principal interest in life was cooking! Not the consuming of good food, but the preparation thereof. With Brillat-Savarin, he believed that the discovery of a new dish does more for the happiness of humanity than the discovery of a star. The big room, or 'studio' in his apartment boasted of a fireplace not unworthy of La Rôtisserie de la Reine Pédauque, and into it he fitted a modern cooking-range. On this the host himself would prepare the dishes that he offered to the few friends whom he honoured with an invitation to supper. Such an honour, needless to say, was much coveted in Parisian society at that time. For, apart from the unusual character of the invitation, the food and the wines were superlative. Henri de Valois was a past-master in his art. But, like other great masters, he was irritable, impatient and impulsive: skilled not only in cooking but in the gentle art of making enemies. One of his numerous quarrels brought him up against a very influential member of the French Jockey Club, and they called each other names ('Sir,' said Mr Tupman, 'you're a fellow.' 'Sir,' said Mr Pickwick, 'you're another.').

This small episode caused so much unpleasantness that Henri de Valois decided to leave Paris for a while and to travel in the East. His professed object was to make a study of oriental cooking. And that is how the story of his life intersected with mine for the brief space of one evening, in Tsi-nan-fu, capital of the Shan-tung province of China. For at that time I too was a young man travelling in the Far East for pleasure and instruction. When I passed through Tsi-nan-fu, Henri de Valois was staying there in the house of the French Consul, and pursuing the culinary studies that he had begun some months before in Canton. On the journey out he had met, on board ship, a pretty and attractive French girl, who was on her way to Java, to join and to marry a Dutch tea-planter, to whom she had become engaged, more than a year before, in Marseilles. It is rare indeed that a long journey by sea, on a modern liner, does not offer the occasion for starting, or for breaking off, a love affair. With his usual impulsiveness, our friend with the royal name begun to make love to the young fiancée. His intentions being strictly honourable, he soon persuaded her to jilt the tea-planter and to become Madame de Valois. The marriage ceremony was performed in the Catholic church at Singapore. After which the happy couple continued on the same steamer, as far as Hong Kong.

I arrived at Tsi-nan-fu one evening late in June, and put up at a small and not very cleanly inn, kept by a German, but run on Chinese lines. I had brought with me an introduction to the British Consul at Tsi-nan-fu, but I was informed on my arrival that he was away on leave, and had entrusted his official duties *pro tem* to his French colleague, as is customary in far-flung consular offices abroad.

The events leading up to the climax in this very long-winded story are so incongruous that I have considerable difficulty in setting them forth in any logical order. And I am especially vague as to what really happened on that summer evening, when I arrived in Tsi-nan-fu, tired and dusty after a tedious journey up from Tsin-tao on the coast.

Unless I am mistaken in my facts, not only the British Consul was away on leave, but also his French colleague has absented himself for a few days. But he had left a compatriot and guest of his in the Consulate, unofficially in charge. This guest had just made an important discovery (or thought he had). He had found the solution of the problem that for many years had puzzled the best culinary artists in Europe: the problem of the *mousse aux champignons*. And he had discovered it by chance (not the dish itself, but a method by which it could be made), while investigating a small eating-house in Tsi-nan-fu, redolent of roast pork and sesame oil.

Such a discovery could only be the prelude to all sorts of interesting experiments (one might almost say *experimenta in corpore vili*). Of these, the most obvious was to invite somebody to a dinner in which the *mousse aux champignons* should figure on the menu, somewhere after the *entrée*. It so happened that I was the first person available, and I was asked out to eat the famous *mousse,* as soon as I arrived in Tsi-nan-fu, on the principle of 'try it on the dog'.

How the experimenter discovered that I had arrived in Tsi-nan-fu I could not say. But I had hardly done so before a message was diverted to me by a Chinese servant, and interpreted by the clerk in the inn where I was staying. I gathered that I was invited out to dinner by a French gentleman called Hua Hsien-seng, and that I should go to the Pavilion of Half Remembered Dreams at eight o'clock. The first of the three monosyllables that formed my host's name was probably the phonetic equivalent of his foreign designation. But it was not of much help in identifying him. The character *Hua* means 'flower'. All I could do when the time came was to put on a white dinner jacket and black tie, and sally forth to find the Pavilion, where Mr Flower was expecting me to dinner.

Despite the glamorous name of this pavilion, I expected — so I seem to remember — to arrive in some Chinese house or villa, temporarily occupied by Europeans, or to some bungalow, such as foreigners build for themselves in the East. But I never entered a house, only a garden on the right bank of the Hwang Ho, separated from the river itself by an expanse of low-lying ground all grown over with whispering reeds. On a small hillock, overlooking the garden on one side and the river bank on the other, was an oriental belvedere or summer-house, with red lacquered columns supporting a sloping roof of tiles.

In the middle of this summer-house (which was open on all sides) there stood a small dinner-table laid for two. A larger table near by, also covered with a white table-cloth, was evidently meant to serve as a sideboard. Illumination was provided by Chinese lanterns, hanging from the eaves of the tiled roof, and distributed on tripods along the garden paths below. Frogs croaked, not unmusically, in the reeds along the river bank. Fireflies glimmered among the shadows.

I was new to China, and when you are new to a place you accept things without question. Not to have been received in a real dwelling, and not to have been welcomed by my host, whoever he might be, would probably surprise me more now than it did then. For 'Mr Flower' was nowhere to be seen. But seated on a chair in the summer-house was a young woman, good-looking and fashionably dressed. She rose and greeted me in French, but she did not explain who she was, or why I should have been invited to dine *tête-à-tête* with her on the night of my arrival at Tsi-na-fu. After all, why explain? The prospect was pleasant. We sat down to dinner together, and the Chinese boys served us with an iced *consommé*.

It did not take me long to observe what was the most peculiar circumstance in that peculiar situation: I mean the extraordinary excellence of the food. The wines were good (they must have come from the French Consul's private cellar, and he evidently did himself well!). But the food was more than good. It was perfect. I have never known such cooking; no, not in Paris itself! This, together with libations that were perhaps just a little too copious, made me begin to doubt that my surroundings could be real, and not the imagery of a dream.

The night air was languid and sensuous; the surroundings exotic; the dinner such as one enjoys seldom in a lifetime. And the lady did not seem to be averse to a mild flirtation (and not so mild as all that!). Is it surprising that, for a few moments at least, I should have lost my head? A compelling impulse moved me to imprint a kiss upon the lady's neck, just half way up from the shoulder. I had half risen from my seat to carry out this amiable intention, when the idyll was suddenly interrupted by a noise of furious quarrelling, somewhere in the garden below. The noise proceeded from some outhouses that must have contained a kitchen, as the food was brought to us from there. Yells, shrieks and curses rent the air, the sound of pots and pans being hurled through space and meeting obstacles in their way.

Then a door opened, showing lights inside, and two figures emerged, one flying for dear life and the other in pursuit. The one who fled was a Chinese coolie; the other a foreign cook with white coat, apron and tall cap all complete. Judging by his language, he was a French cook. *'Vaurien! Canaille! Sacré b———e d'un sale Chinois! Attend que je t'apprenne à . . . !'*

They disappeared into the darkness, in direction of the river.

I watched them till they were out of sight, and then I asked the lady: 'That is your cook, I suppose, Madame?'

She answered simply: 'No. That is my husband.'

At that moment he reappeared along the path, in the light of the Chinese lanterns, fanning himself with his cook's cap. He walked up the steps into the summer-house and bowed to me.

'Monsieur,' he said. 'I offer you one thousand apologies. The supper that I had prepared for you — such a supper as might have been served for Lucullus in the Hall of Apollo, has been spoilt, ruined, destroyed by that ignoble spawn of a Chinese frog. All he had to do was to hand me the silver vase, into which I meant to pour my wonderful *mousse,* delicate as a vapour, aromatic as breezes of Hymettus. It was to have been my triumph and my glory: the dream of my life come true! But he must needs polish the vase. Burnish it, the fool! And with this purpose, what does he do but breathe on the metal with his pestilential breath, redolent of ten thousand generations of garlic-eaters. *Cicutis allium nocentius!* as Horace has it. My dream has been shattered, dear sir, shattered. And I am a broken man!

'You will forgive me, if I do not remain to enjoy your company and your conversation, and if I beg my dear wife to escort me home and offer me the consolations of her affection. Permit us to retire, to nurse our sorrow!'

During this harangue I had not had a chance to get a word in edgeways. And when he paused I was too utterly astonished to speak. I could only gaze at him in silent wonder. But apparently that was all he expected. Just before leaving, he added, in a quieter tone:

'Should you ever visit Paris, I beg you will honour me by accepting a meal in our house. A meal that will not be spoilt by the flavour of a Chinese coolie!'

He took out his pocket-book and extracted from it a visiting-card. And he laid it on the table, among the plates and glasses.

Then offering his arm to the lady, and still fanning himself with his white cap he departed with her down the garden path. And I was left alone in the summer-house.

I sat down again and wiped my brow with a napkin. I was feeling dazed. Then I picked up the visiting-card and read:

Henri de Valois
Palais Royal – Paris

This was the last straw. I gave it up. Sighing wearily, I murmured: 'Some day, I suppose, I shall wake up again.'

Will the reader, I wonder, understand and sympathize?

I am the first to admit that what I have written is too fantastic to be true. Indeed, that is just what I am trying to prove.

For sometimes, even now, I wonder if my life in China has been a real life at all. Can it be that I am still asleep at Tsi-nan-fu, and that some day I shall wake up and see the stars pale in the East, as I shiver in the cool of a grey dawn by a reed-grown river bank, in a Pavilion of Half Remembered Dreams?

THE TEMPLE OF
COSTLY EXPERIENCE

1 The Prince-Abbot

I will give you
Presents from heaven
If you go byeloo,
Mammy's wee lamb.

ELEANOR FARJEON:
Presents from Heaven

It has become a platitude among authors like myself to say that our best books are those that never get written: stories that hover in our minds half told, half guessed at; characters that plead with us to give them life.

I feel that my best book is one that will never be submitted to any publisher. It is a *Life* of Prince Dorbon Oirad, one-time Hetman of Cossacks in the army of the Tsar and later Abbot of a Mongolian monastery, somewhere on the eastern slope of the Great Khingan Mountains.

I met him for the first time in the years of the Great War, but I did not get to know him well. Indeed, I cannot boast of ever having done so, but we met again a few months before his death, in 1928. One day in January of that year, I received a message to say that he wished to speak to me. He was staying at the Lama Temple in the northeastern corner of the Tartar City. The Shuang Liè Ssè, where I lived with my family, is in the southeastern corner. We could hardly have been further apart, within the enclosure of the Tartar Wall.

The Abbot's message was brought to me by a Lama

priest called Baldàn, an old friend of my wife's in the days when she was a *hsiao kuniang*, or 'little girl'. She is still known as Kuniang, but that is because it has become her nickname. There is another *hsiao kuniang* in our house now, aged five, as well as her elder brother, Little Chink, aged seven.

It is characteristic of the old China, in which all foreign devils were given a designation for use among their servants and dependants, that none of us is known by our own name. To my intimates I am King Cophetua, or more often The Maker of Heavenly Trousers (there is a sign with that strange name, hanging outside my study door). Our five Chinese servants, or boys, are 'the Five Virtues', of which Exalted Virtue is the eldest brother.

In my own household, such a variety of names brings no confusion. But I never know what to call Prince Dorbon Oirad. I find myself using sometimes his princely title and sometimes his ecclesiastical one (of the two I prefer the latter – it is shorter!) His double designation corresponded to a double personality. Chieftain of nomad tribes, he was both soldier and priest. And something more besides. For me, the figure of Dorbon Oirad impersonates Asia itself: the Asia that is passing with the passing of her conquerors and her sages. In him there was something of both.

Before the War, he visited St Petersburg and was fêted at the court of the Tsar. The goodwill of a powerful Mongol prince was well worth cultivating. And not only the Russian Government followed this policy. A court lady, famous for her wealth and for her beauty, was similarly inspired. And the resultant love-affair had far-reaching consequences. The lady, known to us as Elisalex, followed him into Siberia and went through some form of marriage ceremony with him, though it was doubtful if this were legal. The ties that bound these two together were not entirely severed when Prince Dorbon Oirad shaved his head and put on the robes of a Mongol Abbot. Even these few fragments of his personal history might justify my own desire to write the life of such a man. Think what a mentality!

Gentle old philosopher as he became in his later years, he still retained the character of his forebears, which was pastoral and nomadic. He and his retainers represented the last of the nomads, whose habitat began where civilization ends, beyond the outermost furrow of the plough, in the desert and the treeless steppes. He disliked what we call 'civilization', which in his own mind was not connected with culture, or progress, or religion. Perhaps his dislike was unconsciously atavistic. His ancestors, and the ancestors of those few retainers that still gathered round Prince Oirad, had swept westward to the gates of Vienna and had taken Constantinople. They were men for whom wealth lay only in the empty grasslands, and to whom any increase in population brought poverty. These were the most terrible warriors that the world has ever seen. No war-scare of our own day can equal the approach of that shaggy cavalry, with no organized state behind it, no finance, no homeland, but only a primitive hunger for space. They set fire to crops and to cities, because they had no use for them, but only for pasturage. They herded their prisoners together and shot them down (and later withdrew their arrows from the still quivering bodies), because they wanted the land that these people occupied. Such was war, as the Tartars knew it – a war of utter destruction. Our gases and our bombs are humane in comparison, for they aim only at breaking down resistance.

And, apart from the mentality, think what a background!

It was only after I got to know the Abbot better and he spoke to me of the lands he once hoped to weld into a mid-Asiatic kingdom, that I realized the enormous size of the country that we allude to comprehensively as 'Siberia': a region that is larger than the United States, and rich in pastures, in land for agriculture, in forests, in minerals and in water. The Abbot was not the type of

25

traveller that writes monographs on butterflies in Yunnan, or the flora of the Amur Basin. Nor could he have given lectures – save in Chinese or in Russian – to the Geographical Society. But he had ranged over half a continent till he considered it his own, from Tibetan monasteries with goitrous monks and buildings out of the straight, to Chinese ports on the Pacific, where East meets West, and they jazz together to Negro music.

Steamy Burmese valleys, sodden with monsoon rains, where the dusk is starred with fireflies and the leaf-mould alive with leeches. Northern rivers, frozen for half the year, where giant sturgeon come to spawn out of Arctic seas. Manchurian forests, humming with summer insects, though the tigers have shaggy coats to protect them from winter snow. Himalayan glaciers that no white foot has ever trodden, and milky streams flowing down from the roof of the world through fields of purple gentian. Riders with jangling bells on lonely mountain passes (where the summit is marked by a cairn and a wind-torn flag). Feudal states where the taxes are paid in butter to an overlord who is the incarnation of Buddha himself. Armies wearing Homburg hats, and carrying rifles, crossbows and umbrellas. The vastness, the incongruity, the comic pathos and the haunting nostalgia . . . the Abbot knew them all.

Even so, the desire to write his story might not have come upon me had it not been for a small episode that occurred when he came to see me, one afternoon during the festivities for the Chinese New Year, in 1928. He arrived about five o'clock in a horse-drawn vehicle, of a type that one sees only in Peking: a brougham, all glass and brasswork, with a step behind on which a groom can stand, when the carriage is proceeding along the straight. At the street corners, the groom (or *ma-fu*) jumps down and attempts to regulate the traffic to his master's advantage, with much shouting and pushing and quarrelling with carters and rickshaw-coolies.

When he called on me, the Abbot was not wearing the

26

robes of a Lama, but a quilted and fur-lined Mongol coat, held in at the waist by a silken sash, with a large silver buckle inset with turquoises. Not having seen him for nearly ten years, my first impression was that he had become the ghost and shadow of his former self. By which I do not mean that he was prematurely aged (he cannot have been more than fifty). His skin was hardly wrinkled; his hair was only slightly tinged with grey. And there was still something soldierly in the tall, slim figure. But he gave me the impression of being a disembodied spirit. Face and form had become ethereal, like the vision of a saint. His hands were so thin as to be almost transparent. One noticed his hands more than with other men, owing to his habit of holding a pair of polished walnuts and playing with them unceasingly in his long fingers.

The Abbot was not easy to converse with. He spoke a little French with an exasperating slowness, and Chinese only a little faster. But, if one did not try to hurry him, he was well worth listening to. Conversation among Orientals is a more leisurely business than with us. They arrive at their conclusions by tortuous paths and linger over ideas and sentences, as if loath to part with them. Unlike the nervous, self-conscious westerners, they are not embarrassed by long pauses and intervals of silence. The Abbot sat in my study for two long hours and only made an occasional brief effort at conversation. He did not seem to expect me to say anything, and it was obvious that he had nothing of any importance to say to me. Apparently he merely wished to enjoy my company and the pleasure of seeing me again after many years. He sat on the sofa, his hands moving under their long sleeves, as he played with his walnuts. And he smiled.

Soon after my guest's arrival, Exalted Virtue brought in a tray with a teapot and two little cups without handles. And he placed them on a low, hardwood table in front of us. In deference to Chinese etiquette, neither of us touched this refreshment till the call was nearly over. For me to have lifted a teacup to my lips would have been equivalent to a gesture of dismissal.

Again, in deference to Chinese custom, Kuniang did not show herself. And she would not have met him, if – much to my surprise – the Abbot had not inquired after her, and expressed a desire to see her again. So I went to look for her, and found her with the children, who were preparing to go to bed, for it was nearly seven o'clock.

Kuniang consented rather reluctantly to come and say a few words to the Abbot before he left. To tell the truth, I think she was a little bit afraid of him. But, like me, she was struck with the change in his manner and appearance. And this reassured her. He was no longer the formidable personage that she remembered, but a kindly gentle priest.

When he drank his tea and rose to go, Kuniang said something polite about hoping that we should all meet again. He answered simply:

'Yes. We will meet again soon, all of us.'

He spoke, not as if expressing a hope, but as if asserting a fact that admitted of no doubt. Yet what could bring us together? Unless he meant only that I would have to return his call!

Kuniang and I escorted him through the courtyards, on his way out to his carriage. Or at least we started to do so. But when we passed in front of the children's pavilion, we heard the most appalling row going on inside. Little Chink's and his sister's voices were raised in a roar, like that of a cageful of lions. Kuniang sprang up the steps and opened the outer door.

The children had expected their mother to stay and put them to bed. When I came and took her away to see our visitor, trouble had ensued. And the amah was incapable of quelling it.

Instead of continuing on his way to the outer door with me, the Abbot followed Kuniang up the steps and into the nursery. And his sudden appearance there had more effect in stopping the noise than the return of Kuniang herself. He stood, smiling down at the children from his great height. And their eyes grew round with wonder.

The amah started to explain with the characteristic volubility of her kind. But though he may have taken in what she said, the Abbot paid no attention. With an unexpectedly supple movement he subsided on to the floor and squatted there cross-legged between the two little straw-bottomed chairs on which Little Chink and the Hsiao Kuniang sat at their supper-table. In this way, the Abbot's head and the heads of the two children were at the same level.

And then, without any preamble, speaking Chinese slowly as he always did (and the children, of course, understood him perfectly), the Abbot began to tell how, when he was a little boy, little more than a baby, in Mongolia, sometimes on summer nights, his mother used to take him out of the stuffy felt hut that was their home, and lay him down to sleep in the open, on a pile of skins.

Little Chink and his sister sat with their eyes fixed on the speaker's face, fascinated no less by what he said than by the slow and almost sleepy cadence of his voice. There was something hypnotic about the Abbot. As he spoke, it seemed to me that our little nursery faded away. In its place he conjured up a vision of the quiet-coloured end of a Gobi eve: grassy Steppes interspersed with stretches of wind-blown sand. There, as the sun sank under the horizon, the eye lost all sense of distance, so that far-off ridges appeared to be mountain ranges at the edge of the world. A group of felt huts near a well, with a trough for ponies to drink out of; threads of blue smoke rising from camp-fires round which the herdsmen gathered. A few dogs, big, black and fierce. Some ponies tethered and others wandering free on the edge of the grass. As twilight fell, all the colours melted into a soft quiet grey. A mother with a Mongol headdress, silver and coral and turquoise, emerged from a hut carrying some skins which she piled up on the sand. Then she fetched her baby and laid him on the improvised couch, while she sat beside him and crooned the weird, haunting lullabies of the Steppes. For a while the little prince lay there awake, and smiled and chortled. As the stars came out, he reached up with tiny groping hands, to catch the Great Bear . . .

What an opening for the life-story of an Asiatic chieftain! Nightfall in the wilderness: a Tartar cradle canopied by the sky. And all the stars in heaven caught among the dimples of a baby's smile.

2   The Eight Trigrams

'. . . Time is an analytical device, which effects the
sharpest possible distinction between subject and
object.'

J.W. DUNNE:
The Serial Universe

When I went to the Lama Temple, to return the
Abbot's call, I found him in one of the outer courts,
bargaining with a fat and argumentative little mer-
chant from Men-to-kou over the price of coloured tiles,
such as are used in North China for covering the roofs
of temples and of palaces. In the days of the empire, all
the majolica tiles for the imperial household were baked
in the village of San-chia-tien, halfway up the Men-to-
kou valley, possibly because there are coal-mines close
by and fuel is cheap. Nowadays, the demand for such
ornamental tiles has fallen off. The hospital built by the
Rockefeller Foundation, north of the Legation Quarter,
and the new University buildings, near the Summer
Palace, were the last to order green and yellow tiles for
their sloping roofs.

For the Abbot's benefit, samples of tiles, in different
colours and shapes, were spread out on the stone flags
in the courtyard of the two bronze lions. The beauty of
their glaze and of their workmanship was being pointed
out by the manager of the Liu-li-chü kilns, who had
come up to Peking expressly for this purpose. I wondered why the Abbot could be wanting so many tiles (he
was ordering them by the hundred thousand!). But,

though he politely asked my opinion as to the colours chosen, he gave me no hint as to the kind of building for which they were destined. Not that such a consideration has much importance in China. Temples, tombs, palaces and gates are all roofed over in similar fashion: the only difference being in the matter of certain colours that not everyone is privileged to use. Also, the imprint of the dragon on terminal tiles and on the supports of the gutters, was once reserved for the imperial palaces. But since China has become a republic, even these restrictions have disappeared.

When we had finished inspecting the tiles, the Abbot and I strolled through the courtyards and looked in at various pavilions. The Lama Temple still represents an exotic Mongol element in the ancient Chinese capital. It is the centre of a religion that changed the history of the world. For it was the advent and the influence of Buddhism, with its numerous monasteries and its celibate Lamas, that checked the increase of population in the northern Asiatic plateaux and put an end to the sporadic irruptions of Mongol hordes westward into Europe itself. Ignorant demon-worshippers as many of the Lamas have now become, they have still a pride of race that makes them look down on the more effete Chinese. And northern chieftains still find a home from home in this, the principal sanctuary of the Tartar City.

It was in the Lama Temple that I had first met the Abbot, nine years before. And then I had predicted that some day he might rule over it, as representative of the Dalai Lama himself. In this I had been wrong. The Abbot was not qualified to impersonate the Living Buddha in China, because he had never had smallpox. Since a Dalai Lama died in Peking of smallpox, during the reign of Ch'ien Lung, only those monks whose faces are marked by a pustular eruption can assume the ecclesiastical succession. Although it is considered fortunate, in China, to have had the 'flower disease', I am inclined to think that the Abbot was to be congratulated on his disqualification. Especially as, in these degenerate days, the ancient glories of the Yung Ho Kung have sadly declined. No longer do imperial grants come in to swell its coffers, or tribute from the Mongolian Banner Corps. Only a few tourists pay for admittance to religious services and 'devil dances', and gape at obscene figures that represent the gods of Desire and Procreation.

A recumbent figure of a jovial, obese Buddha, in coloured clay with life-sized babies clambering over him, reminded the Abbot of the scene in my house, when he had quieted the children with a bedtime story. He asked me if they were in good health.

'Little Chink,' I answered, 'has had two teeth extracted by the American dentist in the Legation Quarter. Because he was very brave about it, his mother has presented him with a watch: a very cheap watch of Japanese make. And he is learning to tell the time by it.'

The Abbot smiled. 'Let us see,' he said, 'if we can find a present for me to send him.'

There are always plenty of things in an Eastern temple to interest a child, though some of them – such as wine-cups made from human skulls – are more like to frighten than to amuse. Though I did not say so, I half expected Little Chink to be given a conch-shell trumpet, or one of the drums that the *chelas* sound in chorus at intervals, during religious services. These drums are fixed on the edge of a stick, and have brass pellets attached to them by short strings. The pellets strike the vellum surfaces, as the stick is twirled in the hand of a *chela* and they make the most satisfactory noise! But fortunately for the peace and quiet of my home, the Abbot was not thinking of musical instruments. He led the way into what, for lack of a better term, I can only call a sacristy, and began turning over the contents of some red lacquer boxes, full of small objects of worship: rosaries, charms and talismans. All around were *objets d'art* that I myself would have given much to possess: gilded bronze figures of Buddha enthroned on the lotus fruit and backed with a flaming aureole; vases of cloisonné; silken carpets from Ninghsia in the Ordos country; Mongol and Tibetan pictures of sages and bhodisatvas, seated on coloured clouds.

The Abbot, so I noticed, moved about the Lama Temple with a proprietary air, as if all it contained belonged to him, to dispose of as he wished. And the priests that we met in the courts and halls of worship, stood by in deferential attitudes. Some of them were not unlike the sacred images on the altars. Their shaven heads shone like polished bronze. Their vestments, flaming orange and brick-red, blended with the backgrounds of gold and rust-coloured lacquer: sunset tints that Veronese or Turner might have put on to canvas.

The Abbot took some time to find what he wanted, and finally handed me a small circular disc of dark-brown jade, almost black with age. It had the most beautiful patina I had ever seen, smooth, cool and translucent. The disc was adorned with the ancient Chinese symbol of the Pa Kua, the talisman supposed to have been invented by Wên, father of the first Chou King, in the age of bronze. Eight trigrams stood out in bold relief and were surrounded by a deep-cut line. At the back of the disc were some Mongol characters (I think they were Mongol: certainly they were not Chinese), long-shaped, like chords of semiquavers in a Western music-score. Except that the disc itself was quaint and shiny, I could not imagine anything less suitable as a present for a child.

But the Abbot explained:

'Some day,' he said, 'when your little boy grows up, he may learn to use this also as a kind of watch. And he may find it useful, if he has toothache, or is otherwise in pain.'

'I have heard that the Eight Trigrams have protective virtues. But how can they take the place of a watch? You cannot tell the time by them.'

'Not the time of the day. But, if the broken lines represent the Past, and the unbroken ones the Future, there you have all Time.'

34

I stared at the disc that I held in my hand, and wondered if the Abbot was speaking seriously, or indulging in some peculiar oriental form of humour.

'There is no middle point,' I objected, 'between the broken and the unbroken lines. Does that mean that there is no Present?'

'Time is all one: Past, Present and Future. It is held within one little circle.'

He traced, with his forefinger, the line that ran around the trigrams. What he meant, I suppose, was that the outer circle represented a cycle in the years.

'And what do these characters mean, at the back?' I asked.

'The shadow of a swiftly flying bird has never moved.'

There is often something deceitful in oriental philosophy: a false simplicity that pretends to be artless and naïve. And their epigrams are like strings of uncut jewels. The paradox of the bird's shadow served to illustrate the oriental conception of the unity of Time.

When you live in the Far East, you are apt to meet this theory in the most unexpected places, and generally mixed up with the theory of metempsychosis. Some of us accept it and find in it the explanation of such things as ghost-stories, and thought-transference and dreams of events that afterwards come true. For my own part, I am content to leave such problems unsolved. *Nescimus, nesciemus* . . . But I enjoy playing with the idea and mentally toying with examples, such as you find in the *Pin Hoa Pao-kien*: a touching story of a gentleman who used to go and make sacrifices at his own tomb – that being, of course, the tomb of his own body in a previous existence.

In one of his various lives, the gentleman in question killed a stag and, not being able to take it home at once, buried it under a certain tree. In another life, he dreamed that he had killed a stag and again had buried it under a certain tree (which happened to be the same tree). And he got up and went to the place. Sure enough, there was a stag, fresh as if it had just been killed. But when the gentleman who had really killed the stag, went back to look for it, he could not find it, and decided that it must all have been a dream (you will find a similar story also – unless I am mistaken – in the Northern Sagas). More than a hundred years separated the huntsman from the dreamer. But the stag was freshly killed, because the two lives co-existed in Time, though separated in the generations. This sort of story is nothing more than a maze: a confusing network of thoughts and ideas, like paths and passages so arranged as to make egress difficult.

I put the little jade disc that the Abbot had given me into my pocket, wondering how many pockets and wallets it had passed through before reaching me, and if other former and future owners were doing likewise at that same moment. And I expressed a suitable gratitude for so fine a present to my offspring.

A few minutes later I took my leave, parting from the Abbot in the central pavilion. Some of the Lama priests accompanied me as far as the outer gates. They accepted as a matter of course the few coins that I distributed among them, but my acquaintance with the Abbot saved me from being pestered for more. In former days it was easier for a foreigner to enter than to leave the Lama Temple. Though it is no labyrinth, he had to buy his way out.

When I got home, I told Little Chink that his friend of the other night had sent him a present. And I handed him the jade disc. He promptly tried to bite a piece off, and was obviously disappointed to find that it was not made of toffee.

3 Igor

Les Archers d'Emèse: 'La fleur de ta veine est
plus belle que l'anémone d'Adonis.'

D'ANNUNZIO:
Le Martyre de Saint Sebastien

If I had read no newspapers and had not gone occasionally to the Peking Club in the Legation Quarter, to hear
the latest gossip, I might almost have imagined that
China, in 1928, was the same as when I first came to
her, nearly thirty years before. The north wind still
carried black and yellow sand from the Gobi desert and
spread it over my furniture. The south winds brought
summer rains and the smell of Chinese cooking from
restaurants on the other side of the Tartar Wall. Itiner-
ant vendors still made the hutungs melodious with
their cries, while offering dumplings boiled in soup (and
cooked in a portable stove that they carried on a pole
across their shoulders), or smoked fish, face powder,
matches, melon and persimmons.

Passing years and changing conditions reduced the
numbers of our foreign neighbours. The Russian family
down the street, whose household Kuniang used to frequent when she was in her teens, had mellowed with
advancing age. The parents, Patushka and Matushka,
were getting white-haired and venerable. The daughter, Natasha, had married and gone away to Harbin.
Only Fédor, the son and heir, remained an intimate of
my family. He had broadened out and become a huge,
powerful-looking man, like his father before him. He

was beginning to get well-known as a painter, and many smart ladies from the Legation Quarter called themselves his pupils, having taken lessons from him in his father's house. Sometimes I wondered if it were only the love of art that took them there.

Then there was the Russian boy, Igor, who, like Kuniang, had frequented the Russian family before he grew up. Later on, he transferred his allegiance to us. I saw very little of him before I married Kuniang and hardly realized that he was there at all. This was because he was shy of me and kept out of my way. It was only after Kuniang gave me her diaries to read that I discovered how much Igor had been part of her youthful experiences. She used to say that he was 'wanting' and compared him to Parsifal, because of a sort of spiritual vagueness, combined with extraordinary physical good looks. Igor's intelligence developed slowly, but he was not stupid. He had a placid disposition and rarely showed resentment or displeasure.

It is not unusual for recently wedded young women, proud of their new estate, to assume a matronly and even motherly attitude towards the boys with whom they used to associate as girls. So I was not surprised when, after she had married me, Kuniang became motherly towards Igor. Indeed, I approved, for Igor, poor boy, needed someone to take thought for his welfare, as Matushka had done in the past. He had no legitimate parents. His mother – so I was told – kept a modest store in what had been the Russian Concession in Tientsin. And when her son was almost grown-up she had married a Chinese. Igor's mother provided him with clothes from her store and allowed him a little money. She would have kept him with her at Tientsin, but he preferred to lead a hand-to-mouth existence under the protection of Patushka's peculiar *ménage* in Peking. To the credit of the Russian family be it said that they were as kind to him as they knew how, and never denied him a meal and a bed.

Igor liked company, especially the company of

people who did not expect him to make any effort at conversation. He soon got into the habit of spending several hours every day at our house, generally playing with Little Chink, who ordered him about despotically. Sometimes he came and sat in my study while I worked. Though I took little notice of him he would remain there quite content, turning over the pages of an illustrated book, or looking at a photograph album. He gave me no trouble, and I rather liked having him there; he was so good to look at!

Kuniang's Peke, Hwang Feng, better known as Uncle Podger, was still with us in those days, and he used to get Igor to lift him into the armchair. Podger could no longer jump up by himself, and he resented having to lie in his basket, thinking, I suppose, that he lost face by accepting the accommodation suitable to other dogs. Uncle Podger always considered that he was born to the purple.

Sometimes, turning round in my chair, I would see Igor lying on the sofa, sound asleep, and I would leave my work to go and look at him, marvelling at a youthful loveliness that had something eerie in it.

One morning, Kuniang came into the room and found me standing by the sofa and staring down at Igor, as he slumbered there, a book still open in his hand. Later on in the day I talked to her about him.

'What surprises me,' I said, 'is that you never fell in love with that boy, when you were together in the Russian family. It must have been difficult to resist the fascination of so much beauty.'

'I did the next best thing. I let him make love to me, especially after Fédor had found someone else to attract him. And I was fond of Igor and did my best to make him happy and to protect him. I think I would have fallen in love with him, if he had been well and strong. But he was delicate, and I felt that what he really needed was a nurse. It is true that it was pleasant looking after him. Beauty in distress!'

'What was the matter with him?'

'There were moments when he saw things, or imagined that he saw things that were invisible to the rest of us. A sort of second sight. When this happened, he was tired and sleepy afterwards.'

'Did it happen often?'

'It used to happen very often. But now his trances, or whatever you might call them, come to him very seldom. I suppose he is getting stronger and more normal.'

'Can you tell me something of what he sees?'

'It is always connected, in some way, with death.'

'He must be what the Scots call *fey*. Why have you never told me of this before?'

'We all had a sort of feeling, I think, that it was kinder not to say anything about poor Igor and his visions. And when he talked about them himself, we used to change the subject. Both Patushka and Matushka were nervous. I think they were superstitious about it in some way. They would fly into a rage if anyone mentioned Igor's trances, or encouraged him to describe what he had seen.'

'It is odd that they should have let him come so much to their house, if they felt like that about it.'

'They were really fond of Igor, and sorry for him. We all were.'

'And was nothing done to try and cure him?'

'Yes. Patushka called in Doctor Folitzky from the German hospital. You remember him: a queer little man and a great talker. The same who, a year later, disappeared from Peking and died on the Hill of Seven Splendours. Some people thought that he was not quite right in his head. But in spite of that, or because of it, he seemed to understand all about Igor without our having to explain.'

'And what did he say?'

'He used a lot of long words, and told us that Igor was suffering from introspective melancholia, alternating with rapturous exultation. And he added that the boy was brain-starved and love-starved, and needed to be taken out of himself. This puzzled poor Patushka very much, though I told him that it was merely the German for chicken-broth.'

'Was that what the doctor prescribed?'

'No. He said that Igor needed an object of fixation.'

'And did he get one?'

'Yes. He got me.'

'What *do* you mean?'

'Just that! The doctor had said that Igor was love-starved. So Patushka and Matushka encouraged us to be together. To flirt with me was part of Igor's cure!'

'That being the case, it was lucky you were not really in love with him. I would have got left.'

'As I said before, I could not really care for him in that way. I admired him, as one admires a beautiful statue. But, as far as I was concerned, the statue never came to life.'

'But he was in love with you?'

'Yes, poor boy. He was very much in love with me. Calf-love, I suppose you would call it, but real enough while it lasted.'

'Are you sure that it has passed?'

'No. I don't think it has. But now he sees much less of me than he did in the old schoolroom days. And I think that his heart, like his mind, is half asleep. He does not make love to me any more. And his thoughts seem always to be hovering, halfway between the real world and a dream-world of his own.'

'I wonder what he sees in that dream-world.'

'Things that happened long ago, and things that are still to come. Do you remember the evening a year ago when Uncle Podger died? I had gone over to the Russian family's house and had stopped to talk with Fédor in the old schoolroom. He had been having a drawing class there, and his pupils had gone because it was getting dark. It was also time for me to go home, so I went out and shut the door behind me. As I did so, something dropped out of my bag, which had come open. It was a key, and it fell to the ground with more

41

noise than I would have thought possible. I stooped to pick it up, but it was so dark that I could not find it at once. So I remained there, kneeling on the floor and groping about. Suddenly a voice, Igor's voice, spoke to me out of the shadows to ask: "Why are you crying, Kuniang?"

'I was startled, for I thought I was alone in the room. Had it been anyone but Igor, I might have shown some annoyance. But I answered, as gently as I could: "I am not crying, Igor. And even if I was, it is much too dark for you to see." But he insisted: "I saw a tear fall. It splashed on to your hand."

'Just then I found the key. When I had put it back in my bag, I went over to where Igor was lying back in one of the black horsehair armchairs. He looked as if he had been asleep. His shoes were on the floor beside him. I helped him to put them on again, and then I went back and told Fédor what had happened. Igor was having one of his trances again. Fédor told me not to worry. He would look after Igor. So I came home.

'Uncle Podger heard my step in the courtyard and got out of his basket to greet me. When I came in through the door, he was standing there, his ears cocked and his head on one side, while his tail moved gently. He ran forward, but even as he did so, he collapsed, a pathetic little heap on the carpet. I went down on my knees beside him, and you stood by. Poor old Podger had died of heart failure. As I knelt there, stroking him for the last time, I felt a big tear fall and splash on the back of my hand. And I remembered what Igor had said.'

4   *Turgenev's Heroine*

... who knows not Circe,
The daughter of the Sun ...?

MILTON:
Comus

In all the years he has been in my service, Exalted
Virtue has never learnt to look after the inkstands. I
suppose this is because the Chinese do not consider ink
as a liquid but as a solid substance, to be watered down
as required. When, as happens after a dust storm, the
contents of my inkstand lose all fluidity and become a
mere ropy sludge, he adds a little water and considers
that there is no more to be done. So now I look after the
inkstand myself. One morning I was busy cleaning it
out and refilling it, when I heard voices outside, and
glancing through the open window, I saw the two Russian boys in the garden with Kuniang. Fédor was
arguing and gesticulating, and Igor standing by with
an expression of pleased expectancy. After a few minutes, Kuniang came running across the lawn and leant
in at the open window. The breeze from outside moved
the little tendrils of her hair. Her eyes glowed with
excitement.

'Do you know what Fédor tells me?' she said.
'Elisalex is coming to Peking!'

'Good Lord!'

'She may be here in ten days' time. Do you think we
might ask her to stay with us?'

'Kuniang,' I answered, in a cowardly attempt to gain

43

time, 'when will you learn to take things quietly? You behave like the rampageous flapper that you were when Elisalex stayed in Peking years ago. Please remember that you're grown-up and married, with children of your own and a rapidly ageing husband.'

'All the more reason for having Elisalex to stay with us. I can't afford to have you grow old before your time, as you certainly will if you sit in your study all day with musty Chinese classics. Elisalex is a beautiful woman. Give her a chance, and she will make you feel younger in no time.'

'I have one beautiful woman in the house already. As the song has it: "With no other Goddess will I face the dawn"!'

'But you never *do* face the dawn, with me or anybody else! You go to bed at half-past ten. Elisalex would make you sit up a bit, and do you a world of good!'

'And leave me a broken-down wreck when she goes. By the way, where is she now?'

'On the French boat, the *Sphinx*, somewhere between Hong Kong and Shanghai.'

'If she is coming to Peking, why does she not stay with the Russian family, as she did when she was here last?'

'I think that is what she meant to do. But there is no-one in their house but Fédor. His father and mother have gone to Mukden to see Natasha, who is expecting a baby sometime this month.'

I kept on asking questions, seeking some loophole of escape.

'How does Fédor know she is arriving? Has she written to him?'

'She wrote to his parents and her letter was forwarded to them unopened. Now they have sent a telegram to Fédor, giving her address: Astor House, Shanghai. The telegram says that Elisalex will be passing through Peking, and may stop for ten days or a fortnight.'

'Passing through to where?'

'It does not say.'

Kuniang spoke almost breathlessly. To her, the

coming of Elisalex seemed too wonderful for words.

'What does Fédor think about it?' I asked.

'He wants her to stay in the house with him.'

'Naturally. And what do you think she herself would prefer?'

'I don't know. But I would love to have her here. I could show her what a delightful home I've got, and what wonderful children, and what an adorable husband.'

'I suppose that settles it. But what about the Five Virtues? They were sworn enemies of Elisalex in days gone by?'

'That was long ago. Besides, we can quell the Five Virtues, between us.'

'Can we? I am not so sure. But have it your own way.'

Such a grudging assent may seem ungracious, but Kuniang literally jumped for joy. She started to climb through the window, to hug me, but thought better of it and blew me a kiss before running off again to Fédor and Igor. She had got the better of Fédor.

A little later, she reappeared to say that she was going to the telegraph office herself to send off a wire. She took no notice of my suggestion to leave it to the *tingchai*. I shook my head in simulated disapproval of so much zeal, and watched her as she went off, one arm through Fédor's on one side, and one through Igor's on the other. They were like a group of happy children. Kuniang's feet danced rather than walked.

I returned to the task of cleaning and refilling the inkstand. But my thoughts were elsewhere. I kept on asking myself: Is she right? Am I in danger of growing old before my time?

There were fifteen years between us, but I had never felt any disparity of age. Nor – I am sure – had she. I liked to sit among my books and to catch glimpses of her through the window, in the sunlight. When she came in to tell me some piece of household gossip, it always seemed as if she carried the sunshine with her.

One of my hobbies is Chinese calligraphy. Not that I

presume to practise it myself. But I love studying its technique and all its various forms that vary so much throughout the ages, yet are still fundamentally the same as they were a thousand years before the birth of Christ. The Chinese will tell you that calligraphy is an old-man's passion, and that the most famous calligraphers only reached the zenith of their powers at a venerable age. I suppose that is why I cannot get Kuniang to take much interest in my stone rubbings.

The other day I showed her the original text of a report from the Viceroy of Nanking to the Emperor Ch'ien Lung. It was written on yellow paper, backed with flowered yellow silk. The characters were most minute, and the Emperor himself had marked his approval by writing the character *Nan* (peace) on the report, with his own Vermilion Pencil. Kuniang stared at it and remarked: 'I wonder how the Chinese can make those tiny characters, with the rotten eyesight most of them have!' And then she added: 'Don't *you* ruin your precious eyesight with all that nonsense. Come and talk to me while I have my bath.'

A report from the Viceroy of Nanking to the Emperor Ch'ien Lung *nonsense*! But it is true that Kuniang in her bath is less trying to the eyes.

When the answer to her telegram arrived, accepting our invitation, Kuniang was overjoyed, though why she should have thought a refusal likely, or even possible, I cannot say.

To tell the truth, I also felt a thrill of excitement. It was no ordinary guest that was coming to stay with us, but a direct descendant of the lady who, under the name of Irina, is described in Turgenev's *Smoke*. The character of Irina in Turgenev's romance was taken from one of two sisters of the Dolgorouki family. They were successively the mistresses of the Tsar Alexander. He married Katia, the younger one, morganatically, after his Empress died. Our friend, Elisalex, was the granddaughter of the elder sister and of the Tsar.

The following paragraphs are from the Preface (signed Edward Garnett, January 1896) to the English translation of *Smoke*:

But Irina – Irina is unique; for Turgenev has in her perfected her type till she reaches a destroying witchery of fascination and subtlety. Irina will stand for ever in the long gallery of great creations, smiling with that enigmatic smile which took from Litvinov in a glance half his life, and his love for Tatyana. The special triumph of her creation is that she combines that exact balance between good and evil which makes good women seem insipid beside her and bad women unnatural. And, by nature irresistible, she is made doubly so to the imagination by the situation which she recreates between Litvinov and herself. She ardently desires to become nobler, to possess all that the ideal of love means for the heart of woman; but she has only the power given to her of enervating the man she loves. Can she become a Tatyana to him? No, to no man. She is born to corrupt, yet never to be corrupted. She rises mistress of herself after the first measure of fatal delight. And, never giving her whole heart absolutely to her lover, she, nevertheless, remains ever to be desired.

Further, her wit, her scorn, her beauty preserve her from all the influences of evil she does not deliberately employ. Such a woman is as old and as rare a type as Helen of Troy. It is most often found among the great mistresses of princes, and it was from a mistress of Alexander II that Turgenev modelled Irina.

Strange how the same type reappears in successive generations, and how attractive it always is! Like her ancestress, the new Irina, that is to say Elisalex, was a woman who claimed the love of men as her right. If only by right of conquest.

5   Guests at the Shuang Liè Ssè

'Quo me cumque rapit tempestas, deferor hospes'
(Wherever the storm takes me I go as a guest)

HORACE:
Epistles

It never rains but it pours.

When the steamer *Sphinx* arrived at Shanghai we heard that another friend was on board, an American, name: Donald Parramoor; profession: painter and designer of scenery and of costume for the theatre – a pupil of Bakst. He had travelled out with Elisalex and wrote to me, saying that he would be coming on to Peking. He begged me to reserve a room for him at the Hotel des Wagons Lits. I telegraphed back, asking him also to stay with us. He would act as ballast, so to speak, and as a counterweight to Elisalex.

We had no inkling as to why the latter should be 'passing through'. Nor could I understand why Donald should be with her, except that he had known her in Paris and doubtless had fallen under the spell.

When the day of their arrival came round, I decided not to meet our guests at the station, but to let Kuniang go, escorted by Fédor and Igor. And I told her on no account to ask the two Russian boys to dinner. I wished to have our guests to ourselves on that first evening.

All day, Kuniang had been in such a state of excitement and suspense that Little Chink and his sister might have fallen into the garden pond, and she would hardly have found time to pull them out. After she had started to the station, I went into the guest rooms, to see if all was well. This is a necessary precaution to take at the last minute in a Chinese household, when you are expecting guests. On this occasion my vigilance was justified by finding that the Boys had put some of the flowers that had been left over from the more ornamental vases into a white enamel receptacle that the French qualify with the words *de nuit*. I was not surprised that the flower vases had given out. There were fresh blooms even in the bathroom that Fédor had decorated (one time when he and his sister were staying in our house) with frescoes representing Susannah and the Elders, and Leda and the Swan. This was to be Elisalex's bathroom. I wondered what she would think of the mural decoration. The recumbent figure of Leda was especially suggestive. . . .

The unaccustomed bustle and preparations had roused me, no less than my household, from our ordinary routine. I sensed that the coming of Elisalex portended something in my life; something in all our lives. And I sighed, for I welcomed no portents and no drama within my house. Elisalex was a charming woman, but not a restful companion. I had no wish to be drawn into the vortex . . .

It had been a fine warm day. The air was still, and though as yet we had had no rain (nor could we expect any for a month, or more, to come) the moisture that rose to the earth's surface after the winter frosts were over encouraged the flowering shrubs to blossom. The yellow briar was out in the garden, and the lilac had swollen buds. Spring was in the air.

There was a smell of incense in the outer courtyards. The Five Virtues had been celebrating some private anniversary at their family altar in the back premises. Golden shafts of light fell from the pavilion windows on to the stone flags of the paths. In the nursery, the children chattered over their supper, before the amah put them to bed. I opened the door for a moment and peeped in. Little Chink was too absorbed to look up, and his sister had her back towards me. The light from the lamp above shone on her golden curls. She had been fortunate to inherit them from the elder 'Kuniang'.

An indignant: *'Poo yow niu ni!'* in a childish treble, showed that there was some disagreement about the bread and milk. I was careful not to interfere, but to let my daughter and the amah fight it out between them. The door closed gently behind me.

Exalted Virtue and a following of kitchen coolies were passing to and from the dining room and the kitchen, bringing flowers and dishes of fruit for the table. Out in the street, someone was beating a gong. A not unmusical cry of *ying mien poa poa* indicated a street vendor, hawking the hard Shantung biscuits that, for some reason unexplained, are only sold at night.

The Chinese divide the passing years into cycles, in which events repeat themselves throughout the ages. As I paced the courtyards and looked in at the various pavilions I had a feeling that it was all scenery in a theatre between performances. Time itself was suspended, as it might be for a brief moment when a cycle in our lives closes and another is about to begin.

It came over me suddenly how fond I had grown of the Shuang Liè Ssè. How much quiet happiness I had found in the old temple under the Tartar Wall! Could I ever tear myself away? Habit and memories had made it dear to me. And it had given me Kuniang. For it was the house and its garden that had attracted her, when she first passed over the threshold in search of her kitten, more than twenty years ago.

I walked round the garden and was coming back towards the house, when a ghost-like figure in a light-coloured dust coat came towards me along the path, and a whiff of perfume reached me that was not the scent of the yellow briar. I exclaimed in astonishment: 'Elisalex!'

And I added: 'How did you get here so soon? It is

only a quarter of an hour since Kuniang started to meet you at the station.'

'We must have missed one another. She probably went in at the main entrance, whereas I came out at the Water Gate.'

'But the train was due at half-past seven, and' – looking at my watch – 'it is only half-past seven now!'

'There was an important Chinese general on the train, and he was in a hurry to reach Peking. We bustled along at quite a dangerous speed, considering the state of the line. And we got here before our time.'

'Well, I'm glad to see you, anyway.'

'It is nice of you to say that, and to ask me to stay. You were so suspicious of me in the old days.'

There was some truth in this. So I asked hurriedly:

'But where is Donald Parramoor? Is he not with you?'

'Yes. He's here. But your Number One Boy took him off to his room. I preferred to stroll about. It is so nice to find myself once more in a Chinese house. Peking and Paris are the only places where I ever want to live.'

'Rue de la Paix with its jewels, and the Liu-li-chang with its jade.'

'I am tired of *le Boeuf sur le Toit*. When will you take me to a Chinese restaurant? I long to go back to that eating-house outside the Ch'ien Men, where they make turtle soup.'

'When you like. Tomorrow, if convenient . . .'

I could hardly have said anything different, whether I meant it or not. But it struck me suddenly that I *did* mean it. It would be amusing to dine out somewhere with Elisalex. Damn the woman! She had hardly crossed my threshold before it came back to me how alluring she was!

I heard the sound of voices under the arch by the entrance. Kuniang and her party were back from the station. I left Elisalex to them, and went off to look for Donald. I found him unpacking his suitcase. After our

51

first greetings were over, I asked him: 'What sort of a journey did you have? The *Sphinx* is a nice boat, I believe.'

'It is. But the cooking did not agree with me. Not after Aden. We came in for something that was not a monsoon, but worse. I threw up everything except my profession.'

'Do you still design costumes for the theatre?'

'Sure. And when I heard that Elisalex was starting for China, I decided I would travel out to the States by the eastern route. I want to get some new ideas – I mean new to me – of Chinese robes under the various dynasties. In these last years, most of the inspiration for *les Arts Décoratifs* has reached us through Russia out of Asia. I thought I would come to the original source and refresh my memories of oriental colouring. Say! Is Mei-lan-fan acting here now?'

'I don't know. The last I heard of him, he was in America. But there are other actors in Peking. Mei is only one of the Wu Chao Teng, the Five Incomparables.'

'And who are the others?'

'Oh! There is Kung Yun-fu, singer in the roles of old women, and Yang Hsian-lou, who portrays generals and military heroes. We might go to the Kin Ming theatre some night. One or other of them is sure to be acting. But now I'll let you have a bath and change. You can leave your unpacking to Exalted Virtue. He's quite a good valet when he's not thinking of something else. When he is, he will brush the sleeve of a jacket for ten minutes at an end, and then put away the suit with both trouser-legs spattered with mud.'

Donald paid no attention. His mind was back in the theatre again.

'I want some Chinese ideas for the scenery of *Le Rossignol* – the opera, I mean. When we gave it in 1914, the *décor* was designed by Alexandre Benois: a great artist. The third act is supposed to be the bedroom of the Emperor of China. He got some wonderful effects of golden lights against a background of dark blue. But the lights, curiously enough, were very like those round the tomb of St Peter in Rome, the bronze lamps around the balustrade, in front of the Baldacchino. If we revive *Le Rossignol*, I would like something more characteristically Chinese.'

I said I would do my best. *Le décor* of the ballet has always fascinated me, even the old-fashioned ballet as described by Halèvy in *La Famille Cardinal* when pretty ballerinas would shed red flannel petticoats to dance in *Don Juan*, like butterflies emerging from a chrysalis.

When I left him to go and dress for dinner, Donald came to the door of his pavilion and stood on the topmost of the three steps that led down into the courtyard. He sniffed the evening air, as if its odours pleased him. Smells from the Chinese town mingled with the incense from the Five Virtues' family altar. Suddenly, Donald clasped my arm and exclaimed:

'Who is that?'

I looked round to see what had attracted his attention. It was Igor, standing under the low eaves of the sloping roof near the *k'ai-men-ti*'s lodge. The strong light from a hanging-lamp shone on his head and shoulders, and threw them into an almost uncanny relief against the background of deep shadows. Igor was on his way out, and had stopped to look back regretfully (I remembered my instructions to Kuniang not to ask the two Russian boys to dinner). There was something wistful in his expression, and this added poignancy to his astonishing good looks. He stood there only for a moment. Then turned and disappeared into the darkness outside.

I explained to Donald who he was.

6 Donald and the Theatre

'Uratur vestis amore tuae'
(Let him be consumed by the love of your dress)

OVID:
Ars amatoria

Even in the old days, when she emerged out of Russia
in revolution, Elisalex impressed me as being the best-
dressed woman I had ever met. Now that she came
straight from Paris, her clothes were a joy for ever.
That first evening she wore a gown of wine-coloured
chiffon, low-necked but hardly *décolleté*, and so plain
as to be austere in its simplicity. It fell into quiet lines
like ripples of water and, as with water, every movement produced new lines of beauty. The dark material
absorbed all light, and against it the white of her bare
arms and neck glowed like Parian marble. Her only
ornament was a massive Byzantine ring.

Kuniang had chosen to dress like a Chinese, all
except her hair. The broad shoulders of her short
jacket, with its ample sleeves, and the still lines of her
well-ironed trousers contrasted with the sinuous grace
of Elisalex's floating draperies. But the glowing satin
of the Chinese robe was overlaid with exquisite embroidery. The rich folds revealed no line, no curve, of the
youthful figure that they clothed. Her rose-coloured
shoes, jewelled even on the soles, refused to follow the
lines of Kuniang's slender feet.

Donald, an expert in costume, looked at the two
women and smiled delightedly. He was sitting opposite

54

to me and I had the opportunity to observe him, as I had not been able to do in the few minutes before dinner. He still wore the heavy tortoiseshell glasses that in the past had made me compare him to an old Chinese scholar. His face was thinner than of yore and his manner less buoyant. Life in Paris had mellowed him.

As he finished his soup, he looked round and smiled.

'Did you ever hear,' he asked me, 'how I first met Kuniang?'

'You were shopping – were you not? – in the Tartar City?'

'Yes. We had no sooner got to Peking, when both my sisters declared they had nothing left to wear, and they must have some Chinese silk to make up into summer frocks. Someone advised us to go to the Clock Store, though why it's called that I have no idea.'

'Because there's a clock over the entrance.'

'Is there? I never noticed. It was the inside of the store that interested me. I was so struck with it that I immediately started to make a sketch, with the idea that it would make a lovely background for a Chinese play: the shelves mounting up into the skylight, like a Jacob's ladder made of rolls of silk. Blue-robed boys climbing up on real ladders, to hand down the wares; little women with the winged Manchu headdresses bending over the multi-coloured silks upon the counters, so that they looked like butterflies along a herbaceous border. I felt I wanted to set it all to music.'

'It would need some sort of a story,' I suggested.

'Of course. Cannot you imagine the store closing at night; the assistants gone home, and all the lights out? And then, at midnight, coming to life again, when the fairy of silkworms waves a silver wand, and all the other fairies come out to dance? There would be the fairy of satin, and the fairy of brocade, and the fairy of silk velvet. Little dwarfs, with round bodies like cocoons, would hold up the train of the fairy of cloth of gold.'

'I don't see where Kuniang comes in,' I said.

'She saved us from the fury of the populace. You see, I had got so excited that I climbed up on to a table and sat on some bundles, sketching. This caused a commotion, as nobody understood what I was doing, and we couldn't explain. Then a lovely girl with golden hair – she might have been our own good fairy – came to the rescue. She talked Chinese to the storekeepers and soon had them all smiling, though what she said to them I have no idea.'

'I explained,' said Kuniang, 'that you were poor, ignorant foreigners from a country where they had no silk and went about dressed in goat-skins.'

'Anyhow, we were so grateful that the girls persuaded Kuniang to come back with us to the hotel for tea.'

'Before that,' said Kuniang, 'they bought up half the shop. And the proprietor gave me a dress-length of blue Shantung, as "squeeze".'

Elisalex listened to this story with a smile of amusement. Then she said:

'My own arrival in Peking was also peculiar. Do you remember, Kuniang, how I was received in the Russian family's house?'

'I only remember that everybody's nerves were in a frazzle for days before you came. The whole house had to be cleaned and furbished up. But they were not very practical about it. It only occurred to them at the last minute that you might like to have a bedroom to yourself. Fédor had been using the guest room as a studio. When they told him to clear his things out, he shoved his canvases into the cupboard, leaving you no room to put your dresses. Matushka flew into dreadful rages with the servants, who had been given the money to buy new cotton clothes and did not have them ready in time. Even Patushka was not safe to approach. But at the actual moment of your arrival, all was peace and amity as far as I know.'

'True, they were all smiles. But, nevertheless, my welcome was a little unusual. After the first greetings

56

were over, they got up a heated argument about the tempo of some music-score, and no one thought of showing me my room. So I went upstairs to explore. On opening a door, I saw my luggage all piled up in a sort of pyramid, and I went in. My dressing case was half buried under the other things and I had some difficulty in getting it out. While I was struggling to lift a heavy suitcase, I was startled to hear a voice close behind me saying:

' "Can I be of any help?"

'I looked round and saw a lovely pink and white boy, sitting up in bed and smiling at me. I had not noticed him when I first entered, because there was a screen between the door and the bed and it was getting dark. It occurred to me that the coolie must have put my luggage in the wrong room. But before I could say anything, the boy jumped out of bed and began to rearrange my boxes for me. He seemed quite unconscious of the fact that he was stark naked.'

Kuniang laughed: 'That, of course, was Igor.'

'Yes. He explained that he had undressed, expecting to act as a model for Fédor. After waiting a bit, he felt cold and got into bed, where he fell asleep. I suggested that he might put on his clothes again, and he did so, while I tried to make some room in the cupboards. They were full of studies in oils or in *sanguigno*. Most of them represented Igor, just as I had found him. Others were of a pretty fair-haired girl, in the same costume. Igor explained that it was a friend of the family. And that was the first I heard of you, Kuniang.'

Donald asked an unexpected question: 'Do you think that Igor could act or dance?'

He spoke to me, but I left it to Kuniang to answer. She thought the matter over and said:

'I wonder . . . Possibly he could be taught. He is an excellent mimic, and can imitate the Chinese actors with their queer somersaults and falsetto voices. Curiously enough, Igor is at his best when he is not himself: I mean, when he is posing for his portrait, or playing games of make-believe with Little Chink. Then he brightens up and is no longer nebulous. But I don't think any of us ever thought of his going on the stage.'

'I know a part that would suit him down to the ground. Especially if his figure is as beautiful as his face.'

'You would not put him on the stage with nothing on, surely?'

'It is not he who would mind, apparently. But I suppose we would have to consider the censor. I was thinking of him as Saint Sebastian. In the last act, when he is tied to a tree, he has only a loin-cloth, as in the pictures by old masters.'

Elisalex intervened: 'As you do not live in Paris,' she said, 'you may not realize that Donald is talking of d'Annunzio's mystery play, *Le Martyre de Saint Sébastien.*'

'That's so,' said Donald. 'They are going to produce it in London, at Covent Garden, and in Milan. The part of Saint Sebastian will be taken by Ida Rubenstein, who created it when the play was first given in Paris before the war. She does it wonderfully well, for she is long and lanky. But it would be much better if we could have a man. Igor would look the part to perfection. Saint Sebastian was supposed to be a sort of Adonis.'

'From what I remember of the play,' I said, 'I am inclined to agree with you. But why are *you* so interested? Are you going to produce it in the States?'

'I might look for a producer, if we could put together a suitable cast. Igor hasn't got any younger brothers, has he? I want a pair of good-looking twins, for the boy martyrs, Marco and Marcellino, in the first act.'

I shook my head: 'No. Igor is an only son, as far as I know. Certainly he would make an ideal Saint Sebastian in a *tableau vivant*. And Kuniang, who knows him better than I do, seems to think it not impossible that he could learn to act. But you, of all people, should know that the technique of acting cannot be learnt in a month or in a year. Effects of natural-

58

ness and spontaneity are achieved only by the most experienced players, after much study and hard work!'

'Sure! Anyone on Broadway will tell you that. But remember: there are plays in which the centre of gravity is pageantry, and not action. In these plays, action is merely secondary, as it is in *Saint Sebastian*. And it is also true that some people, who could not recite a poem, will fall quite naturally into certain parts that suit them. Not long ago they put on a play in New York called *Green Pastures*. It was much less stagy than the *Saint Sebastian*. It represented a darky's idea of religion. The Scriptures put on the stage in Harlem. The cast of that play was mostly of amateurs, but they delivered the goods better than any professional. The old Negro who took the part of God was the best of the bunch and they got him by mere chance, after looking everywhere for somebody suitable. He strolled into an agent's office one day, to ask some questions about Shakespeare readings, and they pounced on him and insisted he should act in *Green Pastures*. He was just what God might have looked like, if he had been a darky. At first, the old man would not hear of it. He had never set foot on a stage in his life, and said it was too late to begin. In the end, they persuaded him, and he thoroughly enjoyed it. You should have seen him handing a cigar to "Gabe", as the Archangel Gabriel was called, or distributing dimes to the piccaninnies that hung on his coat-tails when they were not acting as cherubs in heaven. Poor old God died while the play was still running. They never found another like him.'

Kuniang turned to me. 'You know d'Annunzio's play – do you think that an amateur could act in it?'

'As far as I remember it is one of those plays that Donald mentioned just now, in which there is more pageantry than acting. And the pageantry is magnificent. It begins with a Roman hall of justice. The gouty old prefect is there to try the Christians. His swollen feet are upheld by two slaves. The boy martyrs are tied to the columns. The prefect's own son, their friend and schoolfellow, begs them to abjure their faith. Five young girls, Marco's and Marcellino's sisters, bring in the sacrificial vases and implore their brothers to sacrifice to Caesar. Behind them is the weeping mother and the turbulent, angry populace. Sebastian is looking on, standing in front of his soldiers: the archers of Emesus. He leans on a great bow and watches the scene entranced. In his agonizing sympathy for the two sweet boys, he unconsciously presses the sharp point of the bow-end into the palm of his hand, so that the red blood flows down his forearm and drips on to the marble floor.'

Kuniang exclaimed: 'Igor would be all right as far as that!'

'Certainly, as far as looks go, Donald is right. Igor is made for the part. Sebastian was so beautiful that everyone loved him: the populace, his own archers, even Diocletian, who condemned him to death. After the martyrdom, the emperor had a crown made from the leaves of the laurel to which his friend had been tied. Igor may, or may not, be able to act the principal part in a decadent play, but in that last scene all he would have to do would be to show a white torso against the dark foliage. The gorgeous Eastern archers loose their arrows, sobbing as they shoot. Then the pious women undo the ropes and gently lift the dead body, which a final miracle reveals unscathed. The wounds are bars of light, and a hundred arrows lie embedded in the trunk of the tree.'

7   Conversation Piece

'Colloquio iam tempus adest'
(Now is the time to converse)

OVID:
Ars Amatoria

After dinner, Elisalex and I went and sat near the fire in my study (the nights were cool, though the fire was lit more for ornament than for necessity), while Kuniang and Donald pored over some old photograph albums, which they laid on my writing table at the farther end of the long room. We could hear their voices and little chuckles of laughter, through the silk and camphor-wood partition that hid them from our sight, though it did not shut them off from us.

I put a cup of coffee near Elisalex and held the match while she lighted her cigarette, after which she sank back into her chair with a sigh of contentment. Then she looked at me and smiled:

'Am I wrong,' she asked, 'or is there not a question written in your face?'

I looked at her inquiringly and she continued: 'You want to know why I have come to China.'

I did not like to say that I had my own ideas on the subject. I imagined that she must have come to see Fédor. After they had parted in China, they had met again in Paris, that time when Fédor went to Europe. But to humour Elisalex, now that she was my guest, I answered dutifully: 'It is true that I have wondered.'

'The trouble is I cannot tell you.'

'No need to, if you had rather not.'

'What I meant was that I do not know myself.'

I must have looked incredulous, for she laughed and exclaimed: 'It is quite clear that you do not believe a word I say.'

'It *is* a little difficult to swallow. But I will get it down, if you give me a little help.'

'In seeking a woman's motives, do you exclude caprice?'

'Not if it means someone of the opposite sex. But few people travel half round the world, even for that.'

'I may be one of them. You know what my life was in the past: Russia under the Empire – Rasputin – Siberia, and the rest . . . Shall I tell you how I live in Paris? I have a nice flat: a *rez-de-chaussée*, near the Etoile. Quite nice, but small. My bedroom is tapestried in dove-coloured silk, and the carpet is the same colour. The bed is rococo and can be turned into a divan in the daytime, with huge dove-coloured cushions. Little electric candles are held up by clusters of bronze branches, two on each wall, and at the end of each branch there is a white enamel flower. But the lighting really comes from a standing lamp in a *cracquelé* vase, on the floor with a plain vellum lamp-shade that reaches to my elbow. There are plaques of old Wedgwood on the walls, light blue and white, and vases of the same on two old Dutch consoles. A low hardwood table that I brought from China has my breakfast tray on it in the morning, or tea in the afternoon. It is all very dainty and Parisian, but oh, so small! Even my little garden that I can step out to from my bedroom, is only a few feet square. It is enclosed by an ivy-covered railing, but on the inner side the railing is panelled with looking-glass, so as to make the garden look bigger than it is. So many people envy me my flat: especially my bathroom, which is all gold and black glass. And mine is a pleasant quarter of the town to live in. Donald says that it makes a nice walk, just the right distance from the Travellers, near the Rond Point des Champs Elysées.'

'It does not sound very far.'

'Not if you are used to distances in Asia. And that is just my trouble. It is all so small, so very small. And I am bored. Too much comfort, too much safety, and the future stretching away into the distance in little rooms tapestried with dove-coloured silk. Golf, crossword puzzles, detective stories and street lights (they are very fine, in Paris, I must admit!), and shops and restaurants and theatres, and round it all a well-kept countryside, with motor-roads that lead to lots of places, all much the same. Do you understand now why I wanted to come back to China?'

I looked at her and smiled and shook my head; 'What is his name?' I asked.

She gave an answering smile and a tiny shrug of her white shoulders.

'You are quite right. There is an old friend of mine in China. Indeed once – as you know – he was more than that.'

'I notice that you do not speak of him as your husband any more. But I suppose you mean the Abbot?'

'If you like to call him that.'

'I find it difficult to think of him as Prince Dorbon Oirad. Is he still here, at the Yellow Temple?'

'No. He is staying somewhere west of Liang Ko Chuang.'

'You mean, near the Hsi Ling – the Western Tombs?'

'Yes. It must be in that same region.'

'And what is the Abbot doing there, if one may ask?'

'That is what I have come to find out.'

'He has not told you?'

'Three months ago, he sent me a telegram of five words, besides the signature: *I have found my kingdom.* I wired to ask what he meant, but he answered only with a letter of a few lines, giving me his address. He is living in a temple called The Temple of Costly Experience.'

'That is a translation. What is the temple called in Chinese?'

'The first word, as Dorbon wrote it, was not very clear. It might be Pao-lien Ssè, or Hao-lien Ssè. You may be able to tell me which is right.'

'Not without seeing the characters. *Pao*, in this case, must mean "treasure", and *Hao* might mean "waste". Both words convey the idea of costliness.'

'What a language! But anyway, Pao-lien Ssè, or Hao-lien Ssè, must be easy to find, and that is where I want to go. It should make a pleasant change after Paris, and I would like to discover what Dorbon means by saying that he has found his kingdom. It does not seem to make sense.'

'In China, propositions that don't make sense often come nearest to the truth.'

'I wonder if that is why you refuse to believe anything I say, when what I tell you really makes sense. Now I will confide to you something that does not. I have a curious feeling about the Temple of Costly Experience. The place itself is drawing me, more than my old affection for Dorbon. And its lure is so strong that I cannot resist. Somewhere, south of the Great Wall, at the back of the Hsi Ling, is a Chinese temple with a strange, suggestive name, and something in that temple is calling me. It is my fate that I should go, though I am just a little afraid. I wish someone would come with me: you and Kuniang, for example. I am sure that Dorbon would be pleased to see you. And you always found him an interesting man.'

'Quite true. Since the militant bishops of the Middle Ages, who fished for souls, fought for power and courted pretty women, the world has not seen a man like the Abbot, who is both warrior and priest, chieftain and mystic. I never know how to think of him: as a Tartar warlord, whose home is on the Steppes, or as an Eastern scholar, seeking an ideal king and preaching the return to a golden age.'

'It was not an ideal king, but an ideal kingdom, that Dorbon went in search of.'

'Yes. I remember. What Kuniang called Kingdom

Come. Dorbon was to reign over it, and you were to have been his queen. We were all to go and stay with you, including Uncle Podger. And now the old plan comes to life again, for the Abbot has found his kingdom. It is very charming and quite crazy. I sometimes wonder if you and your friends are real people at all, and not phantoms in a surrealist's dream.'

'It is something of that old craziness that I hope to find once more, as I did when I was last in China. Are you sure that I and my friends are not the only real people left, in a timid, over-civilized world? I feel more real, more alive, among the phantoms you speak of, than among the people who live normal, orderly lives in little flats in Paris. Do you still disapprove of us, as you did of the Russian family? You were very much shocked at some of the things they did.'

'Certainly the Russian family were neither timid nor over-civilized! But I would not have disapproved, if Kuniang had not been sent to them for tuition. Their habits and customs were delightfully picturesque, but unsuited to a Western girl.'

'And you were beginning to be enamoured of the Western girl. So you took her away from them. I foresaw it would end in a love match, and I was right. Later on, having got all you wanted, you became quite friendly with the Russian family.'

'Quite true. I soon grew fond of them.'

'I have always been fond of them, despite their peculiarities. They are the most refreshing people I ever met. But you and they were bound to disagree in the matter of a finishing course for the pretty girl of seventeen who was staying in your house. Matushka once told me that Kuniang was a perfect darling, and they were all in love with her. But she was an awful handful, and much in need of discipline, such as Fédor and Natasha were accustomed to. On the other hand, *you* looked upon Kuniang as an angel in human form, bravely putting up with ill-usage, so that she might not cause anxiety to an absent father, or trouble the kind gentleman who had offered her a home. I don't suppose you would have got so agitated about it, if the shape assumed by the angel in question had not been so attractive.'

'And what was *your* idea of Kuniang, as she was in those days?'

'I remember her as a mischievous, delightful rapscallion, full of devilment and affectionate impulses. It was generally the latter that got her into trouble. I, too, felt that Matushka's young charge was a perfect darling. But I was by no means shocked when I entered the schoolroom unexpectedly and came upon Kuniang, face downwards on the music stool, receiving correction with the family birch. I could not but realize that the Russian *ménage* suited her down to the ground, in spite of, or because of, its lack of modesty and decorum. She must have felt this herself, for she did her best to keep you in ignorance of what went on, lest you should interfere, or tell her father about it.'

'You imply that she is like you, and prefers craziness to convention.'

'We need a little of both, for a change. Even if the change is only from bad to worse.'

Just then I heard a sound behind me and turned to look over my shoulder.

'Here,' I said, 'is Kuniang herself. We will hear what she has to say about it.'

8   Kuniang on Happiness

'La felicità è un modo di vedere.'

UGO OIETTI

Kuniang and Donald had finished looking at the photograph albums, and they joined us round the fire.

'What are you talking about?' asked Kuniang.

'We were discussing your lurid past. Elisalex maintains that, like every woman, you are at heart a rake.'

'That may well be. And what about it?'

'She concludes that you were quite content in the peculiar Russian *ménage*, where she first saw you.'

'When I was fourteen,' said Kuniang, 'I wanted to join a circus. Failing that, the Russian *ménage* was the next best thing.'

'The only circus I ever saw in Peking,' I objected, 'was one that came here in the summer of 1915. It had got stuck in the Far East and could not get back to Europe because of the War. It was a very poor show indeed. You can't have wanted to run away with that!'

'Yes I did. I had never seen a circus before and did not expect much. This one had set up its tents in the open space opposite the Temple of Agriculture. But it happened to be the rainy season, and the plot of land between the Temples of Agriculture and of Heaven was flooded over. The circus horses splashed so much mud around that no one could sit in the best seats: that is to say in those nearest the ring. And the audience was depressing, for the Chinese took it all as a matter of course, and never smiled and never applauded, but just sat in rows in the cheap seats, which were those that disappeared into the upper darkness. Anything more dismal it would have been difficult to imagine.'

'Yet attractive enough to make you want to join in?'

'I had made friends with a girl of my own age, who did wonderful things on the tightrope. So I went behind the scenes, which was fun. I was at school, at the convent, in those days. But there were holidays, so I passed most of my time at the circus. I even started to learn to walk on the tightrope, and so discovered that I had a wonderful head for heights. I began to get on quite nicely, when the show moved on to Tientsin.'

'And left you lamenting?'

'Yes. I had made friends with all the animals. There were two elephants in charge of an Indian. I don't think they got quite enough to eat, so I used to buy apples to give them, but they thought nothing of a barrelful. Then there were some monkeys, and a lion that must have been thirty years old. He had hardly any teeth left and was full of rheumatism, but he could still roar. The programme described him as very fierce, but there was much competition among the performers to sleep in the lion's cage, when it got too damp elsewhere. They nearly crowded him out.'

Elisalex looked at me. 'There!' she exclaimed. 'That is the sort of absurdity that I wanted to come back to. And Kuniang admits that the circus was hardly more thrilling than the Russian family.'

Donald interposed. 'We have been looking at photographs of the Russian family,' he said. 'Certainly they would make a good show. I would like to make a film of them and you. Cinema fans would certainly fall for them. They seem to have gone in largely for *déshabillé*.'

Kuniang agreed, with reservations. 'A film of my young days with the Russian family would never get past the censor: at least, not if it were true to life. Every ten days or so there would occur some catastrophic episode among the younger members of the family, and

68

then Patushka or Matushka would rise up and smite us on our bare behinds.'

Donald smiled. 'That would require careful posing, or a discreet fade-out during the preliminaries. But we could make up a story on the lines of Tom Sawyer and Becky Thatcher. At the critical moment, Igor might act the part of Tom, and take the blame and the punishment.'

'In real life,' said Kuniang, '*I* sometimes took the blame, to save Igor. On one occasion, there was what we call a "yellow wind", that is a wind that brings the yellow sand from beyond the Great Wall. One of the glass doors that led out of the schoolroom on to the veranda blew open and all the loose music-scores on the piano were wafted over the room. Patushka's violin fell on the floor and its bridge got knocked off. Patushka was much annoyed. He gave a snort of rage and sat down on the sofa, where he tried to repair the damage while I stood by and watched him. Then he told me to go and fetch Igor, adding that he would teach that fool boy to mind what he was doing.

'Patushka was right. It *was* Igor who had gone out that way without making sure that the latch of the door had clicked: a silly thing to do, when there is a yellow wind. But I did not want poor Igor to get into trouble, so I murmured something incoherent to the effect that it might have been me. I hoped to get off with a scolding, but I was disappointed. Patushka's violin lay across his knee. He quietly set it aside and put me in its place, so that I found myself staring down at the pattern in the schoolroom carpet, which had the ancient symbol of the Eight Trigrams woven in it. The Chinese say that they are effective as a charm. But they never saved *me* from what was coming.'

'Nevertheless,' said Elisalex, 'I still maintain that you would have found life very dull without the Russian family. Don't you agree that you were happy with them – as happy as any one is in this vale of tears?'

Kuniang appeared to be sleepy. The day's excitement had tired her. She gazed into the embers, her chin cupped in her hands, and stifled a yawn before saying:

'There are so many ways of being happy. My own idea of happiness is to enjoy what is delightful with someone I am fond of and who is fond of me. And if we love each other, almost everything makes for happiness, just because of that. A few passing troubles make no difference. In spite of being chastised, I was content in the Russian family, for they were fond of me, and I of them. Besides, there was always the Shuang Liè Ssè to come back to, with King Cophetua, and the Five Virtues, and Uncle Podger. It is possible that I might not have been so contented if I had known any other world, but I was born and brought up in China. Like the Chinese, I took for granted that everything the foreign devils did was just their little way – one of their peculiarities. Everything the Russian family did appeared quite natural to me. To tell the truth, it does still. So, you see, I continue to reason like a Chinese.'

'The Chinese,' said Elisalex, 'have a wisdom that has taken a long time to mature. Nowadays, people acquire wisdom overnight. Or they think they do. And they appear to have lost the art of living in difficult times.'

Kuniang paid no attention. She seemed to be thinking aloud:

'The Chinese do not expect happiness all the time, even when the rice-bin is full. They do not imagine that happiness is their right, or that it will come to them, or remain with them, all the time. They have a saying: "If you wait for Happiness till the Yellow River becomes clear, how old will you be?" Happiness must be sought after. And when it is there, it must be coaxed to stay, lest it depart . . .'

'I wonder what that means, in practice,' said Donald. 'We all are willing to do our best to ensure happiness, but there does not seem to be much that we can do.'

' "If you don't scale the mountain, you can't view the plain." That is another Chinese saying. You must make some effort to ensure happiness, every day of your life. Otherwise you may lose what you have.'

'And what do *you* do about it?' asked Donald.

'I share things with people I am fond of. Nowadays that gives me all the happiness that I need. But in the years we were speaking of, the Five Virtues were always taking me to some ceremony or other, and consulting their Family Magician about me, or giving me charms to ward off the evil spirits. I suppose that is why, in the end, everything went well.'

Kuniang and Donald went on talking, and now and then Elisalex put in a word or two. But I was no longer listening to them. What had been said about courting happiness had started a train of thought in my own mind, and I wondered if it could be true. If so, I had been very remiss. I had taken things for granted, happiness included. I had attended no ceremonies in Chinese temples. I had consulted no Family Magician, and I had acquired no charms to ward off evil spirits. Yet, now that the responsibility was mine, was it not incumbent on *me* to do something about it? Something more than bask in the reflected warmth of Kuniang's own contentment? It was all nonsense, of course, all superstition. And I smiled at my own thoughts. But in the East superstition often takes the place of religious faith. It shows a willingness to propitiate the gods, and the humble tributes to tutelary deities reveal respect for the nation's ancient culture.

We were then in the Third Moon, the 'Sleepy Moon', during which Chinese scholars make a point of going out to the Tung Yo Miao, a rich Taoist temple outside the Ch'i Hua Men. And they burn incense to their professional god, the God of Literature, who has an altar there. Why should I not ride out, some day soon, and do likewise? I was something of a scholar myself. I might ask my Chinese patron to keep a kindly eye on Kuniang's happiness.

It should never be said that I neglected to propitiate the gods – the old old gods of China.

9 *Le Jongleur de Notre Dame*

Vierge, mère d'amour, Vierge, bonté suprême,
Comme à l'air du berger souriait l'Enfant Dieu,
Si le Jongleur osait vous honorer de même,
Daignez sourire au seuil des cieux!

MAURICE LENA:
Le Jongleur de Notre Dame

We were sitting in the garden, after a rather hectic afternoon. Donald had got tired of the Chung-ho theatre, where Mei-lan-fan acts, and had insisted on being taken to a very old-fashioned playhouse, outside the Ch'ien Men. Even there, the principal actor had been good, in the perennially popular role of the White Damsel – a snake who has assumed human form. Nevertheless, our expedition had been a failure. Donald had been so affected by the lack of ventilation and consequent smells in what for want of a better name he called the foyer, adjoining what for want of a better name I might call the lavatory, that his face had turned green; he had felt very sick and had to be taken out into the fresh air and escorted back to the Shuang Liè Ssè. Poor Donald had still much to learn about stageland in the Far East! But after several dry martinis and a sandwich or two, he felt better.

Fédor and Igor were with us, but as it got late they went off home (I mean to the Russian family's house) for a bath, before joining us again at supper. It was never for long that Fédor detached himself from the side of Elisalex.

Donald watched Igor go, and then he said:

'Do you know, my idea was not so crazy after all! That boy has a gift for mimicry. And I believe he could be taught to dance. With his looks, think what an opening that would be! Also, I believe it would do him good.'

'No doubt about that,' I answered. 'It would stimulate his imagination and develop his intelligence. The theatre is a great educator. But what do you propose to do about it?'

'I would like to take him to Paris. There is always an opening in Paris for beauty in any form. Merely as a painter's model, Igor could make a living there. But he could do better than that. Ever since they gave the first performance of *Boris Godounov* at the Châtelet, in 1908, Paris has become a centre of what you might call *les Arts Décoratifs* applied to the theatre, and this centre is almost entirely dominated by Russians. From the first production of *Schéhérazade*, in 1910, to that of *Les Dieux Mendiants* this year, there has been a flowering of beauty and of talent that even the Great War did not interrupt. And unless I am much mistaken, most of the artists, from Diaghilev and Massine, found their inspiration in Asia: in Asiatic colouring and costume and *décor*. Igor is a Russian, born and bred in Asia. I cannot help thinking that he could find a niche for himself in the world that centres round the Russian Dances. Or perhaps I should say that I could find it for him, if Elisalex will help.'

Elisalex nodded approvingly. 'It is true,' she said, 'that we know that world well, you and I. We might be able to help Igor to set foot upon the ladder. But you may be too ambitious for the poor boy. It was what the French call *une pléiade* of very great artists that followed Diaghilev's lead at the Châtelet and at the Opera. Painters like Bakst and Cocteau, musicians like Borodin, Stravinsky and Rimsky-Korsakov, choreographers like Fokine. The pupils and successors of these men might take Igor in hand and make something of him. But if they failed to do so and discarded him as useless, we should be responsible for one more failure on the stage.'

'I don't believe,' said Donald, 'that Igor *would* fail. A few days ago I gave him the script of Maurice Lena's play, *Le Jongleur de Notre Dame*. That too was staged at the Châtelet, and Massenet wrote the music. After Igor had read the story, I asked him to imagine himself as a juggler, tossing little metal hoops into the air. The hoops were imaginary. Igor had nothing to play with. But he caught the idea and acted the part most gracefully, like a child in a game of make-believe.'

'You hit upon a role that Igor is particularly fond of,' said Kuniang. 'He loves watching the jugglers at the Loong-fu Sseu. And old Yee-ga-lan-tan, the conjurer, is a particular friend of his, and once tried to teach him to do a somersault with a bowl full of water and goldfish under his coat. I had to go down on my knees and help collect the goldfish from off the floor.'

'Are you thinking of staging Maurice Lena's play, as well as the *Saint Sebastian?*' I asked Donald.

'Perhaps. I came upon the idea by mere chance. One day in Paris I went to see a friend of mine, a sculptor, who has a studio in a quiet street miles away beyond the Trocadero and the Eiffel Tower. When I came away, I walked a few blocks, hoping to find a taxi. And I passed a crowd round a juggler, who was trying to earn some coppers at a street corner. He had laid his cap suggestively on the sidewalk for contributions. But, so far, no one had taken the hint. He was a good juggler, a southerner evidently, with a swarthy skin, ink-black hair, and little twinkling black eyes.

'Every kind of show interests me, and if the show is good, and the performers seem to be getting a tough deal, I become almost too sympathetic.

'When the man paused for a moment, I entered into conversation with him. He told me the usual hard-luck story, which may have been true or not. Anyhow, I gave him some money and my address, and told him to come and see me. The sight of that seedy-looking guy, in faded tights, putting up quite a good show on the sidewalk, would not have appealed to me so much, except for a small coincidence. At that same street corner was a big closed *porte-cochère*, and above it a reproduction of a della Robbia Madonna. It was this that reminded me of *Le Jongleur de Notre Dame*.'

'But who was the Jongleur de Notre Dame?' asked Kuniang. 'I don't know the story.'

Donald looked at me. 'You're a story-writer,' he said. 'It's up to you. I'm still feeling too sick to be romantic. It might bring it on again.'

'You will find the story,' I said, 'in Anatole France's *Etui de Nacre*. But I will tell it to you, if you like. It is about a juggler who gets religion and becomes a monk. But he feels out of place in a monastery, where the other friars are scholars and artists. Brother Dominic can write out the loveliest missals, and Brother Joseph can illuminate them with coloured pictures, inset with gold leaf. Brother Daniel can play the organ, and Brother Francis can direct the choir. Between them they glorify the High Mass with peals of heavenly music. But what can poor Brother Jean do, to please the Queen of Heaven? He has nothing to offer. Nothing. Unless . . .

'One night, into the dimly-lit church, there creeps a strange figure in a spangled dress and with his face grotesquely painted. He lights the candles at the high altar and spreads a little carpet at the foot of the steps. First he kneels for a moment in prayer. Then he leaps up, agile, graceful, a creature of fire and flame. Golden balls toss and circle like swallows round a church spire. Bunches of flowers follow them, and little hoops of steel. They dance together in the candlelight and almost touch the feet of the Madonna herself. Brother Jean's eyes glow with happiness. "Holy Mother," he murmurs. "This is the trick I first performed in the market place at Lyons. The merchants stopped chaffering to watch. This was the somersault that pleased the Queen's pages at Compiègne. This tumble drew a smile from the most noble Lord, Guy de Chastillon, Count of Blois . . ."

'Then the sudden alarm as the monks, drawn by the unaccustomed light, enter the church and see a juggler on the steps of the high altar itself. The holy prior calls out against the sacrilege. And the offender cringes and covers his face with his hands. But even as he does so, the church fills with a light that is not of this world, and with a music played by no earthly organ. The friars look up at the figure of the Virgin above the altar, but its lights dazzle them. They feel, rather than see, the softening of the eyes that smile, the moving of the hands that bless!'

Kuniang's eyes were star-like. 'Igor would look lovely,' she said, 'in such a scene.'

Donald agreed. 'That's so, if only in make-believe. But what a strange boy! When you first told me about him, I got the idea that he was a bit loony. But he speaks three languages, or four, if you count Chinese as a language. And he has read a lot.'

'He was never backward,' said Kuniang. 'Only absent-minded, so that he seemed to be living in a very pleasant place, very far away. Sometimes, during a "yellow wind", when Matushka's temper got worse than usual, I would envy Igor this refuge from our schoolroom calamities.'

At this point Elisalex supplied us with some information on the subject.

'When I had been in Peking for some weeks,' she said, 'the last time I was here, Patushka told me how anxious he was about Igor's health. He had visions and heard voices, like Joan of Arc. My friend, Prince Dorbon Oirad, whom you call the Abbot, was staying at the Lama Temple, so I arranged for Igor to go and see him. Dorbon is very deep in the Eastern lore of dreams, and hypnosis and such things. He said that Igor's visions were due to the fact that his mind moved freely in Time. He saw things that were long passed, and other things that were yet to come. Some people might consider him fortunate to be able to do so. Anyway, there was no cure. But the boy might grow out of it later in life. I don't know whether he has done so yet. But he looks healthier and stronger than when I saw him last. And it is true, I believe, that a delicate child will grow out of the obsession of nightmares that spoilt his sleep before he grew up.'

'There does not seem to be much wrong with Igor now,' said Donald. 'He is a nice boy, besides being a beautiful one. And I feel quite flattered at his apparent liking for me.'

'I don't think he can ever have seen anybody quite like you before,' said Kuniang.

'Is that meant to be a compliment?'

Kuniang smiled. 'Of course. Since Igor likes you.'

Donald looked at her suspiciously, but he said nothing.

Elisalex suggested that it might be time to dress for dinner.

10   Walkers on the Wall

'There's rosemary, that's for remembrance.'
SHAKESPEARE:
Hamlet, 4

There used to be in Peking a band of eccentric foreigners – of which I was one – known as 'The Walkers on the Wall'. The name was given to us owing to our habit of taking exercise along the top of the Tartar Wall, built by the Manchus when they took the capital from the defeated Mings.

The first to take their constitutionals on the Wall were those foreigners to whom old Prince Kung gave permission to ascend the sloping ramps from the city below, many years before the Boxer rebellion. The whole circuit of the Tartar Wall is about seventeen miles, but very few people ever troubled to walk the round, for the going is by no means good. Indeed, old China hands like myself use special shoes to walk on the Wall, shoes with Chinese soles made of rags and cordage. These are also the best footgear for walks on the stony paths among the Western Hills. They are not waterproof, but as it does not rain in North China during eight months of the year, this does not matter.

Since the days of the Republic the only section of the Wall that is open to promenaders is that corresponding to the Legation Quarter, and the section east of the Hata Men, as far as the old Jesuit observatory. But the part of the Wall that forms the southwest corner, enclosing on two sides that corner of the Tartar City where stands the Shuang Liè Ssè, has long been closed to the public. The ramps up are blocked by barriers of barbed wire and bundles made of the thorny branches of acacias. Only foreigners seem to resent this limitation: the Chinese were never allowed to walk on the Wall, and apparently they never wanted to. Nor do they now.

It so happened that in the spring of 1928 the barrier on the ramp nearest to my dwelling had partially fallen in with its own weight, aided by the action of winter winds and summer rains. The officials at the nearest police station, whose duty it was to see to the necessary repairs, had not bothered to do so. I half suspect that their negligence in this matter was intentional, and possibly due to a certain friendliness towards myself. My partiality for climbing up on to the Wall was well known. In China, as elsewhere, it is useful to be on good terms with the guardians of the law. Certain little presents that went forth from my back door on the days preceding the Chinese New Year were useful, inasmuch as they served *à entretenir l'amitié*.

So it happened that, at one time, I enjoyed a privilege unique among foreigners in Peking. I had a section of the Tartar Wall practically reserved for my use. I would push aside a bundle of briars with my walking stick, replace it when I had passed through, and go up and down as I pleased. I could not walk very far on the top, for the pathway had almost entirely disappeared among the shrubs and grasses that had forced their way through the crevices in the brick paving.

But from that elevation, high above the highest roof, my gaze could roam over the city and out towards the blue and purple outlines of the Western Hills. I could look down on my own house, with its formal entrance, flanked by marble lions, and with its many pavilions, set symmetrically round the successive courtyards. At the back of the pavilions the garden, and at the back again, the stables, separated from the other buildings by a broad stretch of open ground. Beyond my stables,

with their ornamental gate (The Gate of Happy Sparrows) dating from the time when the Mongol Banner
Corps kept their horses there, came the grey roofs of
the Tartar City, fading away in the distance, towards
the spires of the Catholic cathedral (the Pei-tang). More
to the right, Peking's greatest glory: the golden roofs of
the Forbidden City, and the graceful open pavilions of
the Coal Hill. If I strolled towards the Shun-chih Men
(in an easterly direction), after a few hundred yards I
could look down on the Russian family's house: much
smaller than mine, and built partly in foreign style.

Over the southern parapet I could gaze down at the
Chinese City with its own walls and gates, and beyond
them the never-ending plain.

Sometimes, a great cloud would rise up in the northwest, obscuring sky and hills and gate-towers with a
mighty pillar of grey and gold. The dry air would make
my skin tingle, my eyes smart and my voice grow
husky. A dust-storm was approaching, and the black
and yellow sand from the Gobi desert was about to
descend on Peking.

I always had the impression that, to the broader
physical outlook that I enjoyed from the vantage point
on top the Tartar Wall, there corresponded a broader
mental outlook within myself. And I would climb up on
to the stony path on the summit, to be alone and think.

There was a lot to think about in the weeks that
followed the coming of our guests. There were times
when I felt puzzled.

On the evening of her arrival, Elisalex had told me
how she had heard the East a-calling. She had felt
drawn towards the Abbot's temple, with the strange,
alluring name. But for the moment she showed no
impatience to continue her journey. This was hardly
surprising. Everyone made much of her in Peking,
whereas travelling inland, if not actually unsafe, was
hardly likely to be comfortable. Civil war between
Chang-tso-lin and the Nationalists had not yet broken
out in North China, but it might do so at any moment.

Now that she was there I had no more doubts. I really did enjoy having Elisalex in the house, with all the unaccustomed bustle that it entailed. Although I took no great interest in her love affairs, I watched the skilful play that held Fédor to her apron strings, without allowing him to approach any nearer than she wished at any given time, but even less to stray too far. Fédor himself, if not in the seventh heaven (for the lady was not living in his house), might have been described as standing outside on the landing.

Was it because of Fédor that Elisalex lingered on in Peking? Was it to see him that she had come out again to the Far East? I thought it more than probable. Yet I wondered how, if she were really going to stay in The Temple of Costly Experience with the man who had been known as her husband, she could combine this sojourn with her obvious desire not to be separated from Fédor. This problem, however, gave me no sleepless nights. It did not concern me. But every now and then I felt a touch of anxiety about Kuniang.

Never had I seen her so full of gaiety, even of mischief! She had gone back to that 'rapscalliony' period that had so endeared her to Elisalex and had convinced Matushka that she needed 'discipline'. Kuniang was obviously so pleased with herself that I felt a little conscience-stricken. Had life with me been so dull, in recent years?

Her obvious pleasure in recalling old times seemed to prove that Elisalex was right and that the harum-scarum ways of the Russian family were more suited to Kuniang than my own scholarly style. A life with thrills in it – even unpleasant thrills – offered the spice of danger that young people prefer to the sameness of a contented domesticity.

To revive the past in memory is to live it over again. This is what Kuniang was doing. She had recaptured the spirit of her first youth, almost as if she still had to start off in her rickshaw every morning to go round to the Russian family's house for work or play. Once more she was the Kuniang of *The Maker of Heavenly Trousers*. Only I had grown older.

Yet with me, too, memory pulled at those hypothetical nerves and tendons that are called heartstrings. But if our story were to be told again could I achieve the old whimsical lightness of touch? Could I capture that fluttering heart once more, and cage it between the golden bars of my love?

Donald's idea, serious or not, of putting us on the films, gave Kuniang the opportunity of retelling our life-story in her own way. Mischief prompted her to make out that it was too improper for the screen. But Donald saw through her attempts to shock him, and paid her back in her own coin. So she had to give it up, and to be content with her own characteristic frankness on all subjects.

She gave Donald her old diaries to read. They revealed a young mind that was both ingenuous and precocious. The background was a mixture of old China and young Russia: the former represented by the Five Virtues in the Shuang Liè Ssè; the latter by the schoolroom and Fédor's studio in the Russian family's house down the street. Donald pored over those old copy-books with an amused but by no means breathless interest.

Then one day Kuniang asked me rather dubiously whether she might show Donald the drawings that Fédor had done of her and later on presented to me. In most of those drawings Kuniang's figure is undraped.

'Donald knows all about my posing to Fédor in the altogether,' said Kuniang. 'So I suppose there is no reason not to show him the result.' But she looked at me, as if she expected me to raise some objection.

I might have doubts, but I was not going to show them. For I was determined not to be regarded any more as the narrow-minded Englishman that the younger people had once considered me. So I gave Kuniang the drawings, to show to Donald if she wished.

I had just handed Kuniang the big portfolio that

contained them, when I remembered something, and asked for it back. And I took out four drawings and one sketch in oils (the only study in colour that the portfolio contained).

They all represented Kuniang in the same position, with slight variations. She was lying on her back, in an attitude of complete abandonment, with her head close to the spectator, and her body, much foreshortened, disappearing into the background. One knee was raised and formed the highest point in the recumbent figure. The head, falling back, showed Kuniang's face upside down.

'Why are you taking those out?' asked Kuniang.

'Because they remind me of the Leda in the bathroom fresco. I don't want anyone to think that you posed for that. The nude figure in Fédor's fresco, in conjunction with the swan, leaves no doubt as to what the divine bird is up to.'

But Kuniang was not listening. She had picked up the studies I had laid aside and was looking them over.

'These were the last that Fédor did of me,' she said, 'before you took me away. They were studies for some big picture he was going to paint, and that was to have been his masterpiece. But I never posed to him again, till he did the portrait of me with Little Chink. So nothing came of it.'

It was on such episodes and conversations that I was pondering one afternoon when I had climbed up on to the Wall. And I had reached the point just opposite the Russian family's house when, looking down, I saw a line of rickshaws stopping at the outer door that opened on to the street. There were Kuniang and Elisalex, and Donald and the two Russian boys.

At that time Matushka was still away at Harbin, looking after Natasha, whose baby (a girl) had arrived as per schedule. But Patushka had come back, and his house had become a rendezvous for our party at tea-time. I decided to join the others and made my way down the ramp nearby. I knew that Patushka would have charge of the samovar. And he made tea as only old-fashioned Russians can. For them, as for the Japanese, tea-making is a ritual. And they give you the most delightful jams!

Patushka's beard was growing white, and he was getting bent in the shoulders. But he still towered above us all.

I think it made us all feel younger to have that huge old man with us, and I noticed how fond Kuniang and Igor seemed to be of him; they might have been his own children. His presence allowed Donald to recapture something of the old atmosphere of the Russian family's house. Donald made frequent efforts to enter into conversation with Patushka, but the old man was shy of strangers and did not like being questioned. They got on better when Donald brought and showed him some of the copy-books, in which Kuniang had written her diary of the days when Patushka had tried to teach Russian folk dances to the younger generation.

'Kuniang says that you would pick her up and put her down like a doll,' said Donald.

Patushka was standing in a group with Kuniang on one side of him and Igor on the other. Without any apparent effort he stooped and picked them up, one on each side, and stood there with the two young people seated on his forearms. He smiled, with the pathos of an old man's pride in the strength that is leaving him.

'Fédor is stronger than I am now,' he said. 'But I can still carry children.'

'I suppose,' said Donald, 'that when one is as big as you are, all young people seem to be children that never grow up. Except of course Fédor, and he is Pantagruel.' Then he added in an undertone, speaking to Kuniang: 'But you must have had a rotten time, when you lay across his knee and stared down at the Eight Trigrams in the carpet.'

Kuniang laughed: 'I have other memories of Patushka's knee. He used to put me on it, right way up, and pet me and console me, when I got into trouble. I've often had a good cry into his beard. You were right, just now, when you said that we were all children to him: children that never grow up. If the occasion arose, I believe he would think it quite natural to spank me still!'

'That sort thing is rather popular on the films just now,' said Donald. 'I am told that ladies rather like to see their own sex roughly handled, as long as the story ends – as your story ends – in happiness ever after.'

'Are you sure the story is ended?' asked Kuniang unexpectedly. 'We are all here, and life goes on.'

11   *The Eyelashes of the Swan*

Oh, heart! oh, blood that freezes, blood that burns!
  Earth's returns
For whole centuries of folly, noise and sin!
  Shut them in,
With their triumphs and their glories and the rest.
  Love is best!

R. BROWNING:
Love Among the Ruins

Next day, when I went round again to the Russian family's house about tea-time, to join the others, I found the entrance hall full of boxes and parcels. Like all visitors to Peking, Donald had lost his heart to the Street of the Lanterns and had bought up half the wares of that most tempting thoroughfare. There is no form of illumination so delightful as the silk-panelled lanterns, hand-painted with birds and drooping wistaria and Buddhist symbols and the Chinese characters for peace and happiness and longevity. And they can all be adjusted for our Western electric light. I don't know what possibilities Donald had seen for theatre lighting, but he must have spent a small fortune in that one visit. The lanterns, though neatly folded and packed into the smallest space possible, filled up the anterooms of Patushka's house.

Donald had committed an even greater extravagance by buying half a pound of tea at an emporium, where stately gentlemen, robed in black satin, attend to customers in galleries with gilded columns. This shop has a sign that reads *Ch'i Chih*, or The Seven Passions (I can only remember five of the series. These are: Joy, Anger, Fear, Hatred and Desire). The idea is that they can all be kept under proper control by drinking the firm's tea! The tea leaves that Donald had bought were called The Eyelashes of the Swan. The price for half a pound was a hundred and seventy-five dollars Mex. Each leaf was rolled separately, being much larger than an ordinary tea leaf, and each was tied with a crimson thread. No such tea ever reaches Europe or America.

When I came in most of the party was gathered round Patushka, who was preparing to make an infusion with some of these precious leaves. I stopped for a moment and watched him. The samovar was in the room next to the schoolroom. Patushka took only six of the tea leaves and when I asked him if that were enough, he said yes: the brew would be almost colourless, but strong enough to keep us awake all night!

Elisalex was not there, so I went to look for her and found her sitting on the old schoolroom sofa, smoking her inevitable cigarette. She looked so thoroughly *chez elle* that I could not help smiling. She always *did* look at home wherever she was. And she seemed quite content to sit and do nothing, which most people cannot manage without appearing bored or embarrassed, or merely empty-minded. Elisalex did not adapt herself to her surroundings. She dominated them, creating round herself an atmosphere that was her own atmosphere: an aura of elegance, of charm and of sophistication. How she did it I do not know, but she managed to confer by her mere presence an air of luxury to the most unpromising environment. One might have said of her, as of Roxane, *Elle fait de la grâce avec rien.* She had the grace of a panther, which reveals itself even in a bare cage and behind iron bars.

But what struck me most was that no wind of ennui ever blew into her garden. Underneath the charm and the sophistication there was something exotic, something powerful, even something primitive in its strength. When I came upon her, sitting on the old horsehair sofa, among unfinished canvases and the smell of oil paints, I again recalled the subtle witchery of the princess whom Alexander loved and Turgenev described.

Igor was also in the room, standing near the glass door that opened on to the veranda. He was humming a little tune to himself, and though he was doing nothing but stare out of a window, I noticed, and not for the first time, how much more alert he looked than formerly. He seemed to be living at last in our own workaday world, instead of in the clouds. He greeted me with a smile and then moved off to join the others in the next room. But as he passed her, Elisalex caught him by the sleeve. She too had noticed something new in Igor's attitude, for she asked him:

'What's up with you, Little Brother? You are looking strange in these days. Are you in love?'

Though she used the Slav expression 'Little Brother', Elisalex had spoken in English. But Igor answered in Russian, and they conversed in that language for some moments. Then he passed on, and Elisalex remained silent and thoughtful. I asked her what the boy had said.

She answered: 'He was quoting a song that they used to sing in this room years ago, "I have locked up my love in my heart, under ten locks". I asked him who the lady was, and he answered "Lady Precious Jade". He meant Kuniang, I suppose, but why call her that?'

'A nickname taken from the Chinese fairytale, which tells of a lovely girl, called Precious Jade. She is ill-treated by a cruel stepmother, who has an ugly daughter of her own, called Pock Face. The stepmother gives Precious Jade all sorts of impossible tasks to perform, and whips her when she cannot do so.'

'The analogy is most unfair, especially to Natasha, who was not ugly or pock-marked. But that is just the sort of legend they are making up for Donald's edification. And Kuniang seems to find it great fun.

But Igor is going through some kind of a brainstorm. It may be that Donald is responsible.'

'How could that be?'

'Donald has made to Igor the offer that he spoke about: to have him trained for the Russian dances. It may be possible, of course. Donald knows what he is talking about. And, if Donald is right, then Igor may come into his own. It would be wonderful if he could strike out a line for himself and have a real profession. Perhaps that is what poor Igor needed all along.'

'But what does Donald actually propose?' I asked. 'He isn't going to take Igor with him to America, surely?'

'The idea is that, when Donald gets back to Europe in the autumn, Igor should join him there, to follow some courses in Paris.'

'And who is going to pay?'

'Donald says he'll pay.'

'That's extraordinarily generous of him.'

'Donald has plenty of money,' said Elisalex carelessly. 'And he's always tossing it about in one theatrical venture or another.'

'Still, it *is* generous. And it seems to have made a difference in Igor already. He is not what he used to be.'

'He feels roused and stimulated. Donald has done for him a thing that no-one has ever done before: he has stirred an ambition. And he has inspired in him an interest and a pride in his own beauty. Fédor has painted him innumerable times, but then it was only Fédor. The idea that his face and figure and the grace of his movements could delight the spectators in a theatre had never occurred to poor Igor. I think he feels dazed at having been taken out of his old sleepy environment. The prospect dazzles him, as if he had woken up suddenly in a room full of sunlight. Will he be happier for such an awakening? He is not yet sure. Also the idea of parting from Kuniang is painful, especially now that they are all bent on reviving the past.'

'There was nothing serious between Kuniang and Igor in the past.'

'Serious enough on his part. It is true that Kuniang was never in love with him. But like all girls, she enjoyed being made love to, when she was in the mood ... She was never afraid of Igor, as she was of Fédor. And they were adolescents. As she told us the other day, Igor was encouraged to use her as an object of fixation. I remember that Fédor wanted to paint them together as Cupid and Psyche. I don't know if he ever did so. Certainly those two young things were lovely to look at, when they bathed in the swimming pool, or took sun baths afterwards in the grass.'

Just at this moment Kuniang put her head in at the door and asked:

'Don't you want any tea, you two? And what are you discussing so seriously?'

'We were talking about Igor.'

Kuniang came into the room and stood between us and the glass door. The light from the veranda brought out the softer lights in her hair, and glowed on her summer frock of the palest blue shantung. I thought to myself, as I so often do, how pretty she was.

'Igor,' she said, 'is going through some sort of a mental earthquake.'

'Aren't you partly responsible?' I asked. 'Elisalex seems to think you are.'

'I am merely standing by, in case poor Igor should need me again.'

'To offer him the old cure?' asked Elisalex.

'Yes. Treatment as before.'

'Take care,' I said. 'This time the statue may come to life.'

'That *would* be exciting!' said Kuniang. 'Let's hope it does!'

Just then a delicious perfume of jasmine-scented tea came into the room through the open door.

'Heavens!' I exclaimed. 'Those must be the Eyelashes of the Swan. Let's go and have some. And make

Igor have as much as he can drink, since it is supposed to control the passions.'

That evening we did not dine at home, but went to the Wagons Lits Hotel, where Donald insisted on our having a sumptuous meal at his expense, with lots of champagne.

Old Yee-ga-lan-tan was there, squatting on the floor of the lounge and performing his tricks for the benefit of a party of Americans. He is a Chinese conjurer who has been working in Peking for more years than I can remember. His name comes to him from the utterly senseless but not unmelodious sing-song with which he accompanies his various stunts:

'Lang-tang, lang-tan. Yee-ga-lan-tan. Tui-tui, tui-tu, yee-ge tui-tui . . . ' and so on *ad infinitum*.

He swallowed fire and then drew out yards and yards of paper ribbon from his mouth. He covered up a bunch of flowers with a rice bowl, lifted it up again, and revealed a little white mouse that ran up his long blue sleeve and was never seen again. And he ended up with his usual trick of turning a somersault (no mean achievement for a man of his age), to show that there was nothing bulky concealed about him, after which he brought out from the folds of his robe a bowl of water with goldfish swimming in it.

Igor and Yee-ga-lan-tan were old friends and they soon got into conversation. Donald was introduced and expressed his admiration. I wondered if he were going to offer to take the old conjurer to Paris.

A voice close to me said: 'Say! Look at that young man talking to the Chink in his own language. Wouldn't he make a fortune as a sheik in Hollywood?'

It was one of the American tourists speaking to a companion. Funny that the idea should have come to him too! If it were as obvious as that, how was it that none of us had thought of it before?

Later on, as the night was warm and pleasant, I persuaded the others to join me in my favourite pastime and walk along the top of the Wall. The section of the path that comes under the jurisdiction of the Legation Quarter authorities is better kept than elsewhere. We left our rickshaws at the end of Canal Street, and climbed up by the ramp near the Water Gate. The air was full of willow-fluff that blew up from the trees on the southern side of the Wall (the Chinese will tell you that each of those flakes is a wandering soul). The cries and the murmur of a big town came to us from either side. We proceeded in couples: Fédor and Elisalex in front, myself and Donald close behind them, and Igor with Kuniang in the rear.

We walked as far as the Ch'ieh Men and then returned the way we came, stopping for a moment at the place whence you can best see the towers looming above the ramparts, with their triple series of curved roofs. Both towers were burned down during the Boxer troubles. And when they were rebuilt, wooden shutters were placed in the deep-set windows, and the mouths of cannon painted on them, to intimidate any possible assailant. But originally there were archers, guarding the walls and gates of Peking, and the Bannermen wore uniforms of satin and of velvet.

I stopped for a moment near the transmitting station of the American wireless. The darkness hid the foreign-style buildings in the Legation Quarter. Donald had joined Fédor and Elisalex, and I found myself for a few moments alone, for Kuniang and Igor had gone to look out over the battlements from the projecting buttress that is all that remains of the old lunette. The Peking–Mukden railway has its terminus just there, and a chorus of engine whistles, as well as the glare from the arc lamps below, revealed the proximity of the station.

I think that Kuniang wished to see if there were any signs of the moving of troops, to explain the unwonted activity in the station below.

There is a thick growth of bushes and stunted trees just there, on the southern side of the pathway. I pushed my way through and saw Kuniang some ten yards off, perched on the top of the parapet and looking down. She had her back to me, with her hands resting on the merlons on either side of her as she stood in the embrasure. There must have been a drop of eighty feet on the outer side of the Wall. But Kuniang does not suffer from vertigo. She might well have earned her living as a tight-rope walker in a circus. As she stood there, the strong light from below shone through her thin shantung frock and showed her figure in silhouette.

Igor was standing on the ground behind her, and if she was self-possessed and indifferent to the dizzy height, he certainly was not. The sight of her, like a swallow on the edge of the parapet, produced in him an agony of apprehension. It was *he* that felt the giddiness to which she was immune. I realized this at a glance, from his expression and whole attitude. But Kuniang was unaware of any strain in the situation. Only when she turned round and saw Igor did she understand his terror for her safety. And then some devil of mischief took hold of her. Lifting her hands from the merlons, she began to tap-dance on the broad Tartar bricks.

It was quite safe, really. There was plenty of room. But even I had my heart in my throat as I watched her. Igor held out his arms and gave a little choking cry of sheer pain. The next moment she leaped into his embrace and he clasped her to him. I saw her laughing face look up and heard her mocking question:

'Igor, darling. Was it as bad as that?'

And she kissed him gaily on the tip of the nose.

I turned away, smiling. But her words of that afternoon came back to me: 'Treatment as before.'

Which was best for Igor? A career, an object in life, work and play, failure and success, even as other men, or the old dream-world in which he had grown up with Kuniang?

12 'Caserma Vittorio Emanuele'

> I seem'd to move among a world of ghosts,
> And feel myself the shadow of a dream!
>
> TENNYSON:
> *The Princess*

'Buddy! Watch your step.'

'Buddy' was Donald, who was not looking where he was going, but gazing out over the Lake Palaces, as viewed from the bank of the Pei Hai, where cedars and willows bend over the water opposite a pavilion that is known as The Little Western Heaven.

The speaker was Igor, and it was symptomatic of Igor's gayer, happier mood that he should indulge in Americanisms, which he picked up delightedly from Donald's occasional lapses into the idiom of Broadway.

Igor had accompanied us to The Terrace of Heavy Fragrance on the more northerly of 'the three seas'. Donald had been there on his former visit to China, and he was anxious to see again a side-building that represented in miniature one of the Sacred Mountains of China, where plaster figures and saints and sages people the artificial hills and valleys of what in the West might be called a panorama, but here went by the name of 'Land of Unlimited Happiness' (to me, even after so many years I have lived there, one of the principal charms of old China lies in its names!).

Donald seemed to consider that these plastic representations of landscape in the land of the Blest made up, in some way, for the lack of theatrical scenery,

94

which in China is practically non-existent. Though it is true that some remarkable effects were once obtained in the Empress Dowager's private theatre: such as a lake covered with lotus flowers that opened and gave forth a luminous glow, round the throne of Kuan Yin, Goddess of Mercy (impersonated, in this case, by the Empress herself).

We had come to a temple, which, in the midst of so much flowery nomenclature, is sometimes remembered, even to-day, as the *Caserma Vittorio Emanuele*, ever since this legend was written in large white lettering on the pink outer wall. Although it has been painted over again with a pink wash, the Italian words are still distinguishable. I pointed them out to Donald, explaining to him that those buildings, like all the others in the Lake Palaces, had been occupied, after the siege of the Legations (in 1900), by foreign troops.

Donald was not interested in such recent history, but we passed into the courts of the temple itself and into the various pavilions. In the second of these, at the far end of a shadowy hall, was a huge effigy of Milo Fo, the 'Laughing Buddha', seated on a dais. Donald stopped to look at it and to point out to me how effective was the Chinese custom of hanging narrow strips of tapestry from the ceiling on either side of the temple-altars and of the sacred figures. These draperies, which are not attached to any wall, but only suspended from the ceiling above, give a sense of depth to the twilight behind them, so that the images, framed by them, loom mysteriously in the shadows and seem to rest on clouds of incense.

The obese and ribald image of the Laughing Buddha seemed hardly in keeping with such august surroundings, and Donald remarked:

'He looks as if he ought to be presiding at a cocktail party.'

'In that case,' I answered, 'he would verify an old prophecy.'

'What was that?'

'In the Pali Canon it is said that after the decay of the original religion, another Buddha will arise, who will have thousands of followers instead of the hundreds that the first Buddha had. As you say, the Chinese Maitreya looks as if he might be the god of cocktails, whose followers are legion.'

Igor was standing between Donald and myself. Suddenly he raised his hand, pointed at the image of the Laughing Buddha, and exclaimed: 'But why does he bleed?'

I looked at him in astonishment and asked:

'Does who bleed?'

'Milo Fo. See! There is blood trickling down his paunch and dropping on the floor.'

Donald appeared to be utterly nonplussed. But I understood. Igor was having one of his trances.

It passed off quickly. A few minutes later he was talking gaily of something else, and seemed to have forgotten his question about the statue bleeding. But I thought it best to take him home.

After depositing Igor at the Russian family's house, Donald and I returned to my study in the Shuang Liè Ssè. I got out the old metal dispatch box, where I keep manuscripts, and Kuniang her diaries. With some difficulty I found what I was looking for, and I handed Donald a typewritten document.

'If you will read this,' I said, 'it will explain to you what Igor saw in the hall of the Laughing Buddha. I never published this story. It did not seem good enough. But, after what happened this morning, you may be interested.'

Donald took the pages and went and sat in an armchair to read.

The following is the story, as I wrote it, long ago.

In the northwest corner of the Winter Palace, between the lake and the outer circle of walls, there is a group of temples dedicated to various divinities or to abstract mystical conceptions.

In the late summer of 1900, after the foreign troops that had been sent to succour the foreign Legations had entered Peking, these temples were occupied by sailors and by artillerymen belonging to the Italian contingent. They numbered little more than one hundred men with a sub-lieutenant in command. The bulk of the Italian troops were distributed elsewhere in the Province of Chihli: some in the Summer Palace, some in the Western Hills, and others along the coast.

Near the temples of which the Italians had taken possession were other buildings occupied by the French, while further south, beyond a bridge which divides the lake in two, German troops were stationed opposite the island where for many years the Emperor Kuang Hsu lived, a virtual prisoner of his formidable 'Ancestress', the Dowager Empress Tzu-hsi.

The young naval officer who was in charge of the Italians, having assumed the command of artillerymen on shore, had himself come under the orders of the military authorities. And the latter, being busy with more important matters, appeared to have forgotten his existence.

Our young friend took advantage of the independence that this forgetfulness allowed him, to put into practice certain ideas of his own, which the hidebound conservatism of his superior officers had hitherto kept him from carrying out.

Sentry duty, for example, had been completely transformed by him. A sentinel was posted before the entrance of the temples and another was instructed to keep an eye on the outer walls. But there was no such thing as 'sentry-go'. The two sentinels were allowed to wander round wherever they thought best, as long as they made sure that no suspicious character entered the central pavilions, where cases of explosives and 20,000 cartridges were stored. But this comparative liberty of movement was the price of longer hours of duty. The so-called sentinels might have to remain on guard all day, if their companions happened to be away on a foraging expedition.

To the sentinels themselves, the fact that they could

do what they pleased was sufficient compensation for the long hours of duty. It was not difficult for two men to prevent anyone entering the central pavilions. Very few Chinese were allowed to pass in through the outer gates of the Lake Palaces, and they were furnished with official 'passes', describing them as bearers of messages or provisions for the foreign troops. But if the military duties were not onerous, the corresponding responsibility was by no means light. There was treachery abroad. And this was proved by the repeated and inexplicable breaking out of fire in the German quarters beyond the bridge. Also a couple of Chinamen had been detected while attempting to scale the wall into the courtyards. A fuse laid among the cases of explosives might well have blown up the whole place.

Most of these explosives had been placed under the protection of an image representing Milo Fo, the Buddhist Messiah, as he figures in Chinese temples. To quote Mr Bushell, in whose book on Chinese art this image is described, Milo Fo '. . . is conceived as an obese Chinaman with a protuberant belly and smiling features, holding a loosened girdle in one hand and a rosary in the other and reclining on a bulging sack. He ranks as a bodhisat, having only once more to pass through human existence to attain Buddhahood . . . The common people of China call him simply *ta-tudze*, meaning large belly, in allusion to the enormous paunch which the loosened girdle leaves immodestly exposed.'

The Laughing Buddha in the Caserma Vittorio Emanuele was made of varnished clay, so white and shining as to resemble porcelain. The highlights on his face and paunch seemed to accentuate their jovial plumpness, as though they shone with the glossiness of distended skin.

Although that building bore the appropriate name of The Temple of Extended Felicity, the sailors and soldiers of the Italian contingent had rebaptized it

'Caserma Vittorio Emanuele'. This was probably the first time that King Victor Emmanuel's name had been given to a barracks. For he had only just come to the throne. The assassination of his father, King Humbert, at Monza, had occurred during the month in which the Legations at Peking were undergoing a siege.

One day the little garrison of the Caserma Vittorio Emanuele had gone out into the country in search of fodder for the mules. The sentinel left behind to guard the entrance of the temple was a sailor, by name Nicola Ventura, born in Civitavecchia, near Rome. In accordance with his commanding officer's theories, he had made himself as comfortable as circumstances permitted. He sat on the steps in front of the central door and smoked a terra cotta pipe, which he had filled with the crumbled remains of a 'Tuscan' cigar. It happened to be a Saturday, and Nicola, who was a man of regular habits, was engaged in an occupation which is customary on Italian warships on Saturday afternoons, namely mending his kit. He had provided himself with needle and thread and had begun to mend a tear in the knee of an old pair of trousers.

The heat was tropical, and anyone less impervious to temperature would have made the necessary repairs to his wardrobe in the shadowy stillness of the inner temple. But Nicola sat in the sun and seemed to enjoy its scorching rays as much as the green lizards, who stared at him with beady eyes from the white marble steps.

Every now and then Nicola glanced at the road along the edge of the lake. The view that opened out before him was one of the most beautiful in the Imperial City. A wide expanse of water, fragrant with the sleepy lotus, stretched away to the foot of the Bottle Hill (so called from the strange-shaped building on the top of it). Up the sides of that hill and round the borders of the lake, the summer foliage alternated with roofs of many-coloured tiles that flashed back the sunlight.

With a resounding smack on his own cheek, Nicola killed a mosquito that was preparing to take nourishment, and he muttered a few insulting remarks about the antecedents of the said mosquito. Just then, a coolie with a wheelbarrow appeared at the end of the road, near a pavilion where the Empress once kept her silkworms. It was not the kind of wheelbarrow that one sees in Europe, being designed to carry a burden heavier than that which one man's strength is called upon to bear in the West. The wheel was in the centre, and on each side of it were wooden planks piled up with sacks of coal. The coolie advanced with painful slowness and the wheel creaked so persistently that only a Chinese would have gone on without oiling it. Long before it had reached his immediate vicinity, the squeak-squeak of that un-oiled wheel had got on Nicola's nerves, so that when it passed in front of him he expressed a fervent wish (using a Roman colloquialism that dates from the time of Caesar) to the effect that the wheelbarrow and its motive power might be the victims of an accident. The Chinese coolie shot an anxious glance at the speaker, but did not stop. He plodded on, gasping and perspiring, until he reached the shade of a group of trees, not far distant from the steps where Nicola was seated. Here he decided to take a well-earned rest, and leaving the wheelbarrow on the side of the road, he extracted from his vestments a long-stemmed pipe which he proceeded to fill and to light.

When the coolie had finished his smoke and had started off once more, Nicola noticed with surprise that the wheel creaked less than before. Such breeze as there was came from the direction in which the wheelbarrow was moving off, so that the noise should have been at least as distinct as formerly. The Chinaman had not touched the wheel during his halt in the shade; the only explanation of the diminished noise was a lessening in the weight carried, sufficient to lessen the friction on the axle. But if indeed the wheelbarrow had continued on its way carrying less weight than before, what had it left behind? Nicola was no Sherlock Holmes. But his powers of observation were on the alert by reason of the special requirements of his job as sentinel to the Caserma Vittorio Emanuele.

Animated by curiosity rather than by suspicion, he left the task of mending his trousers and, taking his rifle, moved off towards the trees in the shadow of which the Chinaman had rested. The road was muddy, as it had rained during the night, and Nicola could easily follow the footprints and the mark of the single wheel. At the spot where the vehicle had come to a stand, Nicola noticed two things: first, that the track left by the wheel before stopping was deeper than the track left when it moved on. This proved that the weight *had* been lessened. Second, that in the mud, on the side furthest away from the temple door, was the imprint of an open hand and of two bare feet, smaller than those of the Chinaman who had pushed the barrow. Also there was the mark as of a body that had been dragged, or had crawled, towards the long grass at the side of the road. No need to be an amateur detective to guess that someone had been hidden among the sacks – perhaps inside one of them – and had got down in such a way as to remain unseen by any one seated at the entrance to the Caserma Vittorio Emanuele.

Nicola's first impulse was to run after the Chinaman with the wheelbarrow (he was still visible in the distance), but to do so meant deserting the post he had been left to guard. A rifle shot might have served to give the alarm to the other contingents of foreign troops, but Nicola was reluctant to face explanations in any language but his own. He decided instead to look for the person who had got off the wheelbarrow. For a few yards, the bent grass gave evidence that some one had crawled through it, after which there were no more traces. Obviously the person in question had risen to his feet as soon as he could do so without danger of being seen.

Standing with his back to the lake, Nicola had on his right hand the lateral walls of the compound, inside which were the pavilions, courtyards and porticos of the Caserma Vittorio Emanuele. To his left was a reproduction in miniature of one of the five sacred mountains of China. It was a mound of earth and sculptured rocks, about sixteen feet high, with a tiny path winding to the summit between models of temples and pagodas, the size of dolls' houses. The mound, with its path and its temples, was protected by an ornate roof, supported by four columns, and which served as a refuge for some nesting pigeons. Nicola had the brilliant idea of climbing to the top of the mound, better to observe the surrounding country. But even from that vantage point, he could see nothing of immediate interest.

He noticed, however, that near the wall of the Caserma Vittorio Emanuele the bushes rose to the height of a man, and also that from the wall itself, small pieces of the outer clay had fallen, showing the bricks underneath. To climb over and enter the temple would not be impossible for any one who was fairly agile and who had feet small enough to take advantage of the tiny crevices in the masonry. Was the man who had been hidden in the wheelbarrow hiding now among those bushes, waiting for a chance to climb over?

Nicola came down from the artificial hillock and, holding his rifle ready for a bayonet thrust, began to poke about among the bushes. But meanwhile he had left the place where the presence of a sentinel was really necessary, namely the entrance to the temple. He recalled this fact with sudden apprehension. Starting off at a run, he did not stop until he had reached the central pavilion where the Laughing Buddha sat enthroned, white and shining against the red and gold lacquers of his background. All was quiet. A glance at the cases, piled up inside the big hollow pedestal on which the Buddha rested, was sufficient to show that nothing had been touched. Nicola decided to go in search of his companion, the other peripatetic sentinel, to whose vigilance the Caserma Vittorio Emanuele had been entrusted.

He found him close by, in the temple dedicated to the Buddha with Ten Thousand Arms. He was a gunner and, like Nicola, a native of the Latium, hailing from the capital itself. When Nicola joined him, he was preparing himself a cup of tea, a beverage he had taken to since his arrival in China, but only when nothing better was forthcoming. Every cup was brewed by him to the accompaniment of contemptuous remarks concerning a people who were content to imbibe such a decoction, when they might have imported wine from the Alban Hills.

Nicola told of his adventures and confided his suspicions, but the gunner, like all Romans, was sceptical by nature and did not seem inclined to pay much attention.

'I've been around here till now,' he said, 'and I've seen no one. There's no one in there with the cases, or in the temple. Even if a Chinaman *did* get down from the wheelbarrow, what does it matter to us?'

'You may be right,' said Nicola. 'But till the others come back, I'm going to stay by the cases and watch over them. You never know . . .'

The gunner made no objection, and having partaken of his tea, he went back with Nicola to the pavilion of the Laughing Buddha.

'What do you say to a game of *morra*?' he suggested. This game is popular in Italy among peasants and fishermen, and curiously enough it is played also in China. It involves much shouting and gesticulation.

'I'm ready,' replied Nicola. 'Half a litre up to seven.'

'And where are you going to find half a litre of wine in this benighted country? Do you take that fat old devil with a shiny paunch for an innkeeper?'

'Make it ten cents then, up to six.'

They began to play, and for some time the temple echoed to the cries of: Six – All – Two – Eight, accompanied by much Roman profanity.

The game was suspended when both were out of breath and Nicola had lost twenty-four cents. He

103

turned a malevolent glance on the Buddha. It almost seemed as if the Chinese god were laughing at him.

'I'd like to stick my bayonet into that fat paunch,' he said. 'On the altars at home, they place the Madonna and Child. Here they set up a hat-rack with ten thousand arms, or a half-naked drunkard with a swollen belly. That round paunch of his would make a good target, bull's-eye and all. Shall we have a shot?'

'With a rifle? There is not enough room.'

'With a revolver then. Three shots each, and see who gets most hits right in the navel.' Nicola was a crack shot, and underlying his suggestion was a veiled desire to retrieve his losses at *morra*. The gunner accepted, and they arranged the stakes as before. Nicola went off to get his service revolver, and soon returned with it and with a box of cartridges.

'Who has first shot?' he asked.

'You, if you like.'

Nicola took up his stand in the doorway, facing the Buddha, who continued to smile at him affably. The distance was about eight yards. Planting his feet wide apart, with his gaze fixed on the centre of the white paunch, Nicola raised the revolver swiftly to the level of his eyes and fired.

The detonation echoed and re-echoed under the vaulted ceiling, frightening some pigeons that were hidden among the beams. Nicola raised his arm for a second shot and then let it drop once more to his side. His jaw also dropped, and his bronzed face blanched with fear. His first shot had pierced the navel, and now over the white protruding stomach there trickled a little stream of blood!

The two valiant sentinels glanced at each other and then back at the wounded god. Each had read in the face of the other a terror equal to his own. From the stricken image there came, faint but unmistakable, a dying groan.

'Did you hear that?' Nicola's voice trembled and he made the sign of the cross. The gunner nodded an affirmative and moistened his dry lips.

The stream of blood ran on, making a little pool on the altar. From there it fell, drop by drop, to the floor.

'Holy Virgin, have mercy on us!' prayed the gunner. And then he gave a gasp of relief, as the rhythmic tramp of feet sounded in the courtyard. The two sentinels rushed out to greet their comrades, who were returning with supplies from outside the town. The young officer was the first to enter.

'What is the matter? What has happened? You are both as white as sheets!'

'Oh, sir! The Buddha. The laughing god! We fired at him. That is to say, Nicola fired at his stomach, and he bleeds . . .'

The Lieutenant did not answer, but walked briskly into the temple. At the sight of the blood-stained image, he gave a long whistle of surprise.

'There is more here than meets the eye,' he said. 'Or else it's an Oriental version of the miracle of San Gennaro. Here, you boys, turn the statue over, and be careful of the boxes underneath.'

A few minutes later, the image lay on its side, and from its hollow interior the sailors drew forth a dying Chinaman, dressed in sackcloth. He was black with coal-dust, and coal-dust covered his face, his hands and his bare feet. A fuse was twisted round one arm, and he still held in one hand a small box containing gunpowder. From his belt there fell to the ground a knife and a box of matches. The bullet which had pierced the image had entered the lungs of the man who was hidden within. *His* blood had trickled out over the white shining belly. *His* voice had given the dying groan that seemed to come from the god himself, even though he smiled.

13 Time

'Yes, my Soul went free ... I saw all Hind, from
Ceylon to the Hills; and every camp and every village, to the least, where we ever rested. I saw them
at one time and in one place, for they were within the
Soul. By this I knew that the Soul had passed
beyond the illusion of Time and Space and Things.
By that I knew that I was free—'

RUDYARD KIPLING:
Kim

Donald was still reading my story, *Caserma Vittorio
Emanuele*, when Kuniang and Elisalex came into the
study together. He glanced up at them and smiled. Then
he bent over the manuscript again. Only when he had finished reading did he get up and join us over the cocktails
that Exalted Virtue had brought in by request. I
returned the pages to its place in the old metal box.

'Well,' I said, 'you understand now what the boy must
have seen when he spoke of the statue bleeding?'

Donald was sceptical. 'I suppose,' he said, 'that Igor
could not have heard your story about the Italian
soldiers?'

'Practically impossible.'

Elisalex, who had no idea what we were talking about,
asked what had happened. It took some time to explain.
After which Donald continued his inquiries:

'You assume that Igor has some kind of second sight?'

'What else would you call it?'

Donald took off his spectacles and polished them with

106

his pocket handkerchief. He was looking rather worried. It was Kuniang who guessed what was in his mind.

'I suppose,' she said, 'that you are wondering how such trances might affect his training for the stage.'

'That's so,' said Donald. 'When you're acting or dancing, you need to have all your wits about you. In the part of Prince Charming in *La Belle au Bois Dormant*, Igor would have to stick to Perrault's lines, and not go wandering off on business of his own, through the halls and gardens of the sleeping castle. But if he were half asleep himself, that's just what he might do.'

'I don't think so,' said Kuniang. 'Igor has his visions when his attention is not held by anything in particular. He never had them when he was making love to me. To learn to act and to dance might be the best thing possible for him.'

'How do you explain these visions?' said Donald to me. 'What is second sight, anyway?'

'You will find an article on it in the *Encyclopaedia Britannica*, but no explanation is given. In Igor's case, the Abbot said that his trances were due to his mind moving freely in Time. And this might indeed be the explanation, and the explanation of many other manifestations that we perceive, as St Paul said, "through a glass, darkly".'

'What sort of manifestations?' asked Donald.

'Dreams, especially predictive dreams. And ghosts, and visions. We know very little about the relationship between consciousness and Time. Yet it is obvious that people like Igor have a faculty that we do not all possess: the faculty of lifting their conscious selves beyond the limitations of the present moment. This is not a supernatural but a supernormal phenomenon.'

'If that is an explanation,' said Donald, 'I am afraid I don't understand it.'

'You will find it easier to understand if you approach the problem from more than one angle. Some people have a theory of Time that serves to explain what

trances and dreams are, and what ghosts may be. They
will tell you that Time is not a succession, but that
Past, Present, and Future are coexistent. We should
see them all spread out before us – as a divinity
might – if we could find a suitable vantage point: if we
could look down from Heaven. Yet this is what we actually do sometimes, in our dreams. And so dreams, especially predictive dreams, serve to give us an inkling of
what Time really is. When a sleeper lives through
events that are yet to come, obviously his mind is not
moving in the true "here and now". Yet how often does
it not happen that the events observed by a sleeper in
his dreams actually do occur at a later date? If a man's
mind can move in the future, then the future is coexistent with him, somewhere outside the true "here
and now". The priestesses of Egypt used to learn to
dream, and in their dreams they sought the vantage
point whence they could gaze out over all Time. The
Israelites had schools of prophecy: they may have been
based on the same principle. And it is also possible that
what we call "spiritualistic mediums" are merely people whose minds, as the Abbot said of Igor's, move
freely in Time.'

Donald thought the matter over and then answered:
'If I get your meaning, what happened today was that
Igor's mind, moving backwards in Time, caught a
glimpse of the Buddha's image, as it was after the sol-
diers had fired on it, in the year nineteen-hundred.
What puzzles me is how things like that, seen in a
vision, can seem so real, just as real indeed as you and
Kuniang and Elisalex seem to me now.'

'If you accept the theory that all Time is coexistent,
you can no longer believe that the events experienced
by us here and now are the only ones that are real. The
mere fact that our minds are conscious of certain
events at a given moment does not mean that such
events possess a degree of reality that other events
have lost and others have not yet acquired. It cannot be
the human mind, with its limited perceptions, that

108

confers on objects outside it the quality of reality. The present time or moment, called "now", is an abstraction. Except to our restricted discernment, it is no more real, and no less, than all the other moments in eternity.'

'But what we call *now*,' said Donald, 'is the moment that we are conscious of when we are sitting up and taking notice. In this sense it is real to us, and all the other moments are not.'

'Except in dreams, or in visions such as Igor's. The "self" that moves through Time is one. And the "self" that contemplates existence and its own part in it is another. They move, as the Taoists say, on different planes. From the plane that we reach in our dreams, we may see backwards to moments that, in relation to the "now", are over and done with, and forwards to moments that are still to come. It is as if we saw them spread out, like localities in the map of a country we are passing through.'

'But if they are there all the time,' said Elisalex, 'it means that everything is fixed beforehand, and that there is no such thing as free will. Then the only truth is in fatalism.'

'On a map there are divergent roads and crossroads. We are not bound to follow one of them by any inevitable necessity. We can wander where we choose. Only the past is fixed immutably, and it is immortal. The song that has been sung once peals on for ever, and we could hear it as often as we liked, if we reached the plane on which it sounds.'

'Like an unbreakable gramophone record,' said Donald. And then he added: 'If what you say is true, then the day before yesterday Igor caught a glimpse of events that occurred on the other side of the world, nearly two thousand years ago.'

'How did that happen?' I asked.

Donald looked round at Kuniang and Elisalex. 'You will guess,' he said, 'what I am driving at, for you were there when I spoke to Igor about his taking the part of Saint Sebastian.'

Kuniang nodded. 'I was thinking of that,' she said.

Donald explained: 'I gave him d'Annunzio's play to read, and I showed him some sketches of the costumes. Also some picture postcards of paintings by old masters – Mantegna, Sodoma, and Guido Reni – representing the martyrdom. Igor was enraptured with the play: especially with the last scene, among the laurels sacred to Apollo, and the dialogue between the Saint, who wishes to die, and the archers of Emesus, who wish to save him. As he read bits aloud to us, Igor seemed almost to grow into the character of the Saint. And he kept on repeating:

> "Pour revivre
> ô Archers, il faut que je meure,
>
> Il faut que mon destin s'accomplisse,
> Que des mains d'hommes me tuent!
>
> . . . Vos mains!"

'But when he put the book down and took up the picture postcards of the old masters, he declared that they were all wrong. That is to say, the pose was wrong.'

'What did he mean by that?'

'He said that the Saint should not be tied at all. Or, if he were, it should be by the wrists to a branch above his head, so that his arms would be uplifted. He should be naked, with one arrow deeply embedded between the shoulders. And he should not be facing the archers, but standing with his back to them.'

'Then you would not see his face.'

'We told Igor that, and he answered that you might see it foreshortened and partly from the side, as his head fell back on the shoulders. He added that the Saint should be smiling.'

'None of us agreed with Igor,' said Kuniang, 'except Fédor. And he is going to paint a picture of Saint Sebastian, with Igor for a model, in the pose that he himself describes. I believe they have started on it already.'

Donald asked me: 'What do you think about it all? Does it tally with the theory of Time that you were telling us about?'

The story had left me a little doubtful. 'It does not seem possible,' I said, 'that Igor can be visualizing the real martyrdom of Saint Sebastian. More likely, the pictures you showed him served to recall some other event that we do not know of.'

'Some other event in the past?'

'Or in the future.'

Donald shook his head and smiled: 'I hope you will not mind my saying so, but this sounds to me like pure romance, or like one of d'Annunzio's plays. Here is a boy whose good looks might make his fortune if he could be taught to act and to dance. But he suffers from trances that take him back two thousand years, unless there is some mistake, and it is forwards and not backwards that he is looking. Then, to explain it all, you tell me that I should remember that Time is like a map, with paths through it, like the Bois de Boulogne.'

'You must get used,' said Elisalex, 'to people talking like that when they live in the East. Dorbon used to say that if we could only find the right starting point in a dream, we could carry our minds back over any period of Time.'

Donald shook his head again, as if giving us up as a bad job. Kuniang smiled at him and said: 'You are quite right. People who live out here often get bees in their bonnets. But this discussion about Time is not really as complicated as it sounds.' She turned to me and added:

'You talk as if it were a problem of higher mathematics. But I'm sure the Five Virtues would find these things quite simple. For them Time has little importance, for it exists only in our own minds. The ancestors that they worship on the family altar, and the descendants that some day will burn incense for them, are all one family, living together in the life of the race.'

Donald objected: 'But you don't feel that way about it, yourself, do you?'

'Perhaps not. But I understand the feeling so well.' She turned to me again and said, 'Do you know what this conversation reminds me of? Of that dinner, on Christmas Eve when Monsignor Paoli was staying with us.'

I nodded, and Kuniang explained to the others:

'We were keeping the plum pudding for Christmas Day, and we did not know what to have on Christmas Eve, which is a fast-day. We had to be careful, for there was a bishop staying in the house. I was not feeling very well at the time, for Hsiao-Kuniang was on the way, so I did not look after the matter myself. I merely told Ocean of Virtue – that is the cook – to do his best, which he did. He began by inquiring from some friend of the amah's, who is a Christian, what Christmas meant. She told him that it was the birthday of a sage called Jesus. So Ocean of Virtue made his preparations accordingly. At the end of dinner, a huge cake was served, with chocolate icing and nineteen lighted candles on it.'

'Why nineteen candles?' asked Elisalex.

'Well, we had celebrated Little Chink's birthday with three candles. In this case, each candle represented a century, each of which is as one day, compared to eternity.'

'A pretty idea.'

'But Ocean of Virtue overdid it. There was an inscription in white sugar, on top of the chocolate icing. It read *Hurrah for Jesus!*'

'And what did the bishop say?'

'He said that our boys were wiser than most Christians, for they spoke of Jesus as if he were alive and in the world to-day. Which of course he is.'

14 Cupid and Psyche

Young Adam Cupid, he that shot so trim,
When King Cophetua loved the beggar-maid

SHAKESPEARE:
Romeo and Juliet, II, i.

I cannot remember what it was that took me to the
Russian family's house that morning, about nine
o'clock. I suppose I must have left something there the
day before, or thought that I had left something, when
I went in to tea.

Whatever it was I was looking for, I did not find it.
Indeed I forgot all about it, talking to Fédor.

When I went into the house, I heard Patushka's violin somewhere near, possibly in the room near the
schoolroom.

'Fé-hsien-hseng is in garden,' said the Number One
Boy. 'He catchee picture.'

Fédor was often occupied in catching pictures, but I
wondered what he had found to paint in the garden.
And then, as I walked round a group of lilac bushes, I
came upon him, standing in front of his easel in the
sunshine, with Igor a few yards off, tied by the wrist to
the branch of a flowering acacia, above his head. He
held – or was held in – the pose that he himself had
described as that of the martyred Saint Sebastian.

He smiled over his shoulder at me, and Fédor waved
his palette by way of greeting. I stood and watched
them for a few minutes in silence. I had never seen
Igor stripped, and I thought to myself that he ought to

have lived in Athens, when Beauty was almost the sovereign authority. To the finely chiselled features corresponded limbs that were a marvel of softness and of power, and his colouring might have been that of a girl, rose leaves and ivory. Yet there was nothing effeminate about him. He was no unworthy model for the archer-saint.

Fédor asked me: 'Have you got a match on you?'

'I have a cigarette lighter.'

'That will do. Will you hold the flame on his back, just between the shoulders.'

'Certainly not! What an idea! Why should you want me to?'

'To see how the muscles react to a sudden pain. But it doesn't matter. Most pictures of martyrdoms are anatomically wrong. Look at the crucifixions! How often does one see the Christ with shoulders and hands on the same level, even though the torso may have no other support than the nails that pierce the palms.'

Fédor went on painting, and after a while he asked me: 'You would not care to buy a picture, would you? I may be leaving Peking soon, and am liquidating my stock.'

'I'll buy a picture or two, if you like. Your Saint Sebastian looks as if he might be a *chef d'oeuvre*.'

'It was not of this I was thinking. But you might have it too, if you like. There is a picture upstairs that I do not show to anybody, for I wanted to keep it myself. And Kuniang is in it.'

'Do you mean the Cupid and Psyche?'

'Yes. How did you know?'

'Elisalex was saying, only the other day, that you meant to paint that picture. She did not know if you had done so. And in one of Kuniang's old diaries, it says that you once teased her about a picture that you had kept for yourself, after you gave me the drawings. You made her pose holding a teacup, which was meant to represent Psyche's lamp.'

'That was my first idea of Psyche. But I gave it up.

114

So many frumpy Victorian statues represent her with a lamp.'

'Like Florence Nightingale.'

Fédor stared at me, evidently vague as to who Florence Nightingale was. And he added:

'There is one by Thorwaldsen, nervously clutching with her free hand at the draperies that she tried to hold up in front, though they are slipping down behind.'

'The sort of thing you would put on a tomb in Westminster Abbey.'

Fédor assented, though again I don't think he quite knew where Westminster Abbey was. 'Let us free Igor,' he said. 'If you come with me, I will show you what is really my *chef d'oeuvre*.'

I accompanied Fédor up to what had once been the guest room, and which, in former years, he used as a studio. There was still an easel standing there, and Milo Fo, the Laughing Buddha, smiled meaningly from the mantelpiece, as when Kuniang had occupied the model's throne.

Fédor opened a cupboard and took out a large canvas, which he placed on the easel for me to look at.

My first impression was a riot of gold and white and blue. The gold was Kuniang's hair. The white was her white skin, which glowed against a background of wings – blue wings, Cupid's wings – enveloping her in a caress. And they sprouted from Igor's shoulders.

The recumbent pose was that of Leda, as I had recognized it in the sketches. Igor was bending over her, drinking in her loveliness. How often must he have gazed down on her like that, when they sunbathed together, lying on the grass, after a swim?

The unexpected beauty of the picture, the unexpected pose had startled me, and I felt a little dazed. And at first I paid little attention to what Fédor was saying:

'I got the idea of those blue wings in Paris. There is an allegory by Titian, in the long gallery of the Louvre, before you get to Mona Lisa. The central figure is the

115

Marquess of Avalos. In the foreground there is a Cupid, with open wings. They are light in colour at the base, growing darker towards the tips.'

I said nothing, and after a moment he asked:

'Do you think you would care to buy the picture?'

I answered absent-mindedly: 'Yes. I suppose so.' And I continued to gaze at the two figures: the embodiment of a youth and a beauty in which I had no part. I felt outside it all.

'You don't like it?' said Fédor inquiringly.

I pulled myself together. 'Yes, I like it. More than I can say. It is a beautiful picture. How much do you want for it?'

'Would it be too much if I asked one thousand dollars?'

'One thousand dollars mex is not much, it is not enough, at the present rate of exchange. Your picture is worth more. But how is it that you have kept it hidden all this time?'

Fédor looked uncomfortable. 'I wanted it for myself,' he said. 'And I thought that, if I showed it, I might have to sell it to you. It would only have been fair. You paid me well for the portrait with Little Chink.'

'And now you do not mind selling it to me?'

Fédor smiled. 'No. I do not mind, now.'

I understood, and I smiled too.

'By the way,' I said, 'this is the same pose as the Leda in the bathroom.'

'Well, yes . . . except for the swan.'

'Of course. But the resemblance is there. So do not send this picture round to my house for a while. Keep it here till our guests have gone. But the picture is mine. I will send you a cheque at once. Shall we say two thousand dollars?'

Fédor looked at me in astonishment. 'I understand,' he said, 'what Kuniang means when she says you are the kindest man in the world. And I will keep your picture as long as you wish.'

* * *

As mentioned above, I started home, having forgotten what I came for. I dismissed my rickshaw coolie and walked through the minor hutungs so as to enter the house by the back way, through the Gate of Happy Sparrows.

And I asked myself: why was I so disturbed? Why had the first sight of that wonderful picture given me a sudden stab of pain? It revealed nothing to me that I did not know. Was it that the picture, painted long ago, possessed some in-dwelling meaning, and that this meaning still held good?

I passed through the stable and yard and along the narrow passage that led into the garden. As I stepped on to the lawn, a group of children passed along the path near the lotus pond. One of them was riding a donkey. Kuniang called to me to come and see.

'Donald has given Little Chink a donkey. Isn't it a pet? And Pure Virtue has offered the services of his son and heir as *ma-fu.*'

'Is that little boy Pure Virtue's son? He cannot be more than eight years old!'

'He is getting on for ten, at least the way Chinese make out their age. And he is such a nice little boy. Don't they make a lovely picture together?'

A lovely picture! Yes. Another lovely picture, and I hoped more true to the present than the one I had just seen. Little Chink walked proudly at the donkey's head; his sister in the saddle, no less proud and delighted. She did not hold the reins, but clasped a doll in her arms. Pure Virtue's son walked at her side and held her on. The group reminded me of the flight into Egypt.

Kuniang had just washed her hair and was drying it in the sunshine, a comb in one hand, which she passed now and then through her tresses. Skirts were short in 1928, and she looked like a little girl herself, with bare legs and sandals.

She put her arm through mine and gazed fondly at her offspring.

117

'You know,' she said, 'you ought to be very proud. I've given you the sweetest children.'

'Little devils!' I answered. 'They have all that East and West can offer. And their mother gave them her looks, and their father his brains. They ought to conquer the world.'

'It will be enough,' said Kuniang, 'if they can find one little corner of it, where there is happiness.'

'*Glück im Winkel.* Have you found it, Kuniang?'

'Not I. You found it for me.'

15 Rest Cure

Women I know are dressed in rags,
Women I know in lace,
And one in a dusky robe of gold
With a hooded cloak of mace;
But every robe and every rag
Is a secret hiding-place.

E. L. DUFF:
Not Three – But One

Peking is trying for people who are not used to the climate, and this is especially true during the spring, before the rains come, when the air is surcharged with electricity and one dust storm follows another. It is not unhealthy, but the dry air and constant winds are bad for the nerves.

Elisalex had been – so she said – in correspondence with the Prince-Abbot, and she decided at last to start for Liang-ko Chuang, to join him, at the end of the month. But as the day approached, she began to have doubts, and finally gave it up and retired to bed. It was not that she was ill, but she felt exhausted and unequal to any effort. What she wanted, she said, was a week or ten days' rest.

In any other woman I might have thought that the indisposition and the fatigue were feigned. But not so in Elisalex. She was above small hypocrisies, at least as much as it is possible for a woman of the world to be so. If she had merely wanted to stay on with us a little longer she would have had no qualms. For it was quite evident that everyone was pleased that she should remain as long as she liked.

Though she lay in bed she had plenty of company. We strolled in and out of her room at all hours of the day and night (whether this was compatible with a rest cure, I don't know!) The children would go and sit on her bed and show her their toys. Little Chink offered her, as a special favour, his Teddy Bear to sleep with. And she accepted with becoming gratitude.

It is only the cleverest, most sophisticated of women who know the secret of a graceful silence: that silence which bids you give of your best, and that is almost an invitation to make love to them.

As she lay there, with her hair braided and coiled round her forehead, she could have turned any man's head. Sometimes I felt that her eyes mocked me, as if saying: 'If I liked, I could draw you, as a flame draws a moth.'

Donald, who saw the world through a pair of opera glasses, remarked to me one day:

'What a Schéhérazade she would have made!'

I asked him if he were alluding to her physical attractions, or to her morals. He stared at me for a moment in surprise and then smiled.

'Elisalex,' he said, 'has no more morals than a snake has hips!'

This, coming from an admirer of the lady, seemed to me almost too severe. The mentality of Elisalex was that of the Olympians, for whom good and evil are words without meaning. It was as if she had lived the life and known the passions of the gods. And she breathed a more rarefied air than humbler mortals, such as Donald and myself.

She had her own ideas about morals and was quite willing to tell me about them. They were unexpectedly scientific.

'People's morals,' she said, 'are those of their environment, or else a reaction to their environment. In this, men and women, especially women, are like animals that take on a protective colouring to help them escape the dangers that lurk among their surroundings. My own morals are such as served to ensure survival in the Russian court in Rasputin's time, among nomad tribes in Mongolia, and in the cosmopolitan society of Paris. Naturally they are a bit mixed.'

'It would sound better,' I suggested, 'if you defined them as eclectic.'

'As you please ... But I feel now the reaction to such a feverish existence, and I long for peace and domesticity. I would like to marry Fédor and have children, lots of children ...'

'And why don't you? I'm sure Fédor is of the same mind.'

'Perhaps I will. But Fédor must give me just a little longer ...'

'Yet I cannot help thinking that it would be better if you gave up your excursion to the Temple of Costly Experience, and passed at once into a new incarnation of domestic bliss.'

'I don't think I could do that. I must round off the old life, before I begin the new.'

'I see you have still a hankering after adventure ... You want to have it both ways.'

'Most of us do,' said Elisalex. 'But I do not anticipate that the excursion to the Temple of Costly Experience will be reminiscent of my old life. Dorbon has no more need of me, in the old way ... He has become indeed what you always call him: "the Abbot". And women have no more part in his life. I am so sure of this that I would like you and Kuniang to come with me. Do you think you could manage it?'

I said that I would like to hear something more about the place before venturing there. I knew the region of the Western Tombs, and had often availed myself of the accommodation provided for visitors at the guesthouse. But for this a Government permit was necessary. The temple where the Abbot was staying might be at some distance off. Could it house a party of guests? And would the Abbot be willing to let us camp on his premises?

'I would also like to know if it is fairly safe in those parts. This is the lilac season, when civil war generally breaks out in North China. And I hear that Yen-Hsi Shan proposes to march on Peking. No one out here minds a war more or less, but travelling in the opposite direction to an advancing army is apt to cause discomfort and delay.'

'Dorbon would not ask me to come to him if there were danger.'

'There may not be danger for him, and he may be able to protect his own household. But it is a different thing for a party of foreign devils.'

'Well, I will inquire when I get there, and let you know.'

This conversation with Elisalex occurred on the evening of the last of her days in bed. She had suggested that I should go and have supper with her in her room, while the others dined. Exalted Virtue had prepared a little table near the bed. I remained there while Kuniang went off to change for dinner. She informed us that she meant to put on an old fancy dress that Donald had designed and had made for her when he visited Peking years ago.

To make things easier for the servants, Elisalex and I had our supper before the others began their dinner. Little Chink's Teddy Bear was also with us, leaning stiffly against the pillow on the farther side of the bed. He acted as a sort of chaperone.

'Will you explain something,' said Elisalex, 'that has always puzzled me? Why did you settle for good in China?'

'It is a question that I sometimes ask myself. Perhaps the reason is the same as the one that brought you back. Life in China is just a little unreal to foreigners like you and me. That is its charm. And it never loses that charm, however long we stay here. I have a feeling

122

about China that I think Shakespeare must have had when he wrote *A Midsummer Night's Dream*. He had portrayed so many real people in his plays that he felt the need of characters that were not circumscribed by human possibilities. So he set the scene in a wood near Athens, and peopled it with fairies.'

'And have you peopled China with fairies?'

What I might have answered I do not know, but just then the door opened and Kuniang came in, wearing Donald's fancy dress. It was indeed as if a fairy had entered the room: a sprite out of *A Midsummer Night's Dream*.

The costume, as Kuniang had first received it in a parcel from the United States, included a mask with grotesque, bird-like features. But this mask had lost its shape and colouring, so Kuniang had discarded it. But there remained a wonderful headdress of golden feathers, and she wore it so that it hid her own golden hair. The feathers formed an aureole that undulated as she moved. A shining cuirass of glittering gold scales imprisoned her torso, though leaving the shoulders bare. Yellow trousers of transparent gauze veiled but did not hide Kuniang's bare limbs underneath. The fantastic costume enhanced the wonder of her youthful figure and radiant colouring. Her eyes sparkled with pleasure: the pleasure of dressing-up that no woman ever loses.

Elisalex gazed at her and said softly: 'Poor Igor!'

Kuniang laughed happily: 'Do you think it will impress him?'

'I think it will give him some sleepless nights.'

But Kuniang was not bothering about Igor. She was capricious and full of mischief. Stepping in front of the long looking-glass, she made a pirouette and began to hum the air from *Carmen*:

> L'Amour est enfant de Bohême
> Il n'a jamais jamais connu un loi.

Et si tu m'aime, et bien je t'aime.
Et si je t'aime, prends garde à toi!

Then she waved us goodbye and ran out of the room.

Elisalex turned to me with expressions of wonder and admiration.

'You did not know Kuniang,' I answered, 'in the plumage of a bird of Paradise.'

'*L'oiseau de feu.* I certainly did not imagine she could be so glamorous. She was a lovely girl and now she is a lovely woman. The dress that Donald made for her suits her still. But she keeps it hidden away in a box.'

'She could not very well wear it in the streets of Peking.'

'True. But it is a pity, all the same. She has beauty and intelligence and charm. But they also lie hidden. For you live in a forgotten corner of Old Peking. It sounds romantic, and indeed it is very pleasant. As your guest I might seem ungrateful if I did not admit that yours is an enviable lot, especially in these hectic days, when the world is so full of trouble. But are you going to remain for ever in a backwater? Are your children to be brought up with no knowledge of their own country? Surely the future should hold something different, something better for them?'

'Sometime we will take them back to Europe.'

'And what about Kuniang? These should be the best years of her life.'

'She seems contented.'

'Quite true. But is that enough? And will it last? After a few years, marriage and children cease to be an adventure. And Kuniang's is a nature that craves for adventure. We come back to our old argument about the Russian family. Did she not prefer their unsettled ways to the quiet, orderly life she led in your house or in a convent school? There is something Trilby-like about Kuniang, and Trilby was more at home in Montmartre than she could ever have been in Victorian England.'

'And what do you conclude?'

'That you should take her away from China, at least for a while.'

'Merely to satisfy a taste for adventure?'

'Yes. Though perhaps I would not express it that way. She needs a fuller life than what you can offer her here. It is not enough to be sheltered. Life can be too sheltered. And then it becomes narrow and dull. Kuniang should see more people. She should rub shoulders with all sorts and conditions of men. There is danger in too much safety. When you are continually protected, you forget how to protect yourself. And perhaps you hardly want to ... *I* may yearn for a family life, because I have never known it, and long for children of my own. But Kuniang yearns for novelty and for pleasure. Just now you compared her to a bird of Paradise. Such birds cannot be kept in a poultry-yard.'

'You make me feel that I have been selfish.'

'You have never been anything but kind. But you are a man of culture, with spiritual resources deep down within yourself. Kuniang has a nature that is nearer than yours to the restless spirit of our age. You must try to sympathize and to understand. And you must take nothing for granted. Not even her love for you. Not even your love for her.'

'You remind me of a Chinese proverb.'

'What is that?'

'*A man thinks he knows. But a woman knows better.*'

16   The Singing Cossacks

The last of all the bards was he
Who sung of border chivalry.

WALTER SCOTT:
The Lay of the Last Minstrel

Elisalex left for Liang Ko Chuang at the beginning of
May, and we gave her a send-off at the station, as is
customary among foreigners in Peking. We promised
to follow on if she let us know that there was
accommodation available. I am sure that none of us
really expected that she would do so. Indeed, we foresaw that she herself would be back in Peking in a week's
time at the most. For though Elisalex pretended that
she preferred craziness to convention, it seemed
unlikely that she would put up with the dirt and discomfort inherent to a Chinese picnic with no foreign-
educated Boys to organize things for her. Had she been
going to stay in a Chinese house with a Chinese family,
it would have been another matter.

Elisalex had been a centre round which we had all
circled, like moons around a planet. When the train
steamed out of the station we felt a little lost. Fédor, of
course, was in despair, partly because he was left for-
lorn and partly because he was really anxious about her
safety, all alone in the interior of China under the threat
of civil war. Kuniang regretted the absence of her
friend: for Elisalex had always been, even in the past,
the only woman in whom Kuniang had ever confided.

Donald entered into long and serious conversations

with Igor about his future prospects. But they also missed Elisalex, whose familiarity with the Russian element in Paris made of her a competent adviser even in matters concerning the theatre, which were Donald's special province. And Little Chink missed 'the Beautiful Lady' (as he described her), who had impressed his childish mind with its first glimpse of a cosmopolitan feminine elegance.

The day after Elisalex left, I received an unexpected visit. Patushka came to see me. To do so, he had put on what used to be (before he was pensioned off) his office clothes. He had discarded for the occasion the Russian blouse, bordered with embroidery and belted in at the waist, that he always wore in his own house. In that dress Patushka reminded me of Tolstoy: tall, bearded and mentally detached from his immediate surroundings.

When Exalted Virtue announced the visitor Kuniang and I were in the garden, arguing about how best to replace a tree that showed signs of having succumbed to the rigours of the winter and to the singularly unpropitious soil of gardens in Peking. I could not remember when Patushka had been last in my house. Exalted Virtue said that he had been shown into my study and was waiting for me there.

'Have you any idea what he can want?' I asked Kuniang.

'None whatever. Would you like me to come in and see him too?'

'No. He asked for me. I had best see him alone at first. Later you can give him tea.'

And I went indoors to receive my guest.

Habitually absent-minded as he was, Patushka could be businesslike when his attention was held by something that he had at heart. And he possessed first-hand knowledge of Chinese bureacratic procedure. As soon as we had exchanged greetings he told me why he had come. He wanted to talk to me about Igor.

'Why to me?' I asked.

'Because, now that Elisalex has left, you are the only person who can help.'

'Does Igor need help?'

'That is what I want to find out. I hear that this American friend of yours wants to take Igor to Paris, to make him study for the theatre.'

'Have you any objection?'

'It makes me a little anxious. I am fond of that boy. All the fonder because I feel he has need of care and help. I know nothing of Paris or of Europe. I imagine dangers that perhaps do not exist. But I would not stop him going, even if I could. And I am certain that his mother would not either. She will be only too glad that her son should see the world and have a chance of earning his living. It is very kind of your American friend to offer to do so much. I should like to tell him how grateful we are.'

Patushka was expressing, more or less, what I felt myself: perhaps what we all felt about Igor. It was most generous of Donald to pay for Igor's journey to Paris, to offer to look after him when he was there, and to find him a job in the theatre. But it was a risky business. For Igor was not like other young men of his age (he was then in his twenty-fourth year). His mind was a delicate fabric. Would it resist the buffeting of a world such as Donald lived in? And if not, what then?

Patushka was sitting on the armchair opposite me, his colossal limbs bunched up in the restricted environment. And he gazed at me with his melancholy eyes. I had an unexpected and uncomfortable feeling that he could read my thoughts.

'But that,' he continued, 'was not what I came here to say.'

I looked at him inquiringly, and murmured: 'No?'

'No. I have come to tell you who Igor is.'

I gave a little start of surprise. We had always taken Igor so much for granted that it had never occurred to us to trouble about his identity. This did not seem to be a matter of any interest or doubt. Yet all I knew of him was that he had a mother in Tientsin, who was now married to a Chinese. For once Patushka showed himself more practical and worldly-wise than the rest of us.

'I think,' he said, 'that, if Igor travels abroad, he may have to do so with a Chinese passport.'

I stared at Patushka with astonishment, and asked:

'Would that be possible?'

'Oh, yes. I have been a Chinese employee myself and I have friends among Chinese officials. They will give me a passport for Igor, if I ask them to.'

'Has he no papers of his own?'

'Private papers. I will get them for you. They may be useful later on, to establish his identity if he wishes to become a Russian citizen, or to take up any other nationality.'

'He is an illegitimate son, is he not?'

'Yes, poor boy, though his father and mother meant to marry. They would have done so if things had been easier at that time. But both parents were in Port Arthur, when it was besieged by the Japanese. And the father, Ivan Ivanovitch, was killed on 203 Metre Hill.'

'Igor must have been only a few months old.'

'He was not yet born. His father never saw him. Igor came into the world a few weeks later. A siege baby. That may account for him being a little odd. We had a bad time at Port Arthur during the last weeks.'

'Were you there too?'

'Yes. I and my wife were there. And Fédor was about a year old.'

I stared at Patushka with a new interest. I had never troubled to inquire about his past, or how he came to be in China with his family. But it was not the moment to go into that. We were talking about Igor.

'You say that his father's name was Ivan Ivanovitch?'

'Yes. He was a Cossack, like myself, only a much younger man. We were of the Semiryechensk Cossacks.'

Patushka paused for a moment and then he asked: 'Do you know what a Cossack is?'

'I have a general idea, like most people. But I have never gone into the matter.'

I did not like to tell Patushka that I had always considered Cossacks as picturesque freebooters, who figured in books by lady novelists and Byron's *Mazeppa*.

'I ask you because it is not generally known abroad that, in the old Russian empire, the standard of education among the Cossacks was at a much higher level than among the rest of the population. Ivan Ivanovitch was a poet and a musician. He made up his own songs and sang them. He was a minstrel among the Cossacks.'

I am not attempting to give Patushka's conversation faithfully in his own words. What he said was very much to the point, even though his English (we conversed in English) was not up to the usual standard among foreigners in the Treaty Ports. But his description of the blond northern Tyrtaeus was full of appeal to a literary man like myself. Ivan Ivanovitch must have been to the Cossacks what Körner was to the Germans during their wars against Napoleon: a poet who could fire his comrades to deeds of heroism. His songs were sung by them on the march, round camp fires, even in horse-trucks on the Trans-Siberian railway.

But Ivan's popularity among his comrades was not only founded on his lyric qualities. He was the typical Cossack of his day, like young Lochinvar, riding out of the West, to conquer new realms for the Tsar. It was their dream to give him a double empire, such as Rome had had, East and West, with Siberia to unite them.

When the Russians swept south to Peking, to succour the besieged Legations in 1900, it was Ivan who stuck his lance into a mound of coal near Ching-wan-tao, and claimed the Kai-ping mines for Russia. Later on they became a limited liability company with British capital, but the story of that picturesque imperious gesture lingers on.

Ivan found the lady of his dreams (as he was a poet, we may call her that), at Dalny, near Port Arthur. And they used to meet on a sandy shore opposite some little wooded islands called the Seven Stars. The shore itself was called The Beach of Stars.

Such was the beginning of Ivan's love story. Its end came when he lay dead in the open space between the outer loopholed gallery and the inner parapet of a casemate. The epic struggle between the inner and the outer lines of defence in 203 Metre Fort was one of the last hand-to-hand battles of any magnitude ever to be fought. It continued for more than three days, new Japanese infantry ever pouring in to replace the men whose bodies were piled up to a height of thirty feet. The object of the attack was to conquer a hill from which the town and the port could be overlooked, and the artillery fire directed on to buildings and ships.

Ivan found there a soldier's death, which was the end he would have chosen. And Igor's mother was taken care of – such care as was possible under the circumstances – by Patushka and Matushka. She settled eventually in Tientsin.

'Tell me a thing,' I said, when Patushka had finished his story. 'Some time after the Boxer Rebellion, and before the Russo-Japanese War, the Russians still occupied a fort near Shan-hai-kwan, just outside the Great Wall. It was garrisoned by Cossacks. Was not this Ivan Ivanovitch among them?'

'Yes. Did you meet him?'

'No. But I saw him, when I went up there and stayed a few days in the fort that was occupied by the English (and is still, for that matter). I was the guest of one of the officers. Shan-hai-kwan was full of foreign troops of various nationalities. They quarrelled so among themselves that it is a miracle they did not start another war.'

'What makes you think that you saw Ivan?'

'Because the Russian soldiers were known to their

Allies as "the Singing Cossacks", and there was a poet among them, who made up their songs. They pointed him out to me one night, when the Russian commander drove up to the English fort in an open carriage, with an escort of horsemen each of whom carried a torch, which he held up as he rode. They arrived at a gallop, torches flaring and harness-bells jingling. And when the commander got out of his carriage the escort rode off, singing as they went. It made a great impression on me. I had never seen anything like that before.'

Just then Kuniang came in to say that tea was being served in the garden, and would we come out or have it brought to us in the study?

We decided for the garden and rose from our chairs. Patushka walked on ahead with Kuniang. I followed them leisurely, absorbed in my own thoughts.

For Patushka's story had brought back to me the China I had known when first I came to the Far East. There were wars and invasions and occasional massacres, much as there are now. But they were not broadcasted, and news of them reached breakfast tables in the West too long afterwards for people to get really excited. In China itself there were no railways (there are not many even now) and few telegraph lines. We travelled in chairs, or on ponies and barges. We had no gramophones or refrigerators, and we still possessed, most of us, the characteristic virtue of the East – that of taking things as they come.

Patushka had also recalled to my memory the Singing Cossacks, whose fame, in my young days, had become almost legendary on the Great Wall: a Border Minstrelsy such as a Russian Walter Scott might have collected. The life of Ivan Ivanovitch was a poem in itself.

Why had I not tried to meet him, when I had the chance, in 1902? I had watched him and his companions, admiring their graceful figures as they held aloft the blazing torches. And I had listened to their singing

132

as they rode away in the dark woods that nestle under the Great Wall where it crosses the plain, between the first Manchurian hills and the sea.

I had talked with the commanding officer, and even visited him in his fort, just outside the Wall. He was a soldierly, gallant figure. But what had struck me most about him was his Spartan simplicity. Wishing to make himself agreeable, he had shown me some miniatures – very archaic specimens, done by a painter of ikons – which he kept in a woollen sock. He had no other possessions. The commanding officer of five Sotnias of Cossacks had crossed half of Asia with no other personal luggage than one old woollen sock!

Kuniang was making tea with Patushka, Donald and the two Russian boys standing round her. I looked at Igor and wondered what his mother could have been like as a girl, when Ivan Ivanovitch rode down to the Beach of Stars.

As in *Love Among the Ruins:*

> *And I know, while thus the quiet-coloured eve*
> *   Smiles to leave*
> *To their folding, all our many-tinkling fleece*
> *   In such peace,*
> *And the slopes and rills in undistinguished grey*
> *   Melt away . . .*
> *That a girl with eager eyes and yellow hair*
> *   Waits me there . . .*

17   The Pao-lien Ssè

'Man was lost and saved in a garden'
Pensées of PASCAL

Elisalex had been gone just a week when Kuniang received a letter from her. It had been posted in Kao-pe-tien two days after her departure, but had taken a long time on the way. This is what she said:

KUNIANG DARLING!

Tell Donald that, if he comes here, he will find himself living in *Le Pavillon d'Armide*, complete with *décor* and costumes by Alexandre Benois. Only the music is missing, but the birds do their best to make up for that. This morning they woke me up at an unearthly hour!

You must all come, *all*! Even Little Chink and his sister, if you will let them. There is a courtyard with huge marble stele in it, all covered with Chinese and Mongol characters, and they are supported on the backs of giant tortoises, which the children could ride and climb over. And there is a stream and a little lake to fall into and get wet, without danger of drowning, for the ground slopes down gently. And the woods and the hillsides are gay with wild flowers, to pick and carry home.

The stream is the same as runs through the region of the Imperial tombs, and on the lake there is a tiny island with a pavilion, and wistaria that cascades from the roof down to the water's edge. When the wistaria is over, the roses should begin to bloom: climbing roses: they are all over the place. And there are still some blue irises in the shadow of the trees, and flowering bushes along the stone-flagged paths. The Garden of Klingsor could not be more lovely.

You and the Maker of Heavenly Trousers shall have a pavilion close to me. Donald, Fédor and Igor will not mind being housed in a group of buildings outside the temple itself, on the bank of the stream, about three hundred yards away.

Bring your own cook, boys, camp beds and other paraphernalia, as when you make excursions to the Western Hills.

Dorbon expects you. When I arrived he said to me: "Your friends will be coming here soon." He spoke as if it had been all settled long ago. So don't hesitate. Just come, and start quickly. I am waiting for you. Love,

ELISALEX

P.S. Dorbon would be grateful if you could bring him some kippered herrings. You can buy them (tinned) at Culty's grocery in Legations Street.

E

I thought to myself that the simile of the Garden of Klingsor was a little unfortunate, but the place sounded attractive. And I liked the homely note that was struck by the Abbot's request for kippered herrings.

If we accepted the invitation, we must do so at once. There was no time to lose.

Donald's stay in China was drawing to a close. He had booked a passage on the *Empress of Russia*, sailing for Yokohama at the beginning of June. So it was decided that we should all go down, as soon as possible, to the Pao-lien Ssè. If local conditions appeared to be peaceable, Donald would return to Peking after a few days, leaving the rest of us there, for a more prolonged visit. Possibly I might accompany him, and return to

Liang Ko Chuang once more, if circumstances permitted.

To reach our destination we took the train to Kao-pe-tien, on the Peking–Hankow Railway, and then continued to Liang Ko Chuang on a branch line. The last lap of the journey had to be accomplished on foot or on donkeys.

We were lucky to get through without many delays, even though the train in which we left Peking was so full that we could not find seats. The carriages reserved for passengers were crowded to suffocation. But a friendly guard found us places of sorts in a truck half full of coal sacks. And on these we seated ourselves, having first spread them over with newspapers.

Exalted Virtue, the Number Two Cook, and several coolies accompanied our party, carrying camp beds, pots and pans and provisions, tinned or otherwise. They sat with us in the coal truck, and the coolies beamed with the obvious enjoyment that is typical of Chinese when setting off on an excursion. Only Exalted Virtue kept aloof and looked glum. He did not approve of the expedition, which he considered imprudent in troublous times. And it may be that he still regarded Elisalex with suspicion.

The small local train from Kao-pe-tien was not crowded. It took us comfortably enough to Liang Ko Chuang, where donkeys and chairs awaited us. While our luggage was being sorted on a flat piece of ground that served as a station platform I was surprised to hear my name called out, and to be greeted by a bearded and spectacled Catholic priest, who hailed me like a long-lost brother.

He turned out to be a French missionary, Père Antoine, whom I had known years before at Shan-hai-kwan. His own headquarters were at the Zi-ca-wei observatory, near Shanghai, for Père Antoine was a Jesuit. I asked him what he was doing at Liang Ko Chuang.

'I am studying the folklore concerning the Imperial tombs. And I'm staying with some Italian missionaries, who have built a small hospital here. And what brings *you* to these parts?'

I explained that I and my party were going to stay at the Pao-lien Ssè.

'You don't mean where the Prince Dorbon Oirad lives?'

'Yes. Do you know him?'

'No. I wish I did. He is building a tomb there, for himself, much in the style of the Imperial tombs.'

'Are you sure it's for himself?'

'So I've been told. I would give anything to go and watch the work. But the Prince has a bodyguard of Mongols and Buriats, and they chase me off whenever I go near the place. How is it that you are admitted?'

'We are friends of the family.'

'I should never have thought it possible. Anyhow, if you can get me a permit to visit the tomb, I'll be eternally grateful.'

I promised to do my best.

It was late in the afternoon when we mounted our donkeys and started off from Liang Ko Chuang. At first our way led through an outlying grove that surrounded and sheltered the tomb of the Emperor Huang Hsu (the last of the Manchu dynasty). But soon we emerged again on the open plain, with the forest of the Hsi Ling to our left, like a great green wave that swept up to the foot of the barrier mountains to the south and to the west. Père Antoine had told me that the ride to the Pao-lien Ssè would take about two hours, and it was dusk before we came in sight of our destination. A group of trees stretched out like a spear-point into the plain, and curved roofs showed among the foliage. Except for one small hillock, crowned by a Belvedere, the temple was not built on rising ground, and nothing in its distant aspect revealed the presence of an important sanctuary. If the donkey-boys had not pointed it out to us, when we were still more than a mile off, we might not have guessed that the Pao-lien Ssè was in sight.

To our right was a small village, the typical Chinese hamlet, complete with its backing of willows, its group of tombs and a little shrine to the tutelary god, set out among the well-tilled fields. As we made our way in Indian file along the winding path, we could see on either side the owners of the soil wending their own way homewards at close of day.

We were still in the Third Moon – 'the sleepy moon' of spring, which is the month for fireflies, and in the still evening air they mingled with the first twinkling lights. We crossed a dilapidated camel-backed bridge round and underneath which some bats were flitting. And then I noticed the loop taken by the stream that emerged from the forest, only to return once more into the woods after what seemed a purposeless curve in the plain: as if the waters had meant to flow outward, but had thought better of it and turned back. In the middle of the field that the sharp bend in the stream surrounded was a group of trees, overshadowing another tiny cemetery of sepulchral mounds. From out of the shadows there emerged a solitary horseman, who first scanned us from afar and then raised a horn to his lips, sounding a deep melodious note. And a similar note answered him from the distance. The horseman rode off, and in the darkness ahead more lights began to twinkle. Our donkey-boys, who elsewhere might have forced us to accomplish the last lap at a canter, now as we drew near the Pao-lien Ssè showed signs of reverence amounting almost to fear. They peered anxiously at the lights before them, walked silently, and one and all gasped with sheer nervous terror, when suddenly on both sides of us there loomed up the towering forms of gigantic Tartar warriors.

I had seen such figures often enough in illustrations, by Jesuit engravers, to *The Conquest of Turkestan by the Emperor Ch'ien Lung*, but I had never expected to meet them in the flesh. Yet there they were, taller than any Chinese, broad in the shoulders, massive in shape and heavy in movement. It was too dark to perceive more than their general outline. But some of them wore crossbows slung over their shoulders, others had falcons on their wrists. And one, taller than the rest, stood under the roofed doorway in the light of a hanging lamp and watched us dismount, leaning the while on a long bow. I heard Donald's voice somewhere behind me:

'Say! Is this an Indian reservation or a dude's ranch?'

And then a slim graceful figure in a white frock emerged out of the darkness, and Elisalex hastened out to make us welcome.

I have arrived so often, at close of day, in some far-off Chinese temple, and waited while the boys set up camp beds in a dusky pavilion, smelling of camphor-wood and mould. Generally one has to begin by sweeping away the cobwebs of seasons and the dust of centuries, while a scorpion or two scuttles away towards the door. But here all was swept and garnished, and the camp beds that we had brought with us were soon set up. Exalted Virtue began to unpack without further preliminaries. Even the rice paper on the windows was intact.

As Elisalex had written, the buildings that had been set aside for Donald and the two Russian boys were in our immediate vicinity. I did not visit them, but Kuniang insisted on going off at once to see all there was to be seen. I took the opportunity of being alone with Elisalex to ask her some questions:

'I heard in Kao-pe-tien that the Abbot is building a tomb here. What is that for?'

'He says he expects to occupy it before long, and is most fussy about everything being done according to his wishes. He chafes at any delay. Only good materials may be used, and they have to be brought from afar: the finest lacquer, the best gold leaf, the tallest pillars of sandalwood.'

139

'I suppose that is what he was buying tiles for, when I saw him last, in Peking. He reminds me of Browning's Bishop: "Saint Praxed's ever was the church for peace". But is the Abbot ill?'

'No. Only much aged since I saw him last. You, who met him recently, may not find him changed.'

'Anyway, his digestion must be all right, if he sent me a message to bring kippered herrings from Culty's store.'

'That was my idea, really. Dorbon used to be fond of kippers, and when I asked if he would like some brought down, he said yes.'

'Kippers and premonitions of death don't seem to go well together. But Orientals have a way of mixing up the practical details of their daily life with an esoteric mysticism. I remember hearing about a very miserly old woman in Peking who was convinced that she would die on the third day of the third moon. As the time approached she left her house in the Tartar City and took up her abode somewhere near the Old Hunting Park, where the family graveyard was situated. The idea was to save transportation at the funeral.'

'And did she die?'

'Yes. Though some people believe that her relations helped the premonition to come true, by means of a good thump on the back of the head with a chair-pole. Anyway, she was buried, and there was no need of a costly funeral procession. But I gather that the Abbot is not thinking of economy, if his tomb is to be a replica of an Imperial mausoleum.'

'No. He is spending money like water, and is most popular in the countryside.'

'To build one's tomb is a thing that many people like to get done in good time. But, apart from that, are you sure that he is not speaking figuratively of his own death? He might mean that he is already dead to the world, like the Indian Minister "of no small state", in Kipling's story, *The Miracle of Purun Bagàt*. Such an attitude is quite common among Buddhists who

140

have occupied important government posts. They resign, not merely from their official positions, but from life itself.'

'I don't think that can be Dorbon's idea. But I may be wrong. I have no knowledge of Far-Eastern mentality. It was the Tartar side of his character that I knew and understood.'

'Then you can tell me who are those extraordinary Tartar retainers that he has brought with him to China. We saw them standing round the entrance when we arrived. Donald was much impressed. He said they would look wonderful on the stage, as the archers in *Boris Godounov*.'

Elisalex laughed. 'I heard Donald telling Igor that in Chicago those men would be known as tough guys.'

'And a very good name too! I hope they don't take us for a ride.'

That evening after supper I went to bed some time before the others, for the journey had given me a headache. But I did not get to sleep till past midnight. As I lay awake in the light of a candle that I had left for Kuniang to undress by, when she came, I could hear the sound of voices and Kuniang herself laughing gaily. Then another sound reached me – one that is familiar enough to people who go on excursions in China: the single note of a temple bell. Its vibrations rolled away in diminishing waves and did not come again. I knew they would not, for one hour at least, but unreasonably I wished they would do so. I wanted to hear that note once more, if only out of curiosity. It had not been a beautiful note, but harsh and unmelodious, giving the impression that something was wrong somewhere.

Though two of the rice paper windows were held open by the primitive method of a stick pushing the hanging lattice outward, the room seemed airless, and I decided to leave the door ajar. So I got up to open it. Across the stone-flagged courtyard lights shone in the pavilion opposite: the soft glow that is characteristic of lamps seen through rice paper. Against that bright surface shadows moved, like silhouettes in *Ombres Chinoises*. I recognized Kuniang by her profile and the mass of her hair. Also Fédor's huge bulk.

And then I gave a little start.

On one side of the courtyard, between those lighted windows and myself, were figures barely visible in the darkness. A group of men, watching the windows, as I was. I recognized the Abbot's retainers, 'the tough guys'. They too had their eyes fixed on the shadows, seen against the light.

I stood there and watched them for a little while, even as they were watching the figures seen through the rice paper of the windows in the pavilion opposite. Those men – so I had gathered from Elisalex – formed the Abbot's bodyguard, a bodyguard of archers!

What sort of a place had we come to? Certainly not the usual temple that forms the object of excursions in China, of picnics from Peking. Even in these one steps back in the centuries to a world as old as their ghinko trees, as their groves of white pines, as their strange old ceremonies and services, conducted by priests that keep up a cult that is often neither Buddhist nor Taoist, but a strange mixture of both, or a residuum of older cults half forgotten.

Here we seemed to have entered a world that was alien to China itself: a domain, not of ancient Asiatic religions, but of northern Asiatic tribes.

How had they come there, and why? What was their mentality in the year 1928? Was it no more modern than their weapons? And what would they think of us? Of Elisalex and of Kuniang?

Meanwhile they stood there in the darkness, unseen except by me, who watched them unseen. And from the pavilion opposite came merry peals of laughter.

18   The Western Tombs

'... tongue availeth not to its description, by reason of that which was therein of wonders and of
rarities, which are not to be found but in Heaven;
and how should it be otherwise, when its doorkeeper's name was Rizwàn?'

> *The Thousand Nights and One Night*
> (From the story of Ali-hur al Din and
> the Frank King's daughter)

With picnics, in the East as in the West, the success of
the expedition depends largely on the weather. And the
weather, during a whole week after our arrival, was
uncertain. It did not rain – we all wished it would – but
the north wind blew steadily, day after day, subsiding
only at dusk, and rising once more with the rising sun.
The sky was a dirty grey, tinged with yellow. The
waters of the stream were leaden, and their reflections,
somehow, were untrue. The flowers looked bedraggled
and almost colourless.

There was nothing exceptional in these circumstances. The rainless spring of North China is apt to be
a dusty business.

Fortunately the Temple of Costly Experience lay on
the edge of the forest, and the stream that traversed its
grounds made a wonderland of red-stemmed pines, of
flowers and of running water. Had the sunshine been
stronger, it might have been pleasant to have bathed.
But the water of the stream was still icy cold, and the
dust storms clouded the sky.

As long as we remained in the shadow of the trees, or on the hillsides at the back of the Hsi Ling, the wind troubled us but little. But if we ventured out on the plains, the dry air and the clouds of dust spoilt all our pleasure. For this reason we passed most of our time in the forest, visiting the various tombs.

It took a deal of explaining to make Donald understand the nature of the places he was visiting. To people who are not familiar with the idea that inspires the building of an Emperor's tomb in China, the whole conception is puzzling. For the tombs themselves are just what one never sees. They are buried deep underground and sometimes their whereabouts is purposely hidden. What one does see are the meeting-places for the departed Great Ones.

I take the following paragraphs from a recent *Life of the Dowager Empress Tzu Hsi*:[1]

'The idea of what an Emperor's tomb should be comes down to us from the times of the self-styled "First Emperor", who reigned about two hundred years before the birth of Christ. The tale is told of how he chose a mountain and caused it to be hollowed out, and his Empire reproduced within: cities of jewels and rivers of quicksilver on a floor of polished bronze. In the centre stood the sarcophagus, where he was ultimately laid to rest, and on each side were enormous bowl-shaped lamps, containing oil of dolphins sufficient to keep the flame of a wick alight for two hundred years. The chasm was vaulted by a ceiling on which were reproduced the heavens, with golden stars and silver planets on a background of dark blue. The Emperor's wives, concubines and servants were buried with him, crucified to the walls, lest in death they should assume an attitude disrespectful to their lord.

[1] From *The Last of the Empresses*, by Daniele Varè; quoted by kind permission of the publishers, Messrs John Murray.

'After the burial, the entrance to the mountain-side was closed and covered up with earth. Trees and grass were planted over it. And all those who had hollowed out the mountain, or worked at the tomb, were put to death so that none might tell where it lay.

'Later Emperors have been buried in the mountainside, facing south, or in great mounds, grown over with trees, and called "Jewelled Cities". The wives and concubines did not accompany their late lords except in effigy.

'The successive Emperors of the Manchu dynasty were buried alternately at the Eastern and the Western Tombs (Tung Ling and Hsi Ling) situated in two different mountain ranges, to the east and to the west of Peking. Each group of tombs had a governor of its own, living in a village within the sacred forest, and each tomb had its own guard of archers and halberdiers. In the Eastern and Western Tombs, each mausoleum had a marble-flagged road leading up to it, with colossal marble figures on either side: warriors, sages, elephants, camels, horses and super-natural animals that are no longer seen on earth. In front of the mountain, or "Jewelled City", which contained the tomb, were pavilions like those of a temple, with carvings of sandalwood, whose scent mingled with the pine scent of the surrounding forest. Thrones of yellow satin, embroidered with golden dragons, were placed beside banqueting tables, where, on the day of the annual sacrifice, the departed Great Ones might come and feast.

'There was an extraordinary spiritual appeal in the eerie silence of that realm of the dead, where the only sign of life was the cooing of pigeons under the eaves, or the quick scamper of a squirrel across the marble flags of a triumphal way. In those secluded valleys the Emperors slept on, close to the heart of Nature. The imagery of a life immortal lay around them, less in the complicated symbolism of their costly tombs,

145

than in the slow-moving shadows of the hills, and in
the ever-recurring pageant of starlit nights.'

What struck Donald most was what he himself called
the 'theatricality' of it all. A designer of stage scenery
and costume, he now found himself on a natural stage,
where reality and make-believe were intermingled
through miles and miles of almost primeval forest.

The Chinese idea of a whole countryside reserved for
the spirits of departed Great Ones, which live on among
those hills, those valleys and those deep woods, has
brought into being an imitation world, peopled with
dead emperors, their wives and their concubines.
There, in the forest, within an hour's ride from our door,
were throne rooms, guardrooms and banqueting halls,
scented with fragrant woods and gorgeous with satins
and cut velvets. Real meals were laid out, on certain
days, upon long tables set before the dragon thrones.
Bows and arrows, halberds, drums and bugles were
stacked on red-lacquered stands before the doorways,
for a guard of honour to use when required.

To complete the picture, and to add to our mental
confusion, there rose, close to where we lived, a new
tomb in the making, and almost finished: the tomb that
our host, the Abbot, was building for himself. As yet
there was no triumphal avenue, with marble colossi on
either side. But in their place were the Abbot's retainers: warriors in flesh and blood, wearing the
accoutrements of centuries long dead.

Père Antoine had spoken of them as Mongols, but
that was a generic term. Most of the Abbot's followers
– I mean those who had accompanied him to the Pao-
lien Ssè – were Yakuts, from the Yakut province of
Siberia. I was astonished to see one of them wearing
a military tunic of Western pattern, and on inquiry I
discovered that he had followed the Koltchak army to
Manchuria, when the Tsarist force was driven out of
Siberia by the Communists. He represented recent
history.

Some of the others might have been followers of Tamerlane come to life again. These were smaller men, with flat heads, huge cheekbones and narrow slanting eyes. They were Orotchons from the Barga district in Manchuria (Orotchon, in the Manchu language, means a breeder of deer). Exalted Virtue brought me some gossip about them, which he had collected in the usual Chinese way, and which – as invariably happened with the information that he brought me – was detailed and probably inaccurate. He said that the Orotchons' hunting ground used to be in the northern ranges of the Hingan mountains, where they used reindeer for transport and for hunting. But an epidemic broke out among the reindeer and they all died. After which the Orotchons retired to the central and southern ranges of the Hingan mountains, where they were nearer the Steppes and therefore to the feeding ground of their horses.

I inquired of Exalted Virtue when this was supposed to have happened. But he could not tell me anything except that it was within a century of 'present day' (whether one year ago or ninety-nine, he was not sure). He added that there was a Shahmanist priest among them, who called them to prayer by beating a sheepskin drum with a human bone. If Exalted Virtue was to be trusted, they worshipped a God, in the shape of a horse, called Madairi. And there were also three Buriats and a Russian Tartar, who could charm snakes.

Taken as a group, these men reminded me of the warlike tribes – known as the Three Kingdoms – whose raids had induced the Chinese, under the Tsing dynasty, to build the Great Wall. In those days they were known in China as Shan-nu, and in Europe as Huns.

It would have been natural to have found such men collected round their chief, in the China of Kublai's time. But after my first surprise, I had to admit that they hardly represented an anachronism as followers of the Prince Dorbon Oirad. His day had passed, even as

Kublai's had passed. And he was building himself a sepulchre, in the grand old Chinese manner.

Of all the tombs in the forest this one only was not yet closed (I was not surprised that my Jesuit friend wished to visit it). The entrance was a long, dark tunnel, as broad as a high road, sloping down into the bowels of the earth. The upper structure was a circular building, a mound surrounded by a wall, some sixty feet high, like a large gasometer, half hidden by a network of scaffolding. This was the tomb itself, apart from the usual pavilions (banqueting halls, guardrooms, and the 'Soul Chamber' for the Tablet).

It was the scaffolding that interested me more than anything else. That same type of scaffolding, held together entirely by cordage, must have been used in China long centuries before the birth of Christ. It rose up, eight storeys high, entirely made of bamboo poles, lashed together with overlapping ends. A sloping gangway of boards went zigzagging up the side of the tomb, and the materials – bricks, mortar and tiles (the tiles from San-chia-tien) – were carried up, Chinese fashion, wrapped in cloths. Strange to say, the general design of that archaic scaffolding was similar to that of the scaffoldings set up in Western countries by the most up-to-date contractors. The bamboo was not unlike metal tubing. Only the cranes were missing. The general impression was that of a Piranesi engraving.

If only shades frequented the stately throne room and banqueting halls of the Hsi Ling, here – in the midst of the bustle and confusion occasioned by the building of even such another tomb – there moved another spectre. When I had seen him at my house some months before, the Abbot had seemed to me the ghost of his former self. Now that I met him again, the impression was even more marked. There were no signs of illness about him. He was on his feet from morning till night watching the strings of camels that brought building materials, and the workmen that set them up. But every time I saw him he struck me as being a little more ethereal. It was as if the man were fading away.

He greeted me cordially on our first meeting after my arrival, and to all of us he was smiling and amiable. But he took very little interest in us, and sometimes, when I spoke to him, it became apparent that his thoughts had been far away, and they took some time to come back to earth. Elisalex told me that he had been overjoyed at her own arrival at the temple. And her presence there evidently gave him real pleasure. But when they were not actually together he seemed to forget her existence.

Knowing something of his past history, I would not have been surprised to find in him a disappointed, perhaps an embittered man. But, if he might be reckoned a failure according to worldly standards, it was evident that he had found nevertheless an inner peace, such as is but rarely vouchsafed to success. And it was doubtless symbolic of his state of mind that he should be quietly and contentedly building himself a tomb. He had found his kingdom.

A large long-haired dog of no particular breed followed the Abbot about and accompanied him on leisurely walks in the forest, when he went to look at the Imperial tombs, possibly to get new ideas for his own. Occasionally at meal times (even if the Abbot himself did not put in an appearance), the dog would come and visit us on his own account. He was a nice, friendly dog, and his name – so Elisalex told me – was Rizwàn, after a doorkeeper in *The Arabian Nights*.

19   *Igor at the Temple*

Per speculum et per aenigma

ST PAUL:
Corinthians

From the day of our arrival, when each of us had selected and mounted a donkey at Liang Ko Chuang, a corresponding donkey-boy had seized upon the single members of our party, as his own special prey. I doubt if any of us could have effected a change of mount, even if we had wanted to. Donald's donkey was a large-boned quadruped with an expression of patient resignation and a little tuft of hair under its chin, which gave him – so Donald assured us – a striking resemblance to Abraham Lincoln. Whereupon he was christened 'Abe'. After which all the other donkeys were promptly named after Presidents of the United States. My own mount showed rather more physical and mental vigour than his companions, and was therefore called Theodore Roosevelt. Kuniang's, being thin and taciturn (he remained steeped in introspective melancholy and never joined in the braying parties that the other donkeys indulged in), was known as Calvin Coolidge.

Such not very subtle humour was typical of our conversation, even in that Valley of the Dead. It was more often hilarious than awestruck. This had one advantage. It excluded the shallow sentiment that so often accompanies visitors to the Imperial tombs. I have no patience with people who feel that they have missed something, if they do not rhapsodize over past manners and customs, and dilate with enthusiastic inaccuracy over such small crumbs of knowledge as they may pick up on a weekend's excursion.

So I was content that the atmosphere surrounding our party should be clouded only with the prosaic dust that rose from the hooves of our donkeys. (If our caval-cade had been that of a Chinese emperor, even the dust would have been ennobled by the name of Golden Pow-der.) But, indeed, that very commonplace phrase 'enter into the spirit of the thing' might have had, at least for one of us, a deeper significance than we usually attrib-ute to it. For when we first arrived at the Pao-lien Ssè, I was assailed with a doubt. I wondered if we had not been imprudent in bringing a boy whom we all knew to be 'fey' into a region dedicated to the dead.

If a place existed anywhere, showing the old China as it had been in the past, it was here. To anyone gifted even in a small degree with psychic intuition, it should have been not only visible but vivid.

Material surroundings were there, offering a phan-tom court to phantom emperors. It was difficult, even for me, to gaze on the gorgeous thrones against their background of rich satin and lacquered columns, and not to believe that they were used indeed by those for whom they were intended. I could almost see the Sons of Heaven in their embroidered robes, wearing the Twelve Symbols of supreme power and the flaming jewel of Omnipotence. As a yellow curtain moved in the breeze, it was difficult not to think that an empress would step out, with the high Manchu headdress and the high Manchu shoes, both bordered with fringes and tassels of pearls that undulated as she moved. And if I could visualize them in imagination, would not Igor feel their tangible presence?

Some such thoughts as these came to me one morn-ing when we were visiting the T'ai Ling, which is the tomb of Yung Chen, a group of buildings that blazed with colour, like a covey of golden pheasants, shrined among the red-stemmed pines and backed by a range of mountains that shaded off into the softest blue. We stood upon a terrace, adorned with huge incense burners and with bronze figures of cranes and stags, while the guardian of the sacrificial hall (a feeble old man with a hacking cough) struggled to open one of the brass-studded four-fold doors with a rusty bunch of keys. To reach the highest lock he had to climb a ladder, for it was placed far above the level of a man's head. Just then I happened to notice Igor's face. He was gazing along the avenue that led up to the crimson gateway, and it seemed to me that his eyes followed something that moved. Was he watching the rites of an Imperial interment? Did he see a phantom bier of catalpa-wood towering above the shoulders of a hundred spectres that staggered under its weight? Did he hear the boom of drums, the drone of the *lituus*, and the wail of pipes? Did his eye catch the glint of 'spirit money', as it was tossed into the air?

But even if Igor saw more than we did, this did not spoil his obvious enjoyment. He was taken out of himself by the excitement of 'going places'. And the exuberant spirits of his companions served as a prophylactic.

But that same day, after we had got home from our excursion to the T'ai Ling, Igor had a passing vision – if such it could be called – that we found difficult to explain.

Elisalex had provided a general meeting-place, or living room, in the pavilion that she herself occupied: a big room, sketchily furnished. A row of square, red-varnished tables, set close together, constituted our dining-room table. And there were chairs to match. This type of red-varnished furniture, in the traditional Chinese shapes, is the cheapest obtainable on the market, but for this reason it has the advantage that you can buy it almost anywhere. It is standardized, and the tables and chairs that can be procured in out-of-the-way places like Kao-pe-tien are of the same model as those that Peking offers in precious woods, inlaid with mother-of-pearl. Whatever they are made of, the chairs of this pattern are anything but comfortable. But for a dining room, they serve their purpose. In our 'parlour', as Donald called it, there was a *kang*, or bed, that could be used as a divan. Elisalex had procured some folding chairs, of Western pattern, and a few low tables (also of the red-varnished variety) for cigarettes and ashtrays. There was no carpet, and the cushions that graced the *kang* were hard and uncompromising. In view of the Spartan character of the accommodation, as well as the fact that we were living in a temple, that room would have been more aptly named our 'refectory'.

We met there for meals and conversation. A place at the head of the composite dining table was always left for the Abbot, and sometimes he made an appearance and partook of the kippered herrings we had brought, by request, from Peking. They certainly had the advantage, from the point of view of commissariat on a picnic, that they were easy to cook. All one had to do was to warm the little oval tins, with the kippers inside, and then serve hot.

When the Abbot honoured us with his company, Fédor and Elisalex would sit on either side of him, and talk Russian. Donald sat at the opposite end, between myself and Kuniang, and we talked English. Igor, who sat halfway up, would join in the conversations in both languages. Rizwàn had his meals with us too.

On the day when we had been to the T'ai Ling, and after we had finished lunch but were still sitting at table, Igor rose from his seat and strolled aimlessly off, in the direction of the door. On the way he stopped and looked down at Rizwàn, who lay stretched out sound asleep, after a good dinner of his own. (I may add that Rizwàn thoroughly appreciated the foreign-style cooking that we had brought with us to the Temple of Costly Experience.) Igor said something that I did not hear and would not have understood if I had, for he spoke Russian. But Fédor and the Abbot looked up suddenly, as if what Igor said had startled them. Then he passed on and out. And lunch being over, the others also got up from table and strolled off out-of-doors. Only the Abbot remained sitting at the head of the table, with Elisalex beside him. I moved up and joined them, and I asked:

'What has Igor been saying?'

Elisalex answered: 'None of us quite understood what he meant. He looked down at Rizwàn and exclaimed: "Poor dog! I *am* sorry!" '

'Is anything the matter with the dog?'

'Nothing whatever. He is enjoying a snooze, after eating his dinner. I said this to Igor, but he paid no attention, and went on talking to himself: "That can hardly be a dog's idea of heaven: a shining floor, and jewels, and lighted lamps." '

'What a strange thing to say.'

Elisalex had no explanation to offer, and just then Kuniang called her from outside. As she left us, the Abbot looked at me and remarked, with his characteristically slow enunciation:

'It cannot have been of today he was speaking. His mind was moving on another plane.'

I realized, of course, that the Abbot was using the Taoist phraseology. Igor's mind was moving on another plane, looking down from a higher elevation, so that his glance travelled farther afield than ours and could catch glimpses of what we could not see.

Rizwàn was still asleep and, as I looked down at him, I could not help smiling. For, like the staghounds in *The Lay of the Last Minstrel*, he

> Lay stretched upon the rushy floor
> And urged in dreams the forest race

if not 'from Cheviot Stone to Eskdale moor', somewhere on another plane. He gave little whines and grunts, and one hind paw moved as if he were running.

The Abbot followed my glance with his eyes, but made no comment, and then the spirit prompted me to ask him a question about himself. He might resent my inquisitiveness, but I was willing to risk his displeasure, if I could get only an inkling of what was in his mind.

'Why,' I asked, 'are you building yourself a tomb?'

He did not appear offended, but he gave me the same answer as Elisalex had, when I asked her that question concerning him:

'I expect to be buried there, very soon.'

'What makes you think that? You are not ill, are you?'

The Abbot did not answer, but shook his head in negation.

'But, if you are not ill, why do you expect to die? Can you foresee the future?'

The answer he gave me was a strange one. Yet, in a sense, it was what I had expected:

'There is no future to foresee.'

'And there is no present, then, and no past?'

The Abbot hesitated a moment before answering:

'They are all one.'

It was what he had said to me in the Lama Temple, when he gave me the old jade disc for Little Chink. I asked:

'Can you *see* it all, in one?'

The Abbot shook his head and answered: 'No. Only fragments.'

He looked down at the dog at his feet, and added, smiling:

'So can Rizwàn.'

Hearing his name mentioned, the dog woke up and yawned and stretched himself and shook his head, so that his long ears flapped noisily. Then he looked up at his master and wagged his tail, as if to suggest that it was time they got a move on. The Abbot said something to Rizwàn that I did not understand, and then he rose from the table and smiled a salutation to me. So they departed together.

I too got up and went out to look for the others, but they had all disappeared. So I started off by myself,

155

strolling along the banks of the stream. I was thinking, naturally, of what the Abbot had said, and of how our conversation had started: with one of Igor's visions. Even when the boy was well and happy – as he certainly was now – his mind had no permanent connection with life in the present. It needed an object of fixation. But the difference between Igor's mind and the mind of a normally constituted person was only one of degree. For all of us – within limits – the mind wanders between past and future, and even a dog could pass out of the present moment in his dreams. And that present moment, which we speak of with so much confidence, does not really exist, save as a unit dividing the infinite. We cannot hold it in our minds even if we try to. In the language of Buddhism: 'there is no Being, only a Becoming'.

If Igor's visions were re-evoking and predictive, his mind should be able to look backwards and forwards, as we turn the pages of an atlas to look up a locality in space. It was all there, if one could only see it, or if we could reach the mental plane from which it was visible, as Igor did.

When the Abbot said that there was no future to predict, he expressed this same thought by its opposite, and he might have added that there is no present and no past. It is all one, like a circle, or like the Eight Trigrams, or a flight of arrows. Bergson said much the same thing when he pointed out that, for the future to be really unpredictable, all the Universe would have to be created anew, in every instant of Time. Indeed, some people maintain that this is so. But when I look upon the mountains or upon the stars, I find it difficult to believe.

Still absorbed in my own thoughts, I followed the path till it emerged on to the plain. Clouds of dust moved across it, borne by the north wind, which always grew stronger in the afternoon. The Abbot's Mongol retainers were quartered somewhere out there. Presumably they occupied some of the houses in the

Chinese village. They had their horses with them, and it was just as well that the stream ran down from us to them. I recognized the obvious precaution of one who is laying out a camp. In a hollow to my left were the pavilions now occupied by Donald, Fédor and Igor. I went to see if anyone was there, but I found only a coolie cleaning a pair of shoes. So I turned back the way I came, along the banks of the stream.

After a few minutes, I reached a point where the waters spread out and formed a little lake; the lake that Elisalex had mentioned in her letter to Peking. This was, without doubt, the prettiest spot within the temple grounds. It reminded me of the Jade Fountain, near Peking, which Ch'ien Lung called 'The First Spring under Heaven'. All springs and mountain streams, in North China, seem to hold the dark green and the soft shadows of jade. And in its season, they are framed in fragrant wistaria. Close to the bank opposite where I stood was a miniature island, on which rose a pavilion open in front and overshadowed by a curving roof of amber-coloured tiles. A marble terrace jutted out over the water, with no balustrade to enclose it. This was the so-called Island of Fulfilled Desires. I wondered if, in the intention of whoever designed that sanctuary, 'fulfilled desires' and 'costly experience' did not mean the same thing?

A couple of ducks were paddling about in the water, not far from where I stood. They quacked inquiringly, as if expecting me to throw them something to eat. But the dry wind had made me irritable, and picking up a pebble I threw it at them.

My gesture could hardly have been enough to frighten them, but the ducks suddenly decided to leave the water. They rose slowly, on flapping wings. Then, reaching a higher level, they began to circle round the lake at an ever-increasing speed. At one moment, they flew close to my head, and as they did so, something coming from a quite different direction whizzed past my face. There was a confused whirl of feathers, some

157

of which fell around me and settled at my feet. One of the ducks dropped and lay floating on the water, with its legs upturned. Only then did I see that it had been transfixed by an arrow. Its companion flew away and disappeared.

A huge Tartar, with a shiny head that seemed to be made of bronze, broke out of the bushes that had hidden him from my sight. Without a glance at me, he stepped down and reached for the floating bird with the end of his bow.

From the temple buildings along the path, came Kuniang's voice, calling me.

20 *The Bell and the Road*

A crackt bell can never sound well

THOMAS FULLER:
Gnomonologia

'And what,' asked Elisalex, with affected sarcasm, 'have we here – *le satyre du Bois de Boulogne?*'

We were off for an excursion on our donkeys, to the top of one of the neighbouring hills, whence – so we were told – a fine view could be obtained of all the region of the tombs. Kuniang and Donald had been riding on ahead, and the rest of us in a group together. As we came round a bend in the path we found Donald standing by his donkey, with his shirt lying on the ground beside him. The donkey had its eyes shut and a weary expression, as if it had had enough already of the whole excursion, meanwhile Donald was busy pulling his undervest over his head. When he had done so, he put his shirt on again.

'This would not be necessary,' he explained, 'if I had thought of bringing a woollen sweater with me, to put on when required. The early morning is almost cold. And now – just feel it! The idea of this *déshabillé* is to carry my vest in front of me in the saddle, and put it on again in the evening. I'm sorry if my behaviour shocks the ghosts of Chinese empresses and concubines.'

'They won't mind,' said Elisalex. 'And your donkey-boy evidently thinks it a great joke. I may add that Kuniang does not give you a good example. Does it ever occur to you,' she spoke to Kuniang, 'that you might pull your skirt down just a little? It is almost up to your waist, and your donkey-boy is also grinning delightedly!'

'Little beast!' said Kuniang, making no attempt to pull down her skirt, but rubbing herself behind, with the hand that was not holding the reins. 'He does nothing but whack Calvin Coolidge with that whip of his. And he never looks to see whom he is hitting. Every now and then he gets me by mistake. It's as bad as the old days in the schoolroom.'

'Well! It does not matter much what you do when out on an excursion, as long as you behave with becoming modesty at the temple. Dorbon's retainers are great sticklers for propriety.' Elisalex turned to me and added: 'You have shocked them terribly.'

'*I* have! What have I done?'

'You sleep in the women's quarters, in the same room with Kuniang and next door to me. But never mind that now. Let's get on, or we will be roasted alive in the heat of the day.'

We were about to start off again when, from the path to Liang Ko Chuang that branched off to our right a little farther on, there came what I took to be a trumpet-call. I realized my mistake when all our donkeys, with the exception of Calvin Coolidge, burst into the vocal music peculiar to their kind. The donkey approaching along that path was evidently a relation, pleased at meeting the family, and they gave him a heart-felt welcome. The rider turned out to be my Jesuit friend, Père Antoine, wearing an enormous straw hat of Chinese make. His general appearance reminded me of Don Basilio, in *Il Barbiere di Siviglia*.

When the asinine ecstasy had subsided, I managed to effect some sort of an introduction, and I asked Père Antoine to join our picnic. Exalted Virtue, in the manner of Chinese servants on excursions into the country, had preceded us with provisions. I knew that we would find him, waiting for us at our destination, with a meal ready and supplies amply sufficient, even with an extra mouth to feed.

Père Antoine accepted, saying that he had been on his way to come and see me. But he promptly attached himself to Elisalex. We were riding in single file, and I was behind them. I could not hear more than an occasional phrase, but they seemed to have plenty to say to each other. The clergy have never been averse to pretty women.

And Elisalex looked graceful, even on a donkey. She wore a washing-frock of *crêpe de Chine* which, unlike Kuniang's, did not tend to ride up. Her broad-brimmed hat, loosely held by a silken veil under her chin, protected her complexion and gave the impression of an eighteenth-century portrait.

We left our donkeys halfway up the hill and climbed to the summit. And though there was no shade, the keen air prevented us feeling the heat. Two tall pagodas, dating from a dynasty that reigned long before the Manchus, pierced the blue sky and dominated the plain below. They stood like sentinels, on guard over the past. And above each of them a falcon circled, as if he were part of the general symmetry. The view stretched over the cultivated plain, that ended in a haze on the horizon, and over the forest, at the edge of which flights of mountain pies tinged the air with the blue of their wings. Our party divided itself up so as to find a little shade under the outstanding boulders of rock. I found myself again with Père Antoine and Elisalex. I don't know how the conversation had started, but he was asking her if she had ever been to the Ta Chung Ssè, the Temple of the Great Bell, near the road to the Summer Palace. Elisalex said that she had not.

'They tell a story about that bell, the usual story that appears in the folklore of all nations, where bells and bridges are concerned. The founder's daughter threw herself into the molten metal, because only by such a sacrifice could the casting of the bell succeed.'

I added: 'And now, if you go at night into the hall where the great bell is suspended, you will hear someone in the darkness whispering: "Hsieh! Hsieh!"' (shoe,

shoe). For when the girl threw herself into the liquid bronze, her maidservant tried to save her, but she only clasped a shoe, which remained in her hand. And now the girl's spirit is always asking for the shoe that was left behind.'

'That is a sad story,' said Elisalex.

'I told it to you,' said Père Antoine, 'because there is a similar story about the temple you are now staying in. It is also about a bell. But not so sad.'

'Is there a big bell in our temple?' I asked. 'I have not seen one, though I heard a deep note, like that of a bell, on the night when we first arrived.'

'The big bell is no longer there. What you heard must have been the note of a smaller bell, made out of the original metal. It hangs in the principal courtyard, rather to one side. The original bell – so I am told – used to hang in the principal pavilion, for it was the *raison d'être* of the whole temple. They have put a Pu Tai there now.'

'What is a Pu Tai?' asked Elisalex.

'A Laughing Buddha, Milo Fo. He is represented in various ways, as you may know. The most pleasant effigy is that which is called: "The Buddha Who Loves Little Children", and there are a lot of naked babies clambering over him. But the one that is now in the Pao-lien Ssè is standing up and holding a hempen bag in his left hand, and he has the usual leering smile on his face. The Chinese say that he is the God of Happiness, because his paunch is always full. A very materialistic conception.'

'But a natural one,' I added, 'in this country, where more than half the population is undernourished, even when they are not literally starving. The God of Happiness is one that can satisfy Hunger and Desire. But you were saying that there is a story about the Pao-lien Ssè, a story connected with a bell. What is it?'

'As I said before, there was once a huge bell there. But no young girl had sacrificed herself to ensure the success of the casting. For this reason, I suppose, the

162

bell was cracked. And again for this reason, it was melted down again, and other similar bells, but smaller, were made of the metal.'

'Why was it put up at all if it was cracked?' I asked.

'Give me time, and you shall hear all about it. Several thousand *li* south of Kao-pe-tien, where the passes into Shansi open out into the plain, there lived, in the first days of the Ta Ch'ing dynasty, a mountain chief, whose name I have forgotten. He remained faithful to the fallen dynasty of the Mings, for some time after their star had set. At last he decided to swear allegiance to the new Emperor. Wishing to make his peace, he sent messengers to Peking to say that he had a gift to offer: a great bronze bell, whose voice should be heard at a distance of fifty *li*. He wished to send it north, to be set up in the Forbidden City.

'The Emperor was much pleased, and he charged several important officials to go to the chieftain's fortress, and to inquire how the bell could be brought so far from its place of casting. I don't know if you ever heard how the bell of the Ta Chung Ssè was brought to where it is now. A canal was dug and filled with water. When winter came, the canal froze. And the bell, resting on wooden runners, was dragged to its destination, over the ice.

'But the bell that was to be sent from Shansi as a peace offering was situated in a province where the winters were mild and the canals did not freeze. So the Emperor's envoys decided that a road would have to be constructed, on which the bell could travel. The Emperor approved, and the road-building began at once. As the road was built, the bell moved along it, until it reached the region where we are now, which the Manchus had chosen for the Imperial tombs. And there it stopped. For an order came from the Emperor that the bell could be set up in the region of the tombs and would serve to call his ancestors from the spirit world, on the days when he came to worship them. The mountain chief was much annoyed when he heard of this

163

decision. But, nevertheless, the bell was set up, and a temple built around it: the temple which is now the Pao-lien Ssè. But when it was sounded for the first time it was discovered that the bell, as the Chinese say, was *Mao Ping*!

'You may not be surprised to hear that for many years, indeed for many decades, this unpleasant fact was kept hidden from the Emperor and from his successors. The bell, cracked as it was, continued to hang there during many reigns, till at last someone decided that it was unworthy, and had it thrown once more into the melting pot.'

Elisalex looked incredulous. 'But how could the mountain chief,' she said, 'whose name you have forgotten, dare to send a bell to the Emperor, well knowing that it was cracked. It might have got him into awful trouble. And just when he wanted to make peace, too!'

Père Antoine laid his fingers on Elisalex's wrist, with a gallant gesture that seemed almost out of keeping with his cloth, and said:

'My dear lady. You are very beautiful, and attractive, and even on a picnic among Chinese hills you remind me somehow of the ladies whom I used to see in my native France. But you will excuse my saying that you know very little of China. Otherwise you would have guessed by now that the point of my story does not concern the bell at all, but the road. If the plans of the mountain chief – whose name I have forgotten – had not gone awry, a rebellion would have broken out in the Chihli province, just as the bell reached the marble bridge over the Hun Ho, near Peking. At the same time, the chieftain's own war-chariots would have swept up the road to do battle, which they could not have done before. And the Manchus, taken by surprise, would have been overthrown.'

'A pretty scheme!' I exclaimed, as Père Antoine finished his story. 'And characteristically Chinese in its conception. Even the furrows of the ploughs were made parallel and not perpendicular to the outer wall of

Peking, as to the Great Wall of China, so as to make it difficult for war-chariots to advance. I wonder if the Emperor had merely got tired of waiting, or if he saw through the trick, when he decided to have the bell stopped here?'

'And what,' said Elisalex, 'happened to the spirits of the dead emperors, that the bell should have summoned. Did they answer its voice, though cracked?'

Père Antoine seemed to know all about it. Not for nothing was folklore his speciality. 'People hereabouts,' he answered, 'will tell you that a cracked bell could have summoned only evil spirits. And this has given the Pao-lien Ssè a bad name. Though the original bell is no longer there, the temple itself is supposed to lure people with a spiritual appeal that is inauspicious. Only misfortune awaits those who answer the summons of the Temple of Costly Experience.'

I looked at Elisalex, but she was gazing out over the plain.

Why had Père Antoine told us this story? Was he giving us a warning?

We started back halfway through the afternoon, and as usual when negotiating hill-paths in China the descent was less easy than the climb up. We none of us felt safe riding the donkeys over such rough ground, and there was no possibility, when walking, of looking at the view. All our attention had to be concentrated on our own feet.

Père Antoine left us at the foot of the hills to make his way back to Liang Ko Chuang. After he had parted from us, I found myself riding with Kuniang, and we got a little separated from the others. Elisalex and Fédor went on in front. It was only when we were away from the temple, during some excursion, that those two resumed the old intimacy. Within the Temple of Costly Experience Elisalex kept Fédor at arm's length.

Igor and Donald brought up the rear of the

procession. They appeared to be in hilarious spirits. Every now and then the snatch of a song echoed over the fields. Kuniang explained:

'Donald is teaching Igor the best American lyrics, and keeps on complaining that we haven't got a banjo to take out on a porch and strum the accompaniments to Negro songs. Yesterday he taught Igor "My Country, 'tis of thee", and today it is "The old oaken bucket that hangs in the well", only the words were different.'

'It's all to the good,' I answered. 'Igor is looking extraordinarily well. He is brown with the sun and much more alert than he used to be.'

'Yes. He's a different boy from what he was two months ago. He seems to have grown up all of a sudden. And though he is generally in the best of spirits, he is beginning to be conscious of responsibilities. It is in no light-hearted vein that he has accepted Donald's proposal to take him to Paris. At times he feels anxious about it all. But Donald is wonderful at giving him confidence.'

I pondered over this information and then added:

'Possibly this trip with us has helped: just the pleasure and the excitement. He reminds me of the boy in the storybooks, who has always longed for the sea, and comes out on to the shore for the first time. Has Igor never travelled before, even in China?'

'Only between Peking and Tientsin, where his mother is. The Russian family did not take him with them when they went away in the summer. As Doctor Folitzky said, Igor was brain-starved.'

'More than he was love-starved?'

'Much more. For I did my best in that respect!' She glanced ahead at the couple riding in front of us, and added: 'It is a pity that Elisalex is monopolized by Fédor. She might have taken Igor up where I left off.'

I caught her bantering tone, as I said: 'I believe you are annoyed with Elisalex for poaching on your preserves. Fédor was one of your conquests.'

'My admirers are dropping off. It is sad. Donald has

offered to Igor another point of fixation. And they will be going away very soon, all of them: Fédor, Igor and Donald. It has been great fun. I will be sorry when they leave.'

'So will I.'

I turned in my saddle and looked back at the couple behind us. Igor was leaning out and helping Donald to put on his undervest again, without getting off the donkey. Kuniang and I reined up and waited for them to join us. Igor was singing to himself. And this was the burden of his song:

> The old family toothbrush
> That hangs in the sink.
> First it was father's,
> Next it was mother's,
> Then it was sister's,
> And now it is mine!

21   A Notice Board of Marble

Ambition is no cure for love!

SCOTT:
Lay of the Last Minstrel

The open spaces just outside the temple grounds were littered with materials for the building of the Abbot's tomb. And on the right bank of the stream was a deposit of marble blocks and slabs and sculptured columns for balustrades, all of which had been transported there by water and now waited to be hauled into place. Strings of camels were continually arriving, laden with bricks. The sound of the bells carried by the leading camels formed a distant musical accompaniment to all our activities.

I was busy one afternoon, copying on to a page in my notebook the Chinese characters that were incised on a pillar that lay among the slabs and blocks of marble on the bank of the stream. It was not a stele or tablet, such as celebrate the virtues of some dead hero. The shape was more elongated, and from each side, near the top, two wing-like ornaments spread outwards. They were meant to represent clouds: the idea being that the pillar should appear to be so high as to disappear among the clouds.

The pillar was nothing more than a sublimated notice board. It bore an inscription beginning with the two characters *Hsiao Hsin*, meaning Small Heart. The same characters are used by Chinese railway companies, on the notice boards that warn people of danger at unguarded level crossings. They correspond to our 'Beware!' the idea being that the heart contracts with fear at the possibility of danger. But on the approach to the Abbot's tomb there was no physical danger. The marble notice board that was going to be set up at the outer doors was intended to warn horsemen that they must dismount, as a sign of respect, when arriving at the sepulchre of an exalted personage. The latter's titles, describing him in flamboyant and exalted terms, were inscribed below the warning.

While I was still busy with the Chinese characters, Igor strolled up and joined me. He seated himself on another slab of marble close by, lighted a cigarette and then asked me what I was doing.

I explained, and then added:

'I suppose that some day I will see *your* name on a notice board, but not of marble. It will be that you are acting in *Saint Sebastian*, or dancing in *Le Spectre de la Rose*.'

'Perhaps a marble notice board might not be inappropriate for me too.'

I looked down at him in surprise, wondering what he meant. But he said nothing more. So I continued cheerily:

'Tell me what you feel about it all. It must be a great excitement, but a bit of a wrench as well.'

Igor sat on the slab with his chin cupped in his hands and stared out over the stream. Swallows were circling overhead and dipping to catch the midges that danced above the water.

'I suppose you know,' said Igor, 'that I've always been in love with Kuniang.'

'Yes. We all know that. It must have been great fun for you both, when you were younger. But now Kuniang is the mother of two children, and you are going out into the world. You'll find plenty of pretty women to fall in love with in Paris, and you had better be careful. Love-making becomes a much more serious business as you grow older.'

169

'And then what happens?' asked Igor.

I stared at him in perplexity:

'Well. All sorts of things can happen. Sometimes the lady is unkind and will have none of us, which is tragic. Or she is too kind and wants us all the time, even when we had rather not. And that is more tragic still. If love makes the world go round, it is often as much by flight as by the other thing.'

'I won't *have* to make love to the women in Paris, will I?'

'Not if you don't want to. But some of them are very desirable.'

'More like Elisalex than Kuniang?'

'Well, perhaps . . . But don't you like Elisalex?'

'Oh, she's beautiful and full of charm. But she knows it all the time. And she seems always to be thinking of herself.'

'You have to look after yourself, if you lead the sort of life she's had.'

'That's what I'm afraid of in Paris. Everyone with an eye to the main chance, and nothing for love and kindness . . .'

I had to admit that there might be some truth in this preview of life in Paris. But Igor went on:

'I look forward to the work and to the struggle if there is one. And to the stagecraft that I will have to learn. But at times I feel that without Kuniang to turn to I will be lost.'

'Don't you believe it. You are quite capable of standing on your own feet. And that is what you need: to learn to rely on yourself. And remember: it is not as if you were never going to see Kuniang again. We will come to applaud you in Paris, if you succeed. And if you don't, we will be here to welcome you home when you get back.'

I was rather tickled at the idea of having to console Igor because he would no longer have Kuniang to give him 'treatment as before'. And I was reminded – I don't know why – of a French play called *l'Ane de*

Buridan, in which a young man is in love, at one and the same time, with another man's wife and with his mistress. The young man cannot make up his mind which he prefers. The husband takes a kindly and detached interest in the matter and assures the young man that he is welcome to either of the two women, as long as he does not take both. And the husband even tries to be helpful by pointing out that the problem need not be complicated by financial considerations, for the two ladies cost about the same to keep. I felt sorry that I had not a mistress for Igor to take away with him to Paris. That's the worst of Peking – no music and no women! And I could not spare Kuniang!

But Igor was very serious about it all. I could not hurt his feelings by being flippant and treating his troubles as a joke.

It occurred to me that never before had Igor and I indulged in any weighty conversation. There had never been anything of importance for us to talk about. When he frequented the Shuang Liè Ssè, all that Igor wanted was to sit around with us. He never sought the opportunity of airing his views, as is the custom of young men when in congenial company. His boyish shyness of me had worn off long ago. If now he wished to unburden himself to me, I should encourage him.

'You *are* pleased to go, aren't you?' I asked. 'Even though you may have some natural doubts as to how it will all turn out.'

'Yes. I'm pleased. Very pleased. And flattered. But even if I were not, I would feel it my duty to go.'

Here I recognized something new in Igor. He spoke of a duty, as a man might speak. He had grown up at last, mentally as well as physically. And his attitude, despite his doubts, was more manly than I had expected. Here was no stage-struck youth, full of self-importance because he had aroused an interest in such a connoisseur as Donald. Here was a man, conscious of his limitations, taking up a task because he felt that he owed it to himself and to others. *Hsiao Hsin!* If his

171

heart contracted it was not in fear of what he saw
ahead, but in sorrow for what he was leaving. Not much
to regret, one might be tempted to say, in the life poor
Igor had led up till now in Peking. Nothing, perhaps,
except Kuniang.

Had Donald offered to introduce him to any other
world than that of the theatre, Igor would never have
felt any desire to accept. But he could hardly have
failed to be drawn by the glamour of the Russian
dances, little as he knew about them. It was as if he had
been asked to join an Asiatic pageant, not unworthy of
the Singing Cossack, whose son he was.

I soon finished copying out the Chinese characters, and
having nothing in particular to do, I also seated myself
on a marble slab near the stream. The midges were too
numerous for comfort, and I asked Igor for one of his
cigarettes, and lit it. The wind that had been blowing in
the middle of the day had died down and the air was
still and laden with the perfume of some flowering reed
that grew along the banks of the stream. Fédor
appeared in the distance, coming out of the backdoor of
the temple, and he strolled out to join us. I said to
myself: here is another young man, who is going to
leave China, to try his luck in Paris. But Fédor had
been there before, and was already known – if not
widely known – in Europe as a painter of promise. For
him the future was not such an unknown quantity.

But in those days at the temple he was at a loose end,
moodily resigned to his instructions, which were to
leave Elisalex strictly alone. This spoilt much of
Fédor's pleasure in our trip. And I was not surprised to
notice that, when alone, he was inclined to be morose.

I had laid my open notebook on the slab of marble on
which I was sitting. Fédor picked it up and stared at
the characters that I had drawn. Then he glanced at the
recumbent pillar. 'Is there anything written on the
other side?' he asked.

'I can't see, but probably the same legend is

172

engraved at the back in Mongol characters instead of Chinese.'

Fédor stood up and went over to the pillar, where it lay on the sloping bank of the stream. He put his two hands underneath the marble cloud that stuck out on one side and turned the heavy mass over as easily as if it had been a beam of light wood.

I gasped with astonishment. No effort of mine could have moved such a weight even for one inch in any direction whatever.

'You are right,' said Fédor casually. 'The characters on the other side are not Chinese. They must be Mongol.' And he came back and sat down beside us, stifling a yawn as if he were bored, as no doubt he was.

I made an effort at conversation.

'Igor and I have been talking over his going to Paris.'

Fédor grunted noncommittally. He was not interested. But I persevered.

'What did *you* think of Paris when you were there?' I asked.

'Not bad. There were some good pictures.'

'And which did you like best of the pictures?'

'I liked the portrait of Whistler's mother in the Louvre. Though why it should be there I don't know.'

'Did you not like the Italian pictures? The Mona Lisa?'

Fédor showed signs of warming to a congenial subject.

'Yes. I liked the Mona Lisa, though I think it is about time they cleaned it. I suppose they are afraid to. The Italian picture I liked best was a Madonna and Child by Mainardi. Unless I am mistaken, he was a pupil of Ghirlandaio. It is a lovely painting, with the usual background of arched windows on either side of the central figure. The windows are double arches, supported by a light column in the middle. Through one window you can see the towers and steeples of some Tuscan town, with blue hills melting into the sky. And through the other an inlet of sea with fishing boats.

173

The Madonna and Child have the daintiest of haloes, like threads of golden gossamer, and *her* halo seems to be part of her old Florentine headdress and it mingles with the gold of her hair. She is bending to caress a chubby little St John the Baptist, while three girls, or angels in Renaissance dresses, are grouped in the background, holding long-stemmed Madonna lilies.'

'It sounds lovely.'

'Yes. One of the most beautiful pictures of the Florentine school. And what I liked about it most was that the sweet-faced, fair-haired Madonna was like Kuniang.'

I could not help smiling. Though I might start the conversation on the subject of Paris, it came back inevitably to Kuniang. And I noticed that, infatuated as Fédor doubtless was with Elisalex, he had not found anything resembling her among the Madonnas.

22 *Prince Dorbon Oirad – Past and Present*

'The only difference between the saint and the sinner is that every saint has a past and every sinner has a future.'

OSCAR WILDE

'This is a queer country,' said Donald. 'The more I see of it, the less I understand it.'

'That,' I answered, 'is a feeling that no-one that knows China ever loses. At the time of the Boxer troubles, old Smith, the missionary author of *Chinese Characteristics*, used to say: "What is the use of asking *me* what the Chinese are likely to do next? I have only lived among them for twenty-five years!" But what is troubling *you* at this moment?'

'Well, for one thing, there's a civil war on, somewhere around, or so you tell me – yet here we are, in the path of rival armies, and not a sign of trouble anywhere. The peasants are working in the fields, and the peasant women are sawing wood and hauling water, puddling around on their tiny bound feet and with painted faces. The Abbot is building a tomb. And we are all rubbernecking in the Emperor's private cemetery. People at home have the impression that China in wartime is a terrible place to be in. To me it seems safer than Central Park, where at any moment you may get run into by a kid on a tricycle, rushing downhill on the paths where there are no traffic lights.'

'That's always the way in China,' I said. 'Kuniang and I went through a four-days siege of Peking, and

175

never knew it. We read about it afterwards in the foreign papers.'

More even than by China itself, Donald was puzzled by the Abbot. He had first heard of him when he met Elisalex in Paris and knew her as the wife of a Prince Dorbon Oirad, who lived somewhere on the Siberian Steppes. I suppose that Donald pictured to himself some such Prince as one meets among the *émigrés* in Paris, in company with Russian dancers and the few surviving Grand Dukes. It is true that the Abbot was a refugee of sorts, but not of the kind that Donald had been used to. He still merged into an Asiatic background as if he were part of it.

At the beginning of this book, I said that I would like to write a life of the Abbot. But having lived in the same house with him I know how impossible this is. There was a barrier between us. A wall of incomprehension and perhaps even of distrust. For however kindly the Abbot's manner might be towards me and my companions, he held us spiritually at arm's length. And we remained as 'ships that pass in the night'. It seemed to me that even with Elisalex he stood mentally aloof. And I compared them to Alice in Wonderland asking questions of the caterpillar, as he sat upon the mushroom, smoking a hookah. Yet he had been her lover, if not legally her husband (a matter on which nobody seemed able to offer any reliable information). Those were the days when the Prince Dorbon Oirad came to St Petersburg, to render homage to the Tsar. What a wonderful couple they must have been: he in his black Cossack uniform, with the silver cartridge-cases across his chest. She in the robes of a court lady, with the splendid headdress that they used to wear!

And rooms of looking-glass and gold, with shining floors and pillars of green malachite; flash of diamonds and of gold lace in a quadrille; gipsy musicians in fashionable restaurants; drawing rooms full of roses and cigarette smoke; jingle of sleigh bells in frosty air; people kneeling before ikons at street corners; Italian opera and ballet, organized by a Petipa and directed by a Prince Wolkonsky. Women, wine and song, with somewhere in the background, the expressionless face of the Tsar and the fear-haunted eyes of the Empress.

All this the Prince Dorbon Oirad had known, as if it were his birthright.

Yet the Asiatic in him had never been lost under any veneer of Western custom and costume. The slanting Mongol eyes, half veiled yet burning with unsubdued fires; the long beautiful hands; the air of calm self-possession; the gaze that was ever watchful, wary and remote. These must have been Prince Dorbon's characteristics, even as they were the Abbot's. But in those days, I imagine, he would have brooked no rival. No Fédor. I could imagine him as the Shah Zeman in *Schéhérazade* grasping a curved sword that was red with blood.

The Chinese say: 'If you ferry at all, ferry right over'. The change from the Prince Dorbon Oirad that Elisalex had loved, to the Abbot whom we knew in later years, was radical and complete. He seemed to have passed into a new incarnation, and to have advanced more than one step towards the supreme beatitudes. The love of woman had left him. His mind dwelt on such things as the Eight Trigrams: the root from which had developed all the philosophical teaching in the Book of Changes.

But for me to converse with him on such abstruse subjects was not easy; indeed, it was almost impossible. I tried to do so several times, but we always arrived at an impasse. To make his meaning clearer the Abbot would sometimes write down a Chinese character, or trace it with one finger on the palm of the other hand. Sometimes we called in Elisalex to help, and she and the Abbot would converse for a few moments in Russian. But she found the task of interpreting difficult. And I believe that the Abbot did not like to share with a woman his ideas on philosophical subjects.

In order to follow the Abbot's process of reasoning

some precise definitions would have been necessary, or a mathematical sequence. But all I had to go on with were halting phrases and vague ideograms.

Especially would I have liked to have gone deeper into the Abbot's ideas about Time. Did he consider it as discrete or continuous? Did he believe it existed at all, outside our own minds?

How had the warrior-chief of nomad tribes ever come to dwell upon such subjects? In what Mongol or Tibetan monastery had he been initiated into such mysteries? Never would I learn the answer to these questions.

But I realized that transitions come easily in the East. And so do transfigurations. The step is short from the soldier to the sage; from the libertine to the ascetic. Even in Europe, our saints were generally sinners revised and edited. Perhaps the distance that separates them is not so great as we might think.

But how strange – how eerie even – the change must have appeared to Elisalex! To most of us the past exists only in our memories. But for her the past was there, under her eyes, and so was the future. For to Elisalex the Abbot represented the past, and Fédor the future. Only the present was nebulous and vague. Nothing more than a transition, a transmigration, as if her soul was waiting in some suburb of life, before taking the road again.

Is this a rare phenomenon, or is it not happening to most of us most of the time? I mean those periods of our lives when Time seems to have gone to sleep in the afternoon sunshine.

Despite his new-found saintliness, the Abbot still could show what Browning might have called 'a veined humanity'.

One day I picked up a book that he had left on a chair in our parlour. It was a Chinese book with a backless binding in the thinnest of patterned green silk, the double leaves sewn together with a thick green thread. At first what excited my enthusiasm was the beauty of the characters: a joy to the heart of anyone who loves fine calligraphy. Then I realized that the book was one of the classical accounts of Confucius, called the Lun Yü. A paintbrush, such as in China is used for writing, was placed between two pages as a marker. Just then the Abbot came in to fetch his book. And he told me that the paintbrush marked his favourite story, the story of Confucius and his disciples, and what they wished for.

Another Chinese scholar, very different from the Abbot, had once told me the same thing. I speak of Sir Reginald F. Johnston, whom I knew in Peking when he was tutor to the little Emperor. I used to go and see him in his house in the Tartar City, close under the Drum Tower. I cannot do better than give the story in Johnston's own words, as he once told it to me.

Confucius was sitting one day with four of his disciples and he asked them what they would do if they happened to be in a position of authority and free to follow their own desires. The first said that he would like to be the Minister in a small impoverished state, beset by powerful and rapacious neighbours, and to direct the policies of that country so well that it emerged richer and more prosperous than any other. The second disciple said that it would be enough if he could give the people something to live on. The third was even more modest, and said that he would be content to serve as an acolyte in the temples and learn from observation how the rites should be conducted. Finally the Master turned to the fourth disciple, whose name was Tien, and put the same question to him.

Tien had been strumming on his lute. He put aside the instrument, and while the chords were still vibrating he stood up and stretched out his arms.

'My wish is different,' he said, 'quite different. For it is now the end of spring. I would like to put on light raiment and join a little company of youths and boys.

We would go and bathe in the waters of the Yi River, enjoy the evening breezes and dance among sylvan glades. And we would come home arm in arm, singing in the dusk!'

The Master sighed and said: 'Tien, I feel just like you!'

23 Song of a Lark

'I have seen tears in thine eyes, as when I sang
to thee for the first time: those I shall never
forget.'

HANS ANDERSEN:
The Nightingale

Père Antoine had spoken of Pu Tai, whom he called the
God of Happiness, and who occupied the central pavilion of our temple, where once the great bell had been
suspended. This Laughing Buddha was well known to
us. Indeed, we almost considered him a member of our
party. The outer doors of his pavilion were generally
open, and his mocking face visible from the courtyard,
which was at a slightly lower level. Exalted Virtue was
always in and out of the God's habitation, for he kept
our drinks there, stored in a cool spot under the altar.
The Chinese consider it no irreverence to put the temples of their gods to the most practical uses, for they
include the deities in their own private lives.

The back of the Laughing Buddha's pavilion had one
of those openings that are invisible except from the
side: an inner wall, of the same dark colour as the outer,
masking the passage behind. I might not have been
aware that this opening existed, if it had not happened
that, on more than one occasion, having strolled into Pu
Tai's pavilion, I had the impression that someone was
passing out at the opposite end. And I realized that the
Abbot's retainers used that place as a sort of sentinel's
box (one of many, scattered about the place). There was

one of them on guard there, though he made himself scarce whenever any of our party came near. These men were always around us in the Temple, though almost always unseen. Donald compared them to Red Indians furtively watching a log cabin from surrounding woods. But it is customary, in the Far East, to be surrounded by servants who stand behind screens and silken partitions, ready to minister to their master's wants. And, if I was to believe Elisalex, the Abbot's retainers were more suspicious of us than we of them. She – so I gathered – had warned Fédor on no account to make love to her within the Temple precincts. The Abbot might be indifferent, but his retainers had their own ideas on the subject. Perhaps they regarded the women residing in the house as all belonging to their own lord and master. In the case of Elisalex herself this was reasonable, even though the Abbot, who apparently had outlived his passions, now made it clear that he had renounced them. His renunciation was more complete and thorough than we are used to in similar situations in the West.

Although none of us took much interest in the matter, it was nevertheless true that the relationship between Elisalex and the Abbot represented the most peculiar aspect of a peculiar situation. I imagine that he must have sent her that telegram, saying that he had found his kingdom, much as one writes 'finis' at the end of a story. Possibly he had not expected to see her again. But, as she had come all that way, he was touched and comforted. Her own motives in coming there were more difficult to fathom. I never did believe that it was to see the Abbot that Elisalex had returned to the Far East. Her contention, that she had been drawn by the lure of a Chinese temple more than by any affection for the man who had been her lover, may have contained some truth. And then, of course, there was Fédor ... The only objection to *his* presence in the temple came, not from the Abbot, but from his Mongol retainers.

It was also owing to the prejudices of these gentry that our party, with one exception, carefully avoided approaching the tomb that was in process of construction about a mile from the Pao-lien Ssè. The exception was Donald. He would go off by himself and prowl round the workmen's sheds and the outhouses, even if he did not penetrate into the tomb itself. And he once persuaded me to go with him. This was on the last day of his stay in the Temple of Costly Experience. Next morning we were to leave for Peking, for I had decided to accompany him (I felt it was inhospitable not to do so).

Donald's description of something he had seen near the tomb had puzzled me, and I consented to accompany him to a little dell, through which the stream meandered among the verdure that it created along its banks. Here, on the side of a rough track that passing carts had opened up, some workmen were busy with blocks of white marble. One of these was being prepared to serve as a paving stone, with a strange concavity in the middle. Another block was being cut into the shape of a perfect sphere. A wooden ball, of the required size, served as a model. Only after some conversation with the stonecutters did I begin to understand what they were doing. And I explained to Donald:

'That big paving stone is being chiselled out in the middle, to form a hollow, shaped like a half-sphere, so that the ball may lie in it. To ensure a perfect fit, they will experiment with the wooden ball, as well as with a wooden block, into which the marble ball can go.'

'Is the Abbot's ghost going to play bagatelle inside his tomb?' asked Donald. 'And how is he going to lift that ball?'

'That's not the idea. The paving stone will be placed outside the tomb, under the centre of the door that closes it. As the door is shut, the marble ball will follow it and fall into the corresponding socket, up against the lacquered wooden leaves. Once it is there the ball cannot be lifted out again, and the door must remain closed for ever.'

'Is this usual with Chinese tombs?'

'I only know of one similar closure, and it is not here, but at the Ming Tombs, on the way to the Pass of Nankau.'

We remained there for some time, arguing about the possible effectiveness of this strange method of shutting a door, and then we started back to the temple. We had not gone far before we came upon a group of figures that might have stepped out of a fifteenth-century painting by Kiu Ying.

The Abbot stood on a hillock, with Rizwàn at his feet and three of his Mongol retainers a few yards behind him, but on a lower level. He was talking to an old Chinaman, who carried a bamboo staff in one hand and a birdcage in the other. Clinging to the old man's blue cotton coat was a little girl about twelve years old. She was peering round her companion at Rizwàn, whose presence evidently filled her with awe.

As we drew near, the Chinaman turned towards us, and then I saw that his face was deeply pockmarked. Also that he was blind. (In China smallpox is often a cause of subsequent blindness.)

The Abbot was standing in the middle of the track, and he moved aside to let us pass, and gave us a smile. Then he resumed his conversation with the old blind man.

Donald asked me: 'What kind of a bird was that?'

'Do you mean in the cage? It was partially covered, and the light is waning. I could see nothing.'

'I got a squint at it in passing. And I saw some cinnamon-coloured feathers and a black crest. What could that be?'

'It sounds like a hoopoe, but you don't see them in cages.'

'The colours of a hoopoe would look lovely in *crêpe de Chine* and black velvet,' said Donald musingly. 'I must make a note of it.' And then he added: 'Why should a blind man go about with a bird in a cage? Would not a dog be more useful to him?'

'As a matter of fact, birds in North China seem to take the place of dogs as household pets. In Peking most men go about with a bird in a cage, or perched on a stick, much as in Europe they go about with a terrier on a leash. And the birds that are being carried will call out in passing to the birds hanging in cages outside the shops. And these will answer them.'

'But a bird is no use as a guide for a blind man, surely?'

'Oh, no. That old man talking to the Abbot had the little girl to guide him. Blind men in China are generally musicians. And they teach their birds to repeat certain trills and cadenzas, or to imitate certain calls. I have even known one that miaowed like a cat. There are clubs of bird-owners in Peking, and you will see them squatting in circles in sunny corners outside the city walls, comparing the prowess of their pets.'

'Perhaps the Abbot is a bird-lover?'

'More than likely. But he does not keep a bird himself, now that he has Rizwàn.'

I arrived at the temple entrance alone, for Donald had taken a path across the fields to his own pavilion. He wished to see to his packing for tomorrow's journey to Peking.

When I emerged into the central courtyard I came upon another scene, which this time (except for Western clothes) might have been taken from a Taoist religious picture: a central figure, with others added on either side, in equal numbers, as in an Italian altarpiece.

The doors of the upper pavilion were open and Exalted Virtue was evidently there, getting out our evening drinks. I recognized his lantern, which was lit and stood on the altar at the Buddha's feet and sent a quivering light over his rotundities, so that he seemed to be shaking with unseemly mirth. Below him, in the courtyard, on either side of the door, were the two marble tortoises. On the back of one was Elisalex, resting her shoulder on the stele, while Fédor bent over her. On the other tortoise were Kuniang and Igor, sitting close together. Someone – perhaps one of the Abbot's retainers – had lit some sticks of incense in the big bronze burner, and the perfumed smoke hung about in grey clouds that gave to the scene a touch of unreality. And this was accentuated by the presence in the background of the laughing god.

I turned off into the *k'ai-men-ti*'s lodge to dust my shoes with one of those little dusters of blue rags at the end of a stick that no Chinese household is ever without. Neither of the two couples in the courtyard noticed that I had come in.

That evening, at dinner, I was a little distrait, but it did not matter, as there was no need for me to make conversation. Donald was telling us about another medieval legend which he hoped some day to put on the stage. He had read the story while in Paris (I gather that he passed much time poring over the illuminated manuscripts in the Bibliothèque Nationale), and now he gave it to us in his own words:

'The play should open,' he said, 'at Palermo, at the court of Frederick the Second of Hohenstaufen. I believe that he called himself Roman Emperor. The hero is a Sicilian nobleman, Count Bonifacio: a valiant knight, who delivered the goods every time.

'The services of Count Bonifacio were loaned by the Emperor to some distant vassals, who were troubled by gangsters, called Saracens, that raised hell all along the coast. He left the court just at the precise moment when pages were holding a golden bowl and pouring water for the Emperor to wash his hands.

'Count Bonifacio made such a good job of cleaning up the Saracens that the Emperor's vassals would not let him go. So he remained with them and married and had children. At last, when he was past work, they gave him leave to return to the old folks at home. He reckoned that by that time they must all be dead, but he started off all the same, and got back to Palermo, and went to court and entered the hall where he had last seen the Emperor. And lo and behold, the Emperor was still there on his throne, with the pages holding the bowl and pouring out water. He had not yet finished washing his hands. Count Bonifacio was a sort of Rip van Winkle, only the other way round.'

'It seems to me,' said Elisalex, 'that the best parts of the play would be the Prologue and the Epilogue. But what would come in the middle?'

I don't know what Donald would have answered, for at this moment his attention was distracted by one of the Abbot's retainers coming into the room and bending over his master, to whisper something in his ear. The Abbot had been sitting at the head of the table, partaking of his favourite dish and not giving much attention to anything else. Certainly he had not been following our conversation. He made a sign as of approval, and the Mongol went off again.

A moment later the old Chinaman with the birdcage came hesitatingly into the room, feeling his way with the bamboo staff. His blindness was very evident as he entered an unfamiliar room, and his guide, the little girl, remained outside, perhaps afraid to venture into a dining room full of foreign devils. The old man groped about, looking for something to lean on, and finally took up his stand with his back against the door.

From where I sat I could just see a patch of cinnamon-coloured feathers behind the bars of the little cage, which this time was uncovered. I got up and went and looked at the bird. As I had expected, it was not a hoopoe. It was a crested skylark of the type that is found on the borders of deserts. The pale hue of the plumage is a form of assimilation to the colours on the arid stretches of ground that form the bird's haunts.

I went back to the table and found that, as in the Mad Hatter's tea party, every one, except the Abbot, had moved around. I sat down again in what had been

Donald's place at the end of the table. The others had their backs to me, and were looking at the old Chinaman and his bird. The sight of them all, looking in the same direction, brought home to me suddenly what a mixed lot we were, and how detached from each other. There was the Abbot, with Donald beside him: Samarkand and Broadway. There was Fédor next to Elisalex: the old Russia meeting the new in its lovers. And next to them again, Kuniang with Igor. She was sitting a little behind him, with her arm resting on the back of his chair, which he had turned to face the door. Their heads were close together, and as she leant forward Kuniang's hair almost brushed Igor's ear.

To complete the picture, the blind old Chinaman with his birdcage, and beyond him, in the shadows just outside the open door, the timid face of the little girl, who was too shy to enter.

None of us, except the Abbot, had any idea why a blind old Chinaman, with a bird in a cage, had been invited to join our company. Some of us must have thought that he was a beggar, and that we should give him and the little girl some food. The old man was ragged enough. His blue cotton coat was patched, and it was frayed at the sleeves. But he did not beg. He took a seed, or a bean, out of a little bag that hung on a strap around his neck, and he gave it to the bird to eat. The old man did not bend over the bird, which of course he could not see. He kept his face upturned towards the ceiling. And he emitted a sort of chirrup, evidently meant as encouragement, for after a couple of inquiring chirps in a very similar note, the bird suddenly burst into song.

That song had not been taught it. Birds must have sung like that in Eden, before men sinned.

All that evening I had been feeling uneasy, as if conscious of a happiness that was slipping from me. But the feeling passed, and I gave a sigh of relief. There could be no uneasiness, no anxiety, while one listened to that singing. For here was the song that soars to meet the dawn; the music in a heart that throbs for joy; the clarion call that peals out from the gates of heaven.

My eyes rested on the Abbot. He sat gazing before him, aloof as the Buddha who alone knows and knows no teacher. Serene as an enlightened one, who has found the Path.

24   Return Journey

'The unsymmetrical, the imperfect, the incomplete has become the principle of design. The picture is not filled; it is waiting for our imagination to enter into it. . . .

LAURENCE BINYON:
describing a landscape by the Chinese painter
Ma Yüan

It is a bad workman that quarrels with his tools. And an artist who chooses a means of self-expression and then chafes against its limitations very often has only himself to blame. As the Italian proverb has it: the trouble is with the handle, *Il difetto è nel manico*.

I enjoy making up stories. But when I am writing about China, I so often feel that the medium of a Western language is unsuitable. The reason is not easy to explain. What I feel is that Western languages are too competent (I got this word out of the preface that Somerset Maugham once wrote for a collection of his own stories). They derive, in great part, from Latin. And there is no language in which thought can be expressed and action described more clearly – you might almost say more tersely – than Latin. When I write a Chinese story in English I often feel that I am saying too much: I am being precise and lucid, whereas the story itself should be nebulous and vague. This might not matter, if that elusive quality that is characteristic of Chinese art were not also one of its charms.

This story of ours could be told in Chinese characters

which are merely ideas strung together, or in painting on a Chinese scroll that should be unrolled little by little, showing successive scenes which merge one into another. There would be no captions, and the reader would have to provide a guiding-thread as best he could. Also he would find gaps in the story, and have to fill them up for himself. In most Chinese pictures, there are misty spaces, which enhance the composition.

If this were a Chinese scroll, and the reader were unrolling it on one side and rolling it up again on the other (this would make a good simile to explain the Abbot's theory about Time!), he would come to the moment of my departure with Donald for Peking on the nineteenth of May. I suppose that we would be depicted, he and I, leaving the outer gates of the Pao-lien Ssè on our donkeys, while the rest of our party wished us goodbye. Donald was sorry that his stay with us was coming to an end. His sorrow might be made evident in the scroll by a certain dejection in his attitude, as he turned and looked back over his shoulder, waving a horsehair fly-whisk in a gesture of farewell.

I also was sorry to be leaving the Pao-lien Ssè, and I regretted my decision to accompany Donald to Peking. But I could think of no valid excuse for changing my mind at the last moment. Indeed I could not really give, even to myself, the reasons why I felt somehow that I was making a mistake. The reason was too inconsequent, too elusive, to be put into words. It had something to do with the mountain pies that were flying about the temple grounds shortly before we left. They have blue wings, which are visible only when they fly. Those blue wings brought back to me some of the disquiet that I had felt when I first saw Fédor's picture of Cupid and Psyche.

Donald and I left in the early morning, because I wanted to stop a few hours in Liang Ko Chuang to see Père Antoine. An hour before our departure a storm came suddenly upon us, moving out from a cleft in the hills on to the plain. A cloudburst emptied a cataract of rain on to the temple roofs and the surrounding trees. For a while the thunder rolled and crashed all around us. Water gushed over the gutters and made runnels along the paths. But the clouds lifted as quickly as they had come, and the storm passed off, leaving the stone flags and the marble steps all wet and shining. Big drops trembled on overhanging leaves and sparkled in the returning sunlight.

There is nearly always a storm depicted in a Chinese scroll. It comes as a climax to the story: the story without words.

When we reached Liang Ko Chuang, we found Père Antoine in the building belonging to the Italian mission. And he invited Donald and myself to lunch. He seemed surprised that some of our party were still remaining at the Pao-lien Ssè.

'Is it safe?' he asked.

'You should know better than we. Missionaries are always supposed to be well informed as to the political situation. Is not the countryside quiet?'

'What I meant was: is it safe to leave your wife and your friends in that wild beasts' lair?'

'My dear Père Antoine, you exaggerate. The Mongol retainers may have chased you off, when you came nosing about and trying to get into the tomb. But they represent no danger to the members of our party. And their presence there has the advantage that it keeps away the soldier-bandits. You might consider them a protection!'

'*Quis custodiet ipsos custodes*? That type of untamed nomad is utterly unpredictable, especially when they are taken away from their native Steppes. And the habit of violence seeks an outlet. For the moment they are busy quarrelling with the Manchu guardians of the Imperial tombs. The Manchus consider that no other tomb should be built in this region, which is sacred to the Ch'ing dynasty.'

'The Abbot's tomb is well outside the sacred precincts.'

'For the matter of that so is Kuang Hsu's. The Abbot's ought to have been built farther away.'

'What a strange feud! But the remaining guardians of the Imperial tombs must be a superannuated set of dodderers. The Republican Government has never kept its promise of paying them a salary and providing for the upkeep of the tombs themselves. I wonder there are any guardians left.'

'There aren't many. But, like your Abbot, the dead emperors still have a living bodyguard. And they are armed with bows and arrows. Staying here, I have the impression of having gone back to the China of the sixteenth century or before.'

'With the Mongols archery is a national sport. They are not likely to give it up yet a while.'

'So I gathered . . . One day, when I had ventured as near to Prince Dorbon Oirad's tomb as I dared, I climbed down into a cutting which is being prepared for the stream to flow through – or part of it. And I hung my hat on the branch of a tree. It was rather too broad in the brim to be comfortable for climbing about in, especially among brushwood. All the time I was there I saw nobody and heard nobody, except a sort of nasal sing-song in the distance. But when I scrambled out again, there was my poor old hat transfixed with a dozen arrows set in a perfect circle. I took this as a gentle hint to keep away.'

Donald had been listening to this conversation, and he remarked: 'In my uncle's place in Virginia one still finds Indian arrows in the ground. But not in one's hat. For that sort of thing you must go to joints in New York City or Chicago, where they throw slugs about as a protest against bad liquor.'

Père Antoine looked puzzled, but he did not ask for an explanation. And, as we had a few hours left, before the train started, Donald went off to explore the amenities of Liang Ko Chuang. I remained at the

Mission, talking to Père Antoine, whose views on things Chinese were always interesting and generally unexpected. I asked him if he could explain a circumstance that had been puzzling me during the time I had spent at the Temple of Costly Experience. Why had the Abbot come there? Why was he building himself a tomb in that locality? It was not his homeland, and nothing led one to suppose that his death was imminent. He was not an old man.

Père Antoine listened to my queries and shook his head. 'It is not always easy,' he said, 'to follow the activities of an Oriental. And when you try to fathom their motives the task becomes almost impossible. Who was the Englishman that called the East a university in which one never takes a degree?'

'I have a notion that it was Lord Curzon.'

'He knew what he was talking about. You and I do not, when we try to follow the working of a mind that is both Tartar and Oriental.'

'I think,' I said, 'that there may be a touch of arrogance, which has prompted the Abbot to choose for *his* tomb a region sacred to the dead emperors of a fallen dynasty. But why he should have chosen this particular time to start building is more than I can tell.'

'People who build mausoleums for themselves don't wait till they feel their end approaching. Remember also that your Abbot is a mystic and a soldier: a strange combination anywhere. When the chieftain's day is over he sometimes prefers to die, rather than decline into a tremulous old age.'

Père Antoine thought the matter over for a few moments, and then he concluded:

'One thing is clear: the Abbot has outlived his times. So he builds himself a tomb in the grand manner, and near those of the Manchus, who came from the same part of the world that he does. It is this assumption of equality and perhaps even relationship that annoys the Manchu guardians to the Imperial tombs. Only for us is the whole thing an anachronism. Not merely because a

poor missionary cannot walk in the woods without
having his hat pierced by arrows, but because they are
building a tomb, in the year 1928, as they built such
things in Kublai's time, without using a saw, a hammer
or a nail. To understand what it all means, you must
recapture the mechanics and the mentality of the
Abbot's remote ancestors.'

'I can tell you something of that mentality. Like the
Chinese mandarins of former days, the Abbot believes
that all the troubles of China come from our Western
civilization.'

'He is not far wrong.'

'What a thing for a missionary to say!'

'I come from a class of missionaries that has been in
China for centuries, and we have never interfered in the
political affairs of Asiatics. To do so only retards inevitable solutions and makes things worse than they need
be. Bring them the consolations of our religion, but let
them work out their own political salvation in their own
way. Foreigners interfered in Gordon's time to sup-
press the Tai Ping revolt, and to bolster up the
Manchus. In 1911 they interfered again, this time to
help the Republicans do away with the empire. What
business was it of ours? Who are we to decide which is
the legal government of China? Only a tiny percentage
of the Chinese themselves care about it one way or the
other, though you would not think so if you read the
newspapers.'

'Then you agree with the Abbot!'

'No. I have no special animus against Western civilization as such. I consider that the source of all the
trouble in China is the lack of trees.'

'Of trees?'

'Yes. "*Un peuple sans forêt est un peuple qui
meurt.*" Remember what Eastern Asia was like in
primitive times. The forests of Siberia came down the
coast, to meet the tropical jungles. If ever a country
needed forests it is China. Yet nowhere in the world has
deforestation been so cruel and so senseless. Old Abbé

Huc pointed it out nearly a century ago. And if you travel in the province of Shansi that drains into the Yellow River just south of here, you can see for yourself what conditions have been brought about by the wasteful cutting of trees. I am told that the last of the old virgin forest is being destroyed in these very days at the Tung Ling: the Eastern tombs that correspond to these, and are much finer. The fauna up there was the old primitive fauna, up till a year ago. That is where the Reeve pheasant came from. Now there is little more left than a forest of tree stumps. The whole north of China has been stripped of its trees, and the desert is encroaching even inside the Great Wall. That means droughts and floods and famine, and these mean revolution and civil wars, and these bring foreign invasions. And all because they have cut down the trees.'

Donald was impressed by the Catholic missionaries whose hospitality we enjoyed at Liang Ko Chuang. He talked to me about them during our journey to Peking. Those missionaries were so unlike their opposite numbers in the Protestant field. Which is only natural, as most of the latter are burdened with family cares. The Fathers who directed the hospital at Liang Ko Chuang were dressed like Chinese, and one, older than the rest, mentioned casually that only recently had he cut off his pigtail, 'though I might have continued to wear it here for the guardians of the tombs still wear theirs'.

The express from Hankow was no longer running, but only a train from Chen-chow, which for some unexplained reason was almost empty. On the station platform at Pao-ting-fu (where we waited an hour or two) Donald got into conversation with the stationmaster, and they talked in laborious French. The stationmaster said that, as a boy, he had been to a missionary school in Shensi.

'And are you a Christian?'

'*Oui. Un peu.*'

This answer pleased Donald very much.

'None of us are a hundred per cent Christian,' he said, 'but merely *un peu*. Why not admit it? How many religious wars and massacres might have been prevented if mankind would only recognize that it can only be good in parts!'

Though the sun had long set before we reached Peking, the heat and the stuffiness were oppressive. And the smell from the canal outside the Tartar Wall was reminiscent of the small cemetery nearby. I wished I were back in the Temple of Costly Experience, listening to the old blind man's lark. Would Kuniang miss me, I wondered, when she woke soon after daylight and stepped out into the open air to breathe in the fresh scents of the morning?

25   Saint Sebastian

L'Empereur:
> Mais comme il est beau!
> Il est trop beau. Je veux qu'il chante,
> Qu'il change son extrême chant,
> Tel le cygne hyperboreén

D'ANNUNZIO:
Le Martyre de Saint Sebastien

Donald's travelling arrangements caused us considerable trouble after we arrived back in Peking, for his 'reservations' on trains and steamers took no account of Chinese politics. Not only was there a civil war on, but the Nationalist army, advancing from the south, had clashed with the Japanese at Tsi-nan-fu, and the line was cut between Tientsin and Nankin. There was not time enough for Donald to catch his ship at Shanghai, if he took the alternative route by a coasting steamer from Tang-ku. It ended in his having to travel in the opposite direction, via Mukden and Shimonoseki, so as to embark in Japan. It was lucky for him that, just on this one line, the traffic was not yet congested.

A week after our return to the Shuang-liè Ssè I saw Donald off by the night train to Mukden. During those few days I received one letter from Kuniang. She said that they were all well and that they were expecting me back: unless, of course, the children needed her, in which case she would return at once to Peking. (The children, as I had already written to her, were perfectly

198

well and could think of nothing but their donkey, which they had named Donald after the donor, or Donny for short.)

I accompanied our guest to the station to see him off, and installed him in a compartment, which – rather to his disgust – he was to share with a plump little Chinaman, who spoke some English and seemed conversationally inclined. Indeed, he was brimming over with friendliness. I stood on the platform, talking through the open window, and Donald asked me if there were a bookstore in the station. I answered that there was not, upon which the little Chinaman pulled an enormous tome down from the rack and thrust it into Donald's unwilling hand, telling him that he could read it during the journey; that it was very interesting and instructive. It was called *Swas to Zyri*. The last I saw of Donald, as the train moved off, was his astonished face as he stared down at the book that lay open on his knee. It was an isolated volume (the last) of *Chambers Encyclopaedia*.

I watched the train until it passed through the tunnel in the outer lunette of the old Hata Men. And then I got into my rickshaw to go home. As we padded along the Tartar Wall and stuck for five minutes in the traffic just inside the Shun-chih Men (where a camel had got entangled in the long rope traces of a country cart), I asked myself what I should do next. Donald's departure had kept me longer in Peking than I had foreseen. Was it worth while going back to the Pao-lien Ssè, or should I await Kuniang's return to Peking?

As usual I entered the house by the back way, through the Gate of Happy Sparrows, and I did not go indoors at once. Dark though it was, I paced the garden paths leisurely, enjoying the cool evening air. Ten minutes must have passed before I made my way through the courtyards. A blue-clad figure emerged from a doorway and disappeared into the back premises. Though I could barely see him I recognized Exalted Virtue. I was so used to his flitting through the evening shadows

199

that for a moment I felt no surprise. Then I gave a sudden start. Exalted Virtue was back in Peking! I had left him with Kuniang at the Temple of Costly Experience.

Exalted Virtue had vanished before I thought of calling him. I hurried forward with a sudden sense of anxiety. And then I saw Kuniang herself. She was standing at the door of the children's pavilion, her hand on the doorknob, just about to go in. Seeing me, she stopped and waited. A little light came through the door itself, which in its upper half was made of latticed wood, with rice paper pasted over it. This light shone on Kuniang's summer frock, but left her face in shadow. I was on a lower level than she, for she stood at the top of the three steps that led up to the pavilion, and close to one of the red-lacquer columns that held up the overhanging eaves of the heavy-tiled roof.

'Kuniang!' I exclaimed. 'How is that you are here?'

She continued to look down at me, her hand still on the doorknob. If she answered anything I did not hear it.

'Has anything happened?' I asked.

No answer. I gazed up at her and a strange dread filled my heart. At last she spoke, in a low voice with no life in it:

'Yes. Something has happened. Let me go in and see the children, before I tell you.' She paused again for a few seconds and then added, always in that lifeless voice: 'Wait for me in your study. I won't be long. The children are already in bed.'

As she passed in through the door I heard shouts of 'Mummy! Mummy!' Shadows moved and crossed each other in the rectangles of subdued light that were the curtainless windows. I made my way to my study. The armchairs were still disposed round the fireplace. Though the grate was empty I went and sat there and waited. It seemed a long time before she came.

When at last she did so she passed by me and went and laid her elbows on the mantelpiece and buried her

200

face in her hands. She was not crying, but I noticed, as she came in, that her eyes were heavy with pain, or with fatigue, or both. She spoke through her hands, so that her voice sounded muffled.

'Igor is dead.'

'Good God! How?'

'I will tell you. Give me time.'

The impulse came over me to take her in my arms and comfort her, but when I made a motion to get up out of my chair she signed to me with her hand to stay still. And when she lifted her face she did not look at me, but kept her eyes on her own hand, as her fingers toyed with a little amber snuffbox on the mantelpiece. When she spoke it seemed as if she were telling a story about other people than ourselves, and about something that had happened a long time ago:

'The weather was very fine when you left. All the spring seemed to burst out at once, like a jet of water that leaps suddenly into the sunlight. We all know how the air in North China affects us in the spring: how it makes us irritable, or gives us a sort of mental exultation, as well as a physical exultation. It used to be that way in the Russian family even here in Peking, so that I never knew what they would do next. Well, it was like that, only more so, and more than I had ever felt it before. We were all light-hearted and light-headed, as if we were walking on air. Fédor said he felt the strength of ten men, and he lifted the great bronze incense-burner from its pedestal and put it back, just to let off steam. Igor was in a state of rapturous delight over everything or nothing at all. He had an expression on his face that Fédor said was what was required for the picture of Saint Sebastian.

'Yesterday morning – no, it wasn't yesterday, it must have been the day before – I was woken up by the birds. The air vibrated with their voices. I got out of bed and stepped to the door to look out. Nobody was about – there never was at that hour. And I could see the stream all sparkling in the sunshine. The morning scents greeted me as usual, but they seemed fresher and sweeter. I walked down to the edge of the lake and slipped off my nightie. And then I waded in with little gasps, for the water was cold. I swam down as far as the bridge and back again, and across the lake. A kingfisher kept darting past me, close to. He was not in the least afraid. I came out near the opposite bank on to the Island of Fulfilled Desires, and I lay on the white marble parapet, which was already warm in the sun. I wondered vaguely why the birds were singing so much at that hour. Why weren't they looking for food? Then I leant over the edge of the parapet and tried to see the reflection of my face. But the water was too shallow. All I could see were little fishes hovering above the sandy bottom. I held out my arm and compared the lights and shadows in the stream with those in my jade bracelet.'

Kuniang's voice, and the expression on her face as she described this scene, were so utterly at variance with her words that I stared at her with ever-growing anxiety. I felt that she was turning a knife in an open wound. She was making the description beautiful, in order to enhance some horror yet to come. After a while she continued, never looking at me, but always at the snuffbox that she held in her hand:

'I heard a voice call "Kuniang" over the water. And there was Igor, swimming towards me from where the stream flows out of the lake. If the place and the hour were beautiful, Igor's was the crowning beauty. At first I noticed only the grace and vigour of his overhand stroke, as he cleaved the calm waters. Then the sunlight caught his hair, and his face seemed to glow with a light of its own. As he drew nearer his craving for me brought a look of anguish into his eyes. And at last it found an answering desire in me. He must have guessed it, for his expression became radiant. He found his depth and stood close under the parapet with his face close to mine. His hands caressed my shoulders and our lips met.' Kuniang paused and added:

'That was the end.'

'But you said he was dead! What has this—'

'Even as he stood there a shadow flew through the air. There was a sickening thud, and I saw his face grow blank and pale. He gazed round slowly, with a soft wondering look, as if he were saying goodbye to the sunlight, to the spring, to life itself. But when his eyes met mine he smiled, and tried to say something. I think it was "Lady Precious Jade". Then he fell back slowly, slipping out of my arms.'

Again a pause, and again she went on: 'For a few moments I lay there dazed, and watched his white body floating, with the arrow deep embedded between his shoulders. The water grew all red with his blood. And always, in the trees, the birds were singing, singing, singing . . .'

Kuniang bent her head and lay her face on her arms, as they rested on the mantelpiece. And she murmured, more to herself than to me: 'I think I could bear it, if only he had not smiled . . .'

I wanted to lay my hand on Kuniang's shoulder, or to take her in my arms. But again something retained me. Her nerves were strained to breaking-point. Not yet could I soothe them.

Then I heard a noise behind me. Someone was turning the door handle. Kuniang lifted her head, and we both looked round to see who it was. My thoughts were far from Peking, and when the door opened and a gigantic figure filled it, at first I hardly realized who the old bearded man could be, towering almost to the ceiling. Patushka's face wore a look of misery that matched Kuniang's own. He stood gazing at her, and his lips parted to ask the question that was already in his eyes.

'Is it true?'

Kuniang nodded without speaking, and he came forward into the room, staggering a little as he walked. When he sank down into a chair the tears were running down his furrowed cheeks.

The sight of those tears broke the spell that held us. Kuniang gave a little cry (I can hear it, even as I write!), and she ran across the room to fling herself in Patushka's arms.

She had never known a father's care. And this old man had cared for her, in his own queer way. So she sat on his knee, encircled by his arms, with her face buried in his neck. And she sobbed as if her heart would break.

I got up from my chair and went out of the room, closing the door softly behind me. And I stood there in the darkness, and gazed with unseeing eyes upwards at the stars.

26 Travellers' Tales

On pardonne tant que l'on aime

LA ROCHEFOUCAULD:
Maximes

I was still standing outside the door of my study, stunned by the news of Igor's death and the manner of it, when Exalted Virtue came across the courtyard with a telegram on a little brass tray.

Though such a thought did not cross my mind at that moment I may mention here the characteristic fact that nothing in the words or in the demeanour of my Chinese boys, either then or later, ever betrayed that they were aware of anything untoward having occurred at the Temple of Costly Experience. When a thing ought not to have happened it is well to behave as if it never *had* happened. As the Eastern proverb says: 'To know the truth and to speak it is good. But it is better to know the truth and to speak of date-stones'.

I took the telegram from the tray and made a sign to Exalted Virtue not to wait for an answer (I was in no mood to answer telegrams, whoever they might be from), and I tore open the covering flap. But the Chinese lantern that hangs outside my study door was not lit. To read the text I had to hold the written sheet up against the window of my study, where a little light filtered through from inside. At first, all I could understand was the signature and the name of the place whence the telegram had been sent off (this was Kao-pe-tien). I had to read the contents over and over again before I began to have some inkling as to what it was all about. It ran as follows:

HAVE TELEGRAPHED TO BETINES IN THE HATA MEN FOR DRUGS URGENTLY NEEDED STOP PLEASE SEE THAT THEY ARE SENT TO ME WITH ALL POSSIBLE SPEED, OR BRING THEM YOURSELF STOP – CANNOT TELEGRAPH WHAT HAS HAPPENED BUT BUILDER OF THE TOMB IS NO MORE AND LADY POISONED BY OVERDOSE OF OPIUM STOP.
STILL HOPE TO SAVE HER.

PÈRE ANTOINE

As I said before, it took some time for the meaning of the telegram to penetrate to my brain. But I understood at last that Père Antoine had ordered some drugs from Betines (the German chemist in Peking) and wanted them in a hurry. The builder of the tomb was no more. That must be the Abbot, and he was dead. But how? The lady had taken an overdose of opium. Although it sounded most unlike her, that must be Elisalex. Yet she was no drug addict. Nor was she likely to be overwhelmed with grief if the Abbot were no more. Père Antoine still hoped to save her, but was not sure of doing so. She must be still in danger.

Most people in China know something of the effects of opium-poisoning: the glassy unseeing eyes, the leaden pallor of the skin, the state of coma, with breathing growing ever slower, so that at last the victim will only take a breath every few seconds till breathing stops altogether. Poor Elisalex! How could she have come to such a pass?

It occurred to me that perhaps Kuniang could explain.

When I re-entered my study with the open telegram in my hand, Kuniang was standing with her back to the mantelpiece. Her eyes were without light, and there was something hopeless in the droop of her shoulders. She reminded me of some poor bird that has been stoned, lying on the ground with broken wings. My heart ached for her, but I thought it best to give at once the news that had reached me. I handed her the telegram, saying:

'There appears to have been another tragedy in the Temple of Costly Experience. It is indeed well-named!'

Like myself, when I first read the telegram, Kuniang was slow to take it in, and no less puzzled than I had been. Nothing had happened before her departure from the temple that could make clear why the Abbot should be dead and Elisalex in danger of her life. Kuniang said nothing, but shook her head and looked at me, dazed and uncomprehending. Neither of us paid any attention to Patushka.

'What I don't understand,' I said, 'is how this can have happened all in one day: that is, if you left Liang Ko Chuang this morning.'

'I did not leave this morning, but the day before yesterday, in the evening.'

'And you have been all this time on the way?'

'They are moving troops up the line. I began to think that we should never get here. And at moments I felt that it might be better so . . .'

'My poor darling! Forty-eight hours in that train! After all you had been through.'

Kuniang looked at me and again her eyes filled with tears. She had not expected sympathy, nor a term of endearment. It occurred to me to ask when she had eaten last. She shook her head vaguely and said she did not remember. Then she added as an afterthought:

'It must have been at Pao-ting-fu. There were some Mahommedan soldiers on the platform, frying cakes in oil. Exalted Virtue persuaded them to sell me some, but the oil was rancid . . .'

'You must go to bed, and I'll have something brought to you at once.'

'No. No. I cannot go to bed. If what that telegram says is true, something must be done. I must go back to Elisalex.'

'*You* go back! Impossible. I must go, if any one.'

We gazed at one another for a while in silence. And

then I added, speaking slowly and quietly:

'Listen. This is what I will do. I will go round to the German Hospital. I want to know if they can procure me a nurse. It sounds as if Elisalex needs one. I shall also pass by the station and see if it is possible to travel on the Kin Han line. It is odd that there should be so much confusion south of Peking and none whatever on the Mukden line. Donald got off without any trouble. Perhaps it was only a temporary block. If possible, I shall start again tomorrow for the Pao-lien Ssè and take the drugs with me. The *tingchai* can go round to Betines for them the first thing tomorrow morning.'

'Are you sure I ought not to come too, if Elisalex is ill?'

'Certainly not. I have only to look at you to see that you are completely done up. Stay here with the children. And Patushka will look after you. Won't you, Patushka?'

I turned to the old man in the arm-chair but perceived, to my astonishment, that he had fallen asleep. I smiled and said to Kuniang:

'It looks as if you might have to look after *him*!'

And then at last I did what I had wanted to do all along. I took her in my arms and kissed her. She clung to me with a little sob and buried her face in my coat. She would hardly let me go. When she did so, I left her there, with Patushka asleep in the chair. Oddly enough, I was thinking what a pity it was that Uncle Podger was no longer with us. He always used to console Kuniang when she cried.

Our troubles that evening had not come 'as single spies, but in battalions'. Perhaps it was better so. One had served to counteract the other.

Twenty-four hours passed before I could start off for Liang Ko Chuang. I might have given up the idea, for I hated to leave Kuniang, but it was obvious that if Père Antoine was to get the drugs he had asked for they would have to be taken to him by hand. The postal service in China carries on in the most adverse situations, but it could not cope with a disorganized railway service and deliver parcels in the face of an advancing army, even if there were no fighting. It was up to me to do my best.

And if I did actually succeed in starting at all, I owed it in part to Patushka, who as an ex-employee of the Kin Han Railway succeeded in getting me a compartment in a train that was about to make the best of its way south in the direction of Kaifeng and Hankow.

I had a nurse with me, as well as Exalted Virtue. I got the nurse thanks to old Doctor Ehrhardt of the German Hospital – one of those people to whom half the foreigners in China must have appealed for help at one time or another (and always got it!). I found him in the corridor on the ground floor of his clinic, with his eye fixed on a very old microscope that he held up against a windowsill. The instrument, which looked as if it had been doing service since the days of Pasteur, was not one of those belonging to the hospital itself, but Doctor Ehrhardt's own private property, which he carried about with him in his bag and preferred to any other. He continued to examine whatever it was that he had got there on the glass slides, while he asked what he could do for me.

'A nurse? You can't have any of our nurses. But perhaps Nurse van Bosch is free and would go with you. She is a nice, blonde, efficient, large-bosomed Dutch woman, and lives in the Ma Ta Hu-tung, opposite the French *glacis*. I will send round and ask. A case of opium-poisoning? Well. Missionary doctors get plenty of practice in that among back-sliding converts. Your patient is probably in good hands. And how is your lady wife?'

'Just back from Liang Ko Chuang – the place I am making for. She is much upset. A young man, a Russian, who was with her party, has just got killed there.'

'By bandits?'

'You might call them that.'

'You might call most people that in China, or so I am told. But who was the young man?'

'You may have known him. Igor was his only name. At one time he was a patient of Doctor Folitzky's.'

'I remember. A perfect Adonis. Suffered from hallucinations: probably due to worms. I'm sorry he's dead. There are so many ugly people in the world and so few beautiful ones. Tell your wife to take a sedative: bromide, or something. They will give you one in our pharmacy if you ask for it. Most returned travellers come here for one in these times, when it's not a bullet that has to be extracted from a thigh or a shoulder.'

It took us three days to get down to Liang Ko Chuang. We had brought plenty of food and we drank tea intermittently all day. The time passed sleepily on the sidings of country stations in the plain. It was very hot, and we had to keep the blinds drawn and sit in partial darkness, in order not to be devoured by flies. The nurse had a placid disposition and seemed to be enjoying it all. I suppose it was like a holiday to her. Even Exalted Virtue appeared calm and resigned, far more so than on our first journey down to the Pao-lien Ssè. The sight of trainloads of soldiers, horses and guns, all moving on Peking did not alarm him. Strange to say, it did not seem to alarm anybody. There had been none of the terrified exodus from the capital towards the foreign concessions in Tientsin that as a rule accompanied any movement of troops in the vicinity. The soldiers that we saw along the way were friendly, smiling creatures, ready to pass the time of day with any one that came along. They alternated in the railway trucks with their own ponies and field guns. But whereas the men and the ponies travelled unprotected in the open trucks, the guns were carefully covered over with tarpaulin.

These were the troops of Field Marshal Yen-Hsi Shan, 'Model Governor' of the 'Model Province' of Shansi. He was moving north to oust the Mukden forces, and the main Nationalist army was moving up behind him, but leisurely, doing much propaganda and no fighting. All of which made it clear that the railway was not likely to be free for any active civilian traffic for some time to come.

Like our own, the military trains stuck in stations for interminable waits, but this did not trouble the soldiery. One place is as good as another, and it is pleasant to be able to get out and stretch your legs and steal something from a neighbouring farm. The ideal, of course, is for your train to remain in a nice cosy siding for years on end. This happens when your general – the one that took you away from your native home – is dead, and you are conveniently forgotten or ignored by everyone else. Then you can really settle down, planting a vegetable garden in the vicinity of the railway track. And you can marry and have children. That was what occurred to the 'Blue Train', somewhere between Tientsin and Pukow.

There is something very restful about war in such conditions, though you might not think so from the headlines of newspapers in the West. I could imagine them announcing hysterically: 'Marshal Yen advances on doomed city!'

To Kuniang the long waits in the train coming north must have been nerve-racking and painful beyond words. To me those delays were almost soothing. When I have nothing to do but fold my hands and wait, the quiet philosophy of the East enveloped me like a grey mist, through which the trials of life loom like phantoms and fade away like ghosts. For what is patience but the art of hoping?

27   The Passing of a Chieftain

Ut non ex vita, sed ex domo in domum videretur migrare
('So that he seemed not to pass out of life, but out of one home into another')

> CORNELIUS NEPOS:
> *Atticus*

The congestion of traffic was limited to the main line. Between Kao-pe-tien and Liang Ko Chuang we met with little difficulty apart from that of persuading the stationmaster to get the local train to start at all. He did not seem to think it was worth while.

When we finally arrived at our destination we found Père Antoine not in the old Mission house, where I had seen him on a former occasion, but in the new buildings that had been set up recently for the care of the sick and the infirm. He was standing in a small courtyard, strangely occupied in making a study of bows and arrows. Some of these had belonged to the Abbot's Mongol retainers, and how Père Antoine had got hold of them I don't know. The bows were spread out on the ground before him, and he was so busy comparing them that he hardly paid any attention to us.

'Strange,' he said, 'how these northern Chinese and Mongols all make composite bows. It may be a proof that there are circumpolar elements in their culture. Hence traces of the bear-cult, the use of pit dwellings, rectangular stone knives, and so on. . . .'

'For goodness' sake, Père Antoine, leave Chinese folklore alone for one minute and tell us how Elisalex is.'

'Elisa—what? Oh, you mean our fair patient! Well, she is definitely out of danger since yesterday. I never thought she would live when I first saw her.'

'I have brought her a nurse.'

Père Antoine glanced amiably at Nurse van Bosch and smiled.

'That was a good idea. I don't know who will be more pleased, the doctors or the patient. She, poor thing, is tired of missionaries and Chinese peasant women to look after her.'

The nurse answered something indistinct. But it sounded like 'I don't wonder.'

Père Antoine asked: 'Have you brought the drugs I asked for?'

'Yes. They are all here.'

'Well, the doctors – there are two of them – are both busy. This is their hour for attending to the Chinese patients. You may have seen them all lined up outside as you came in. But I know what the nurse might do, and that is to give the patient an injection of caffeine. She needs that badly.'

Nurse van Bosch asked: 'And where is my patient?'

'Along that passage. First door to the right.'

He pointed to the opening of an outdoor corridor at the opposite corner of the courtyard. The nurse bustled off to begin work.

'And now, Père Antoine,' I said. 'Pull yourself together and tell me what has happened. I understand that there has been a tragedy here. Indeed, more than one.'

Père Antoine shot a keen glance at me through his steel-rimmed spectacles. 'You are right about that. How much do you know?'

'Only that Igor, the Russian boy, was killed while bathing with Kuniang in the stream. Nothing about the Abbot and Elisalex.'

213

Père Antoine led the way to a bench in the shade, near a door that, as I subsequently discovered, led into a dining room or 'refectory'. We sat on the bench and talked, while Chinese servants passed backwards and forwards through the courtyard. After the manner of their kind they shouted at one another as they passed, though there was an invalid close by and though they could have made themselves heard equally well, even speaking in normal tones.

'It has been an unlucky week,' said Père Antoine. 'After the Russian boy, the next to pass out was the Abbot's dog.'

'Rizwàn?'

'Is that his name? He died in a strange way: bitten on the tongue by a poisonous snake. He was out walking with his master, and his tongue must have been hanging out because of the heat. These dried-up beds of artificial rivers – there is one close to the Pao-lien Ssè – are full of snakes. The dog's tongue was probably the nearest thing for the viper to strike at, as the dog was nosing about among the bushes. He must have died within half an hour. The snakes about here are not often poisonous, but when they are they are deadly.

'The Abbot – I call him that because you do – picked the dog up in his arms and carried him home, possibly to get help. The poor brute must have been a heavy burden and the poison would give him convulsions. Nobody quite knows what happened, but we suppose that by the time that the Abbot passed by his own tomb the dog was already dead.

'Some stonecutters and other workmen, who were busy putting up a marble pillar near the entrance to the tomb, saw the Abbot emerge from the forest, carrying his dog. The opening of the tunnel that leads down into the interior of the tumulus was close by. The Abbot passed in, and was never seen again alive.'

'Good heavens! What do you mean?'

'Just that. The Abbot had been alone in the forest, but when he entered the tomb some of his Mongol retainers saw him and followed him down the tunnel. Twenty minutes later they came out again, carrying his dead body, which was immediately dressed for burial in new robes that had been prepared long beforehand, and which lay in one of the pavilions of the Pao-lien Ssè, together with a lacquered coffin of catalpa wood.'

'What an extraordinary business!'

'Yes. It might serve as the basis of a detective story, except that it all sounds far too improbable. To begin with, it is not at all clear why the Abbot should have chosen to carry the corpse of the dog down into the tomb. Did he want to bury him there? As for the Abbot's own death, his Mongol retainers say that, when carrying his dog down the steep incline, he did not see where he was going and tripped over a transversal beam of wood that lay on the ground, striking his forehead on another beam higher up.'

'Would that be enough to kill him?'

'I should very much doubt that it would kill him outright.'

'But you say he was dead when his retainers carried him out into the open again.'

'You raise doubts that only the Mongol retainers themselves could set at rest. We may give them credit for loving their chief. But they knew that his day was over and that he could never recover his strength and his power. Orientals – some Orientals – believe in and practise those mercy killings that are just beginning to become fashionable among suffering humanity in the West, though so far it is only in law courts that one hears of them. The Abbot's tomb was waiting for him. We can only guess at what happened to him as he lay there, stunned by his fall, in the darkness of the tunnel that descended into the bowels of the earth. In the absence of any reliable information, we must fall back on conjecture. The Abbot's death has to be explained somehow. For now he lies buried in a "Jewelled City", as he had always planned. And they buried the lady there too.'

'Buried Elisalex? But she was alive and well!'

'I know. But it is an old Asiatic custom. In the days before they thought of doing so in effigy they used to bury the wives and concubines, and the servants and dogs and horses, all together in the tomb with the emperor. They crucified them to the wall, so that they should not assume a disrespectful attitude in dying.'

'You don't mean to say that they crucified Elisalex?'

'Something very like it. She was tied to the wall, with her arms outstretched. But they gave her an overdose of opium first, so that she should not suffer.'

'And who got her out? You?'

'Oh, dear me, no! I knew nothing about it till afterwards. It was that young Russian giant. And he brought her here, carrying her in his arms, to see if we could save her.'

'Where is Fédor now?'

'Somewhere around. You will see him at lunch.'

'And where are the Abbot's Mongol retainers?'

'Gone home.'

'Home where?'

'How should I know? Wherever it is that they come from. Somewhere in the north.'

Anything so bald and unadorned as Père Antoine's account of these incredible events would be difficult to find outside a school textbook of medieval history. But I was grateful to him for not reminding me of his own warning, not to leave any one of our party in that 'brigand's lair'.

As he volunteered no additional information, I continued to question him:

'Where is Igor buried? The Russian boy, I mean.'

'In the tomb with the Abbot. So is the dog. They are all buried in there. Plenty of room, though I would have preferred a Christian burial for that poor boy. By the way, your Abbot must have been a very rich man.'

'What makes you think so?'

'At last I was able to penetrate into his tomb, just before they laid him to rest there. It is lucky for me that

216

the Mongol retainers were busy elsewhere, or I might have shared the fate of the lady. And I'm sure the Russian giant would never have bothered to get *me* out. An emperor's tomb could hardly be finer. In the central hall, where the coffins lie, there is a shining brass floor, which is really a map. It represents, I suppose, the Abbot's home in the north. The rivers are in quicksilver and the towns in precious stones. The ceiling is dark blue, with constellations in gilded metal.'

I remembered Igor's words, when he saw Rizwàn lying at his feet:

'A shining floor, and jewels, and lighted lamps . . .'

Père Antoine picked up one of his composite bows again and began to examine it once more.

'By the way,' he said, 'where is your friend the impresario?'

'What impresario?'

'That American who was here with you. He could talk of nothing but the theatre, and theatre scenery and costume. He asked me if the guardians of the Imperial tombs wore any special uniforms, when on duty.'

'That was Donald Parramoor. He has gone to America. Why do you ask?'

'Because I bought a coat off one of Prince Dorbon's retainers, before they left. It is made of brown silk, faded to the colour of the brown earth before the rains come. It is belted in at the waist with an ivory buckle, carved to represent two dragons rising out of the water. And the coat is lined with plates of steel.'

'Do you want to sell this to Donald?'

'I would not mind, if it were useful to him as a model for the Russian dances he talked about. If not, I will give it to Père Licent for his little museum at Tientsin.'

I thought it about time to inquire after more practical matters.

'Can you put me up here?' I asked.

'If you don't mind roughing it. At any rate, we will not bury you alive.'

I gave him up, and went off to inquire about Elisalex.

28　Ballets Russes

Anon they move
In perfect phalanx, to the Dorian mood
Of flutes and soft recorders.

MILTON:
Paradise Lost

As a rule, when you arrive at a place where something extraordinary has happened, you find scores of people willing and even anxious to give you their version, with comments and impressions. This was not the case at Liang Ko Chuang. Elisalex of course could tell me nothing. She was barely out of danger, having lain, hovering between life and death, in the very modest little hospital that the Italian missionaries had so fortunately opened there a few months before. It was not a real hospital, for as a rule they took no in-patients. The founders called it, in their own language, an *Ambulatorio*. Chinese suffering from every imaginable disease came or were carried there between ten and twelve in the morning; if they could not come one or the other of the two missionary-doctors went to visit them at home. The doctors' task consisted for the most part in waging a not very successful war against dirt and superstition. These two missionary-doctors were our hosts, and being used to succour only the humbler class of Chinese, they found that to be responsible for a beautiful and fashionable European lady was a truly alarming experience. For this reason they welcomed the arrival of the Dutch nurse with unconcealed relief.

218

Strange to say – for country priests, as a rule, are great gossips – they appeared to know very little about what had happened to bring their patient to such a pass. From them I elicited even less than from Père Antoine, who treated the matter as a mere sidelight on oriental folklore, interesting only inasmuch as the attempted immuring of Elisalex within the Abbot's tomb showed how the atavistic conception of a chieftain's burial still persisted among certain North Asiatic tribes.

Even Fédor was uninformative and absorbed in his own thoughts, which concerned the future, not the past. He had broken the bonds that held the fainting form of Elisalex to the inner walls of the sepulchre, and he had carried her to Liang Ko Chuang. When I asked him how he had overcome the opposition of the Abbot's Mongol retainers he brushed my question aside, and spoke only of how the patient should be tended and how and when she could face the fatigue and the uncertainties of the journey home.

A general unconsciousness of, or indifference to, any atmosphere of tragedy was apparent from the first moments of our arrival. The local train that plied between Kao-pe-tien and Liang Ko Chuang had no longer any timetable. It brought us to our destination about eleven in the morning, and our first meal was lunch. There were six of us at table: our hosts, Père Antoine, the Dutch nurse, Fédor and myself. A huge bowl of spaghetti disappeared in a twinkling. And the wine (which Père Antoine had brought with him from Shanghai) was Chablis of the best. It helped to put us all in excellent spirits. From the jokes and the laughter you might have judged us all utterly heartless. But I noticed how cleverly Père Antoine directed the conversation into easy channels. He knew more than he wished me to guess. Père Antoine was a tactful man, with the mental suppleness and subtlety of the true Jesuit, and a nice perception of what it was advisable to say and to do in awkward circumstances. On this occasion his careless indifference was assumed. And yet it was contagious.

Most Catholic missionaries in the interior of China, when detached from their 'mother' houses in the provincial capitals, must needs live very poorly. I remember one poor padre, in an out-of-the-way hamlet in Honan, who wished to do me honour and brought out, with great pride, a bottle of champagne that had been presented to him by a marauding Chinese general (in exchange, I believe, for some remedy against indigestion). But the Padre possessed no glasses to drink out of. So we drank the champagne out of cheap china teacups.

I suspected Père Antoine of bringing a certain luxury into the modest household at Liang Ko Chuang. After lunch they served us the most excellent coffee. When I say 'they' I should explain that Exalted Virtue helped the local boys and coolies in preparing the table and handing round the dishes. And his ministrations conferred style and dignity on that simple meal.

While I sipped my coffee I inquired whether there could be any objection to my going to the Temple of Costly Experience.

'None whatever,' said Père Antoine.

'Whom will I find there?'

'A few Manchus, such as guard the Imperial tombs. The Abbot's death put an end to the feud between them and the Mongol retainers. When the latter moved out to go home, the Manchus moved in. I could give you a letter for them if you like. But there is no need. A silver dollar or two will serve better than any introduction.'

'And what about the tomb?'

'It is closed up. You cannot get into it any more, as I did the day after the Abbot died. But you can walk round outside.'

'And are the arches and the bridges and the outer pavilions all finished?'

'I am not sure. I meant to go and see what was happening, but there has not been time. At one moment there was a certain amount of confusion, and the local Yamen had to interfere to prevent disorder among the workmen, who were afraid they were not going to get paid. I think I shall go this afternoon to see the Mandarin – he does not call himself that, of course, in Republican times, but I cannot think of him as anything else. He will be able to tell me what has been arranged, and if he has cut off a few heads. Anyhow, the Prince-Abbot has been buried and the outer doors are closed. Probably the next thing we shall hear about it is that the tomb has been broken into and looted by some rabble army. That is likely to be the fate even of the Imperial tombs, if civil war continues much longer. There may not be much fighting, but the sacking of tombs and cities will continue as before.'

'Is there to be no peace in China, even for the dead?'

'Not till some new dynasty comes into its own. They tell me that Prince Dorbon Oirad once dreamt of founding one. And the clansmen of the northern Steppes supported him. But the days of a Gengiz Khan and of a Tamerlane are over. From East and West, the Japanese and the Russian pincers are closing in. I suppose it will end in an invasion from the north, as when the Mongols and the Manchus invaded China. History repeats itself.'

'And will that mean the founding of a new dynasty?'

'Possibly. It would be the twenty-first.'

So, riding a donkey – it was Kuniang's old mount, Calvin Coolidge – and with no other company than the donkey-boy, I went once more to the Temple of Costly Experience. As Père Antoine had predicted, I met with no difficulties. The old Manchu caretakers were quite friendly. I might have been a tourist, visiting the temples in the Western Hills near Peking.

I made my way to the banks of the lake within the temple grounds and gazed across the water. There was the place where I had stood when the duck flew past me and was struck down. From the same bushes that had hidden him from sight the same gigantic Tartar must have loosed the arrow that killed poor Igor. Why had they killed him? I can only guess at the reactions of an Oriental mentality. I cannot analyse them.

The scene itself had been pictured in Igor's mind, long before it occurred. What Donald had taken to be a vision of a remote past had been an unconscious fore-knowledge of the future. It was not a re-presentation, but a pre-presentation, of an event in Time. What might be called an unconscious precognition.

Though he knew it not, Igor had described *himself* in the martyrdom of Saint Sebastian, when he insisted that the saint should be struck down by one arrow between the shoulders. The vision had come true, and Igor had smiled, as he said the saint would smile, even in death.

Who, I wonder, had taken the part of Les Adionastes in d'Annunzio's mystery play and carried the beautiful body to its last resting-place? The soul of Igor may have entered Paradise, as do the souls of children. Could any one doubt a Divine forgiveness?'

The Manchu caretakers hovered round, hoping to ren-der me some slight service that might bring about a repeated distribution of largesse. Wishing to be alone, I left the temple for the neighbouring forest, and sat down in the shade of a flowering acacia, near the empty bed of a stream that should have flowed past some emperor's tomb, but had returned to its natural course. Probably it was there, or thereabouts, that poor Rizwàn met his death, by being struck on the tongue by a poisonous snake. I can imagine him, snuffling round among the rank grasses, and then the sudden yelp of pain. And the hideous convulsions that shook and twisted his body, while his master tried in vain to help.

Close to me fat lizards sat on sunbaked stones, motionless save for their heaving sides. The hot air vibrated to the song of cicadas. In some pond nearby frogs croaked in chorus. My thoughts should have dwelt sadly on the events to which my present surroundings had formed a background. But incongruously enough I found myself visualizing those events as tableaux in a Russian ballet! I felt ashamed of my own levity, but still the idea lingered.

Silly little episodes came back to my mind, from the days of our stay at the Pao-lien Ssè. As when Donald had appeared one morning at breakfast with a swelling the size of an egg on his forehead. He explained that, in passing from the room where he slept to a little cubicle at the back that served as a bathroom (we had brought some India-rubber tubs for our ablutions), he had miscalculated the height of the door.

'I realize now,' was his comment, 'that Elisalex was wrong when she said this place was nothing but a *décor* for *Le Pavillon d'Armide*. It is built of real masonry, as I have found out to my cost.' And Kuniang had added: 'Costly experience!'

Yet Elisalex had been right in saying that it required almost an effort of will to believe that the place was not a piece of stageland, but the material background of our lives. And I imagined a ballet, in which the Pao-lien Ssè might be the home of an artist's soul, as in the old Chinese story of Wu Tao-tzu. He painted a landscape, much like that of the Imperial tombs: groups of trees, little temples, and a background of blue mountains. When he had finished he clapped his hands and a grotto opened in his own picture. Whereupon Wu Tao-tzu walked into it and disappeared. And he was never seen again on earth. Had not something of the kind happened to the Abbot, when he walked home with the dying dog in his arms and penetrated into the tomb?

That might be the last scene in my ballet, but there would be lots more besides. And all our party would be in it, except myself. For me there would be no cue to call me on the stage. And for Igor it would be a dance of death.

I was feeling dazed by the heat and the glare. Except

223

under my flowing acacia there was little or no shade, for I was still only on the outskirts of the forest. And the long journey of the past few days had tired me more than I realized at the time. It is not surprising that my thoughts became confused and inconsequent. When you are writing a story you can make it clear and logical. But when you are living in one, and you are drowsy on a hot summer's afternoon, the edges get blurred and everything dances, like the sun-flecks, before your eyes.

I must have slept about two hours, for when I woke up the shadows were lengthening. There was just time to walk round the Abbot's tomb and to gaze on the pavilions and the tumulus that were now the home of his spirit. The buildings were like those of the Imperial tombs, only smaller. The outer door of the tomb itself was closed by the huge marble ball that Donald had taken me to see, when it was being shaped by the stone-cutters. Above it and above the door, the Eight Trigrams shone in golden lines upon a tablet of black lacquer, symbolizing Past, Present and Future co-existing in that mystery that is absolute Time.

As I gazed upon them I asked myself: Was each moment immortal in the Abbot's life, in Igor's, and in Rizwàn's (I mention them all, as they were buried together)?

Was that one instant no less eternal than the surrounding hills, when Igor's lips met Kuniang's, on the Island of Fulfilled Desires? Or was it the infinitesimal segment of an unending line, uniting life and death – love and oblivion?

Such queries are no less idle than those of Titania, after Oberon had squeezed the magic flower on to her eyelids. But if indeed the world's a stage and all the men and women merely players, then the dramas that are our lives may indeed have eternity for their run, when produced by the great stage-manager of all things.

29 *Curtain*

'Come, children, let us shut up the box and the
puppets, for our play is played out.'

THACKERAY:
Vanity Fair (Conclusion)

Supper that evening was a frugal meal, but good of its
kind. We had a large bowl of minestrone, followed by
bread and ham and finishing with fruit. Exalted Virtue,
on his own initiative, had decorated the table with wild
flowers, an idea that pleased the doctor-missionaries
very much. Apparently they had not thought of decora-
ting anything with flowers, except the altar in their
little chapel.

When the repast was over the others dispersed, only
Père Antoine and I remaining in conversation. I was
always glad to talk to Père Antoine, when he was willing to do so. He seemed to combine the exact knowledge of a scientist with the ancient wisdom of the Holy
See, tinged with the even more ancient wisdom of the
East. The dining room in the Mission's *Ambulatorio*
was a plain whitewashed room, like all the others, with
a rough earthen floor (my hosts told me that they
hoped, someday to pave it with coloured tiles). The
walls were adorned with enlarged photographs of religious edifices in Italy, such as the Duomo of Milan
and Santa Croce in Florence. Other photographs were
portraits of ecclesiastical dignitaries, bishops and car-
dinals, having authority over the Franciscan Order
from which the Mission itself depended.

We had dined under a hanging kerosene lamp, but this drew so many moths and other insects into the room that Père Antoine and I moved out into the courtyard and sat on the usual bench against the wall. It was almost pitch-dark there, but at least the insects did not bother us. Père Antoine asked me how I had got on at the Temple.

'Oh, all right. But I was rather surprised to see that they were still working here and there on the outskirts of the tomb, putting up pillars and balustrades.'

'Yes. I was told today that an order had come from the Lama Temple in Peking, to finish the work that had been begun. The money will be forthcoming to pay for it, though I should not be surprised if half of it does not get lost on the way. Also the priests of the Lama Temple have let it be known that once a year one of their number will go to the Pao-lien Ssè and will accomplish the ritual sacrifices at the Abbot's tomb. So his altars will not remain desolate. As far as I can make out, all this is in conformity with some sort of last will and testament that he himself left in Peking. He seems to have prepared for every imaginable contingency.'

'Except the one that you mentioned today: the possibility of the tombs being broken into and looted.'

'If he had foreseen that, he would not have built the tomb here – though really I don't know where, in China, it would be any safer.'

'The Abbot seems to have foreseen most of the things that happened up till now, his own death included. It is too much to ask that he should see further. And for all we know, the tombs may *not* be looted. What makes you so sure that it must happen?'

'Only that China is getting poorer and hungrier every year. *Malesuada fames . . .'*

'China always has been a catastrophic country.'

'All interesting countries are. And when they cease to be catastrophic, they pass, like Holland, into the limbo of those happy countries that have no history.'

'Then the only chance of happiness for the world is

that there should be no more history anywhere. Which means no more change.'

'That is what it amounts to. And it is not likely to come about in our time.'

'Yet some people thought that we had reached that consummation at the end of the Great War.'

'In France they say: *On croit si facilement ce qu'on espère*. And the Latins put it more crudely: *Mundus vult decipi* ... Yet the Christian religion might have brought about even such a consummation, but for the fact that every minor sect insists on serving Christ in its own way, instead of in His. Good Catholic that I am, I believe that even Buddhism might have brought us nearer to peace and goodwill among men, if humanity had conscientiously followed the Path of the Buddha. All great religions are manifestations of God. And all truly religious people, East and West, feel much the same about life when they come down to essentials. They strive to carry out a doctrine of loving one another. But most of us, all over the world, will only love our neighbour if he behaves as we want him to. In this respect, people in the West are more intolerant than they are here. You would think that they are not really satisfied unless they have somebody to abuse. In the East, at least, outside their own interests, people are willing to live and let live.'

I did not quite agree with this dictum of Père Antoine's. And I objected: 'Even the Chinaman looks down with contempt on the rest of humanity. If he does not go up into the Temple as often as we do, to thank God that he is not like other men, it is simply because he considers that as so obvious that there is nothing to thank God for. Though of course he may pray that, in another incarnation, his sins may not condemn him to be reborn in the shape of a pig or a foreign devil.'

'Well, perhaps you know these people better than I do. But I was thinking that the Abbot, for example, always struck me as being a very tolerant man.'

I glanced at Père Antoine, though I could hardly

see him in the darkness. What did he mean? Was he thinking of the Abbot's attitude towards Elisalex? And how much did he know of his past?

Just then the Dutch nurse came across the courtyard. She appeared to be looking for something or somebody. At first she did not notice Père Antoine and me. She entered the lighted dining room and came out again. It was then that she saw us.

'Oh, there you are,' she said to me. 'My patient seems better tonight. And I think she would like to talk to you a little. Will you go in and see her? But don't stay too long. And be sure to agree with everything she says. She needs encouraging and cheering up.'

'Right you are. I'll go and talk to her. And if you think that I'm staying too long, come into the room on some excuse, and I'll clear out.'

I got up from the bench, crossed the courtyard and groped up a little side passage (the *Ambulatorio* did not boast of any outside lights, except one at the outer door), to the convent cell that was now Elisalex's room. There she lay, very still and quiet, under a plain wooden crucifix that hung on the wall. As I went in, I was struck, as so often before, by that air of elegance that never failed her. I had seen her already, for one moment only, in the morning. Then, the daylight had revealed a yellowish tinge in her skin, possibly the after-effects of the poison, and a marked dilation of the pupils. But these symptoms were no longer visible in the subdued light of a cheap little oil lamp of the kind that Standard Oil once used to distribute gratis all over China. The nurse – or someone else before the nurse arrived – had made an effective if unconventional lampshade of bamboo strips and rice paper.

Two enormous eyes in an almost transparent face were turned towards the door when I entered. Elisalex lay resting against the piled-up cushions, her arms stretched out in front of her. This was no longer the beautiful woman who had taken a 'rest cure' at the Shuang Liè Ssè. Here was a real invalid. But still an interesting one.

I was conscious of a touch of anxiety in the silent gaze that met me. And I wondered what could be troubling Elisalex. The alarums and excursions of the past days were over. She was no longer in danger. All she had to do was to rest and to recover.

I sat down on a wooden stool beside the bed and stroked the hand that lay near me. And I said:

'The nurse tells me that you are better tonight. That is good news.'

She did not answer, but kept looking at me, as if there were something on her mind. And then she asked:

'Where is Kuniang?'

'Kuniang is in Peking. She offered to come here again, to look after you. But I advised her to remain behind and to look after the children instead. She was worn out by all she had gone through.'

It seemed to me that Elisalex looked relieved, but not yet satisfied that all was well. And I guessed her thoughts. Evidently she knew what had happened on the Island of Fulfilled Desires, and she was wondering whether I did too. She was asking herself: 'If he knew, would he have forgiven?'

Is it a curse of all literary men – or only mine? – never to be able to think of any episode or situation, even those that concern them most intimately, without reducing it all to some form of literature? Heaven knows that my reactions to Kuniang's story had been utterly spontaneous. When I had thought of comforting her, and of that only, I had been entirely unselfconscious. But now, when Elisalex scrutinized my face with anxious eyes, wondering how I had taken it all, or still might take it, I felt all the literary appeal of my own kindness and generosity! And I thought of the verses in *Guinevere*:

> And while she grovelled at his feet,
> She felt the king's breath wander o'er her neck,
> And in the darkness o'er her fallen head,
> Perceived the waving of his hands that blessed.

229

I could not answer directly an unspoken question. But I might assure Elisalex that all was well.

'Poor Kuniang! She is more to be pitied than you. For she is haunted by remorse. She feels that she is responsible for Igor's death. One brief moment of vertigo on her part cost the poor boy his life. The memory of his dying smile will remain with her as long as she lives. But we must stand by her, all of us, till that memory becomes less harrowing. I have done, and will do, all that is possible on my part. But you must help. And in order to help, the first thing you must do is to get well. Do not trouble yourself about anything else but that.'

She did not answer. But two great tears welled up into her eyes and ran down her cheeks. Poor Elisalex! She was very weak. I had never seen her shed tears before.

My own eyes were wet in sympathy. But I said:

'Here! You must not do that. The nurse told me that you had to be cheered up: not reduced to tears!'

The ghost of a smile passed over her wan face, and she said: 'Do let us go to Paris, all of us!'

'Ah, yes – Paris! I think you are right. The dear old crazy East can be a bit too crazy at times. Then we feel we need a change, just as we need a change after the other thing. So happiness consists in alternating between streets and hutungs, salons and pavilions, ceilings and the sky . . .'

I spoke at random, thinking only of bringing Elisalex to the contemplation of other things than recent events. I must have succeeded, for she added gently: 'And either way, there is the feeling of going home.'

So she was looking forward to living in her little flat again, panelled in dove-coloured silk, with plaques of old Wedgwood. It would be nice to be near the Etoile, and only twenty minutes' walk from the Travellers' in the Champs Elysées. Fédor should take her back there.

I stayed a little longer, talking about Père Antoine and our hosts, the Italian missionaries. Then the nurse came in with a cup of warm milk, and I rose and took my leave.

There was no-one sitting on the bench as I passed through the courtyard, so I strolled out on to the road. The mission buildings stood just outside the village, on the way to the Imperial tombs. I could hear the beating of a drum and a voice declaiming: a night watchman was doing his rounds and prudently warning malefactors and evil spirits of his approach.

There was a new moon, the Fourth Moon of the Chinese year, the 'Peony Moon' of summer. The gleaming sickle hung in a clear sky over the ink-black shadow of the forest. I accepted it as an omen, a promise of better days to come. Though I could barely see my way, I started slowly along the path that would bring me to the Imperial tomb of Kuang-hsu. I met no one, for Chinese in the country do not like to go out at night. Yet how quiet and peaceful it was. Not even an owl hooted in the darkness. And just the right temperature for a little stroll before going to bed. Donald was right. It was hard to realize that a civil war could be going on somewhere near. But 'nearness' is a relative term. China is so big that wars and floods and famines, affecting provinces that are larger and more populous than many European states, get lost in the immensity, as if they were of no more account in the general scheme of things than the little events that had come upon us in the Temple of Costly Experience.

30   *Dawn on Taku Bar*

All farewells should be sudden, when forever.
> BYRON:
> *Sardanapalus*

The reader, if he has followed me thus far, may have gathered that the plot of our story was not the only *raison d'être* of this, the last book I shall ever write about China. The central theme loses itself in the 'atmosphere': that quaint and (to us) illogical atmosphere of China, to which the Western mind adapts itself so that in time it hardly feels at home in any other. My thoughts, as I wrote, were not so much on the story itself as on the country to which, in these pages, I was saying goodbye. If I have been diffuse, it is because I lingered over details of Chinese life and landscape that I might never see again, except in memory.

And now I have little more to add.

We got Elisalex up to Peking in due course, and she convalesced in her own room at the Shuang Liè Ssè. I imagined that the next item on her programme would be to marry Fédor. But no. She was in no hurry. To my inquiries on the subject, she answered carelessly: 'Someday, if we have children.' Certainly Elisalex had the most practical ideas about marriage. Unless you have some good reason to marry, or to get divorced, why bother? It will all be the same a hundred years hence.

At one time or another I had bought several of

Fédor's pictures. He asked me if he might take them to Paris, to the studio that he meant to set up there. After some demur, I consented. We arranged that he should give them back to me when I asked for them. Fédor departed with Elisalex about the middle of August on the same ship, the *Sphinx*, that had brought her out to China. I felt sorry for Patushka and Matushka, left alone in their old age. But that is the way of the world. The old schoolroom would be very empty, and no young voices to break the silence, unless Natasha came down, with her babies, from Harbin . . .

I also was preparing to leave for Europe with my family, as Elisalex had once advised. Kuniang would not discuss plans. She left it all to me and raised no objection to anything I proposed. But I know that she was glad of my decision, despite the wrench that it implied. I had only the vaguest projects as to where we might settle down. Perhaps somewhere in Kent . . . My father had owned property at Birchington-on-Sea, and though the house had been sold and none of my family lived there any more, my childish memories took me back to Kentish gardens ablaze with flowers in June; to the flash of lighthouses where ships from all the world passed up the estuary of the Thames, and a sandy shore, fragrant with seaweed under white chalk cliffs – a wonderful place for Little Chink and his sister to dig castles, which the incoming tide would wash away! I had also an idea of taking Kuniang to the land of her forebears, that is to say to the Tuscan Apennines and the chestnut woods under La Verna, where Saint Francis preached to the birds.

Coelum non animum mutant qui trans mare currunt. Other skies, other climes, other hopes and fears. But Kuniang and I and the children still together. How near had we been to losing that, the best of all!

Good for us to be out of China for a few years at least. That is what I say now, but I doubt if we will ever come back. *A Midsummer Night's Dream* is over with Puck's leave-taking:

> So, good night unto you all.
> Give me your hands, if we be friends . . .

I have sublet the house to the nuns of Kuniang's old convent school. They were looking for an annexe of some sort, as a hostel for sisters from other convents in China. But I have taken away the sign that hung over my study door: I mean Ah-ting-fu's old sign *The Maker of Heavenly Trousers*. It would hardly do for a convent.

The nuns have promised me never to remove the marble stele on Uncle Podger's grave. Will his little brown ghost patter through the courtyards, I wonder, when they ring the convent bell for supper?

The Five Virtues are pensioned off, but fully intend to take charge of us again, should we ever reappear in Peking. During the weeks before our departure, I noticed that they were preparing to have a sale of all the rubbish that accumulates in a big house during many years, and that the owners discard as useless. When the day of our departure came round, they gave us a grand send-off with crackers and farewell presents. For Kuniang there was a lovely headdress made out of the tiny blue feathers from the kingfisher's breast. And the children were half smothered under Chinese toys, including gilded swords of peach-wood, to keep off evil spirits.

I wrote to Donald, telling him as much as I could of what had happened. And he answered with the following letter:

New York City,
September 1928

DEAR MAKER OF HEAVENLY TROUSERS,

I call you that again, as when I first read the little tailor's sign that hangs outside your study door. The name brings China nearer. But looking out from my windows in the Sherry-netherland, down on to the Saint Gaudens' Sherman group and out over Central

234

Park, it is difficult to believe that such a place exists as The Temple of Costly Experience.

Still more difficult to believe that the beautiful boy, to whom I had thought of giving the part of Saint Sebastian, can really have been shot down with arrows. It is as if Red Indians were to lay in wait for motorcars, travelling south from Washington D.C. and up the Shenandoah Valley.

Nowhere on *this* continent could I take you back to the old covered-wagon days that knew no petrol or canned goods. But bits of century-old Asia still linger on. And it seems only a few days ago that we were living together in one of these. The Pao-lien Ssè is farther away in Space and Time than my poor mind can grasp.

I do not know if any of you caught the contagion of my passionate urge to put Igor on the stage. There are many young people that hover like moths round the lights of Broadway, of Shaftesbury Avenue and of the Boulevard des Capucines. But some of us get stage-struck vicariously. And I am one of these. I would have given anything to have seen Igor on the boards of the Châtelet or the Opéra, in the costume that Bakst designed for *L'Après Midi d'un Faune*, with pointed ears and leopard-like spots on his bare arms and thighs. What could not Fokine have made of Igor! For it was he that foresaw and inspired the emergence of the male dancer from the background of the ballet and from the indignity of the role of *porteur* to pretty ballerinas. The male dancer should enhance the grace and charm of the feminine. But I am lapsing, as usual, into technicalities . . . whereas Kuniang, I know, could not speak or write of Igor without being blinded by her tears. Believe me that I, too, cannot bear to think anymore of putting your story on the films – what the Chinese call "the shadow pictures". Death has cast too grim a shadow on the old gay companionship, as on schoolroom memories of the Russian family. But I still keep a few

235

leaves of The Eyelashes of the Swan. We must have tea together and consume them, when next we meet.

That will be, I hope, some day soon, in Paris. Please tell Little Chink and his sister that there are donkeys and goat-carts to be hired in the gardens between the Champs Elysées and the Avenue Gabriel. I hope to offer them a ride or two. Please talk to them occasionally about me, lest they forget.

Yours ever,
DONALD

We embarked for Europe on a German ship, the *Saarbrucken*, at Taku Bar, going out from Tangku station on a lighter. This savoured somehow of an anti-climax, especially as it was raining. Kuniang took several hours to distribute us and the luggage to her satisfaction in the fine family suite. The amah came, too. She had agreed to stay with us in Europe till we found a suitable nurse for the children. Exalted Virtue was also of the party. He would accompany us as far as Hong Kong.

Though we went on board at 6 p.m., the ship was not due to leave till next morning at sunrise. There were very few people on board. Most of the passengers expected to embark at Shanghai.

Taku Bar is a God-forsaken place, albeit on the threshold of so great a country as China. All the night through, I heard no other noise but the lap of waves on the ship's side, and the buzz and hum of electric fans in the cabins. It is hardly surprising that I should not have slept well that night:

> For Lochaber no more, Lochaber no more,
> We'll maybe return to Lochaber no more.

Also there was a mosquito in my cabin.

About half-past three, I slipped on a dressing gown and went on deck. It was still dark and there was no breeze. The air had that dank smell that is characteristic of swampy flats at the mouth of a river. The lights of two other ships, also lying at anchor, shone murkily in the darkness between us and the invisible coastline. As I passed under the light of an arc lamp near the gangway, I was hailed from below by a fisherman in an open boat, who held up a large shining fish which he asked me to buy. I did not want the fish, but I felt in my pocket for some money. As I was wearing a dressing gown, it was natural that I should not have any on me.

A ship's officer was standing by. He said to me:

'These people don't want to be paid in money. It is no good to them. I can get you some ship's biscuit, if you like, to exchange it for that fish.'

'How is it that money is of no use to them?'

'They trade by barter, for they hardly ever go on shore. And you can do no shopping on Taku Bar. They bring us their fish, and we give them something in exchange. But, I warn you, the fish here taste strong of mud. We take them on for the Chinese crew, who cook them with honey and vinegar, which, I suppose, is an improvement.'

The officer leant over the rail and said something to the fisherman, who nodded and grinned. He would take ship's biscuit in exchange for his catch.

The stars still twinkled above me, but a faint glow was beginning to lighten the sky in the East. It revealed no sign of land. The coast is low-lying and cannot be seen from Taku Bar. One of the principal gateways of North China shows only an unbroken line of sky and sea.

Suddenly I was aware of Kuniang standing beside me, with her elbows on the rail. She also had on a dressing gown, and her hair, loosely tied with a ribbon, fell on her shoulders. We stood there together for a while without speaking, and slowly the sky grew clearer. But all was grey and empty of life. Only in imagination could we picture the land, and all that lay beyond the skyline. Except for the muffled throb of engines getting up steam, and the cry of a seagull, all was silent.

I wondered what was in Kuniang's mind, as she left the country where all her life had been spent, where she had been born, and married and had children. Was she thinking of the Shuang-Liè Ssè, or of the Russian family schoolroom, or of the Temple of Costly Experience?

It was some time before she spoke. Then she said:

'Today is the Sixth Day of the Lotus Moon.'

'Yes. What about it?'

'It is the day that Uncle Podger used to have his bath.'

She did not mean, of course, that it was the only day of the year on which poor Podger performed his ablutions (or had them performed for him!). But the Sixth Day of the Sixth Moon is set aside for 'the airing of the classics'. The sacred books in temples and the scrolls in the Imperial archives were taken out into sunny courtyards, opened, dusted, and their pages interleaved with fragrant herbs that kept away the insects. Women washed their hair, and dog-owners and cat-owners gave their pets a bath.

The Five Virtues always saw to it that Uncle Podger got washed on that date. And he would accept his ceremonial bath, with gravity, as his due. Were not the Imperial elephants also taken out from their stables near the Shun-chih Men, to have a swim in the moat, outside the Forbidden City?

Uncle Podger's memory helped us over a poignant moment, as he himself had done so often in the past. Meanwhile the stars had faded and the sea had blanched, as the light grew stronger. The anchor was hauled up and the ship began to move. For a little longer, Kuniang and I stood gazing out towards the China we were leaving. Then we turned and looked into each other's eyes.

The Maker of
Heavenly Trousers
Daniele Varè

'A book of unselfconscious charm in so high a degree that to
take up the average novel after reading it is like turning away
from a window through which one has seen an enchanted
landscape'

The Maker of Heavenly Trousers is one of the best loved books
ever written about China. First published in 1935 to wide
critical acclaim, it was reprinted many times. It tells
evocatively and charmingly the story of a foreign
correspondent living in a forgotten corner of the old Imperial
City of Peking. The young Kuniang, the homeless daughter of
an Italian railway engineer, enters his life and he watches her
grow from a young girl into a full-grown woman while all
around China is in rebellion. Soon his feelings turn from that
of a guardian to that of a suitor. Across the exotic tapestry of
the decaying Imperial City flit strange characters: Rasputin's
mistress, a Mongolian Abbot, a dying young millionaire. As a
backdrop to the intense historical drama there is the gentle
humour of the narrator's battles of will with his inscrutable
Chinese servants.

'The chief charm of the book lies in its atmosphere of serenity,
its flavour of ancient things, tranquil and beautiful in their
decline'
THE OBSERVER

'A delightful story, in which the author's fancy imparts new
and whimsical aspects to familiar things and scenes'
TIMES LITERARY SUPPLEMENT

'Delightful, one of the few readable tales of Chinese life'
GLASGOW HERALD

'Mr Daniele Varè has a delightful light touch. The story of the
waif who marries her benefactor has been done before, but it
has not been told for some time and it has not hitherto been
told, I think, with Mr Varè's amusing and decorative setting'
BOOK SOCIETY NEWS

0552 99240 2

BLACK SWAN

The Gate of Happy Sparrows
Daniele Varè

'Signor Varè's style is that of the cultured cosmopolitan, leisurely and gently humorous, with a happy knack of casual, unexpected and whimsical turns of thought'
J.O.P. BLAND, THE OBSERVER

The Gate of Happy Sparrows is the sequel to that classic account of life in China, *The Maker of Heavenly Trousers*. The story takes up with the narrator's early married life amongst the Europeans in Peking at the turn of the century. In the same charming, anecdotal manner as in the previous book, Varè describes the tragic and humorous, drawing with unerring accuracy a wide array of exotic characters: his unvirtuous servants the Five Virtues, the German doctor who kills himself knowing that he has contracted leprosy, a foreigner who dies in the deserted pavilions and temples of the Summer Palace during the Boxer Revolution and Lieber Augustin, the German soldier who walked all the way from Siberia to China during the First World War.

Once again, Varè describes the world of Old China in unforgettable wit and style.

'Romance, sentimental, sceptical, civilised, with an irresistible dash'
THE BYSTANDER

0552 99241 0

BLACK SWAN